**HER FINGERS SHOOK AS SHE LIFTED THE
RING OF EMERALDS AND DIAMONDS
FROM ITS VELVET SLOT.**

He took her hand and pressed her fingers to his mouth.
"I was afraid you wouldn't accept it."

"It's incredibly beautiful," she whispered.

"It has an inscription. "It says, *First you are a woman.
Kurt*."

Erin lowered her eyes from his. "I see, it's a message."

He forced her eyes to meet his. "Not a sermon, just a
message. First I am a man; then I am a captain and all
the other things I am. But first a man. And you are first
a woman; then you are a physician and all the other
things you are. But first we're together, man and woman,
or, if you prefer, woman and man. I don't care about
the order, I just care about what we are."

He took the ring from her and placed it slowly back on
her finger. Then came the gentle touch of his lips tingling
on hers. When he drew his head back to look at her, his
eyes were bright and flashing with desire. "I may lose you,
Erin," he said hoarsely, "but I will never do it gracefully."

CANDLELIGHT ECSTASY SUPREMES

SOMEWHERE IN THE STARS

Jo Calloway

A CANDLELIGHT ECSTASY SUPREME

Published by
Dell Publishing Co., Inc.
1 Dag Hammarskjold Plaza
New York, New York 10017

ISBN: 0-440-18157-7

Printed in the United States of America

First printing—April 1984

To Our Readers:

Candlelight Ecstasy is delighted to announce the start of a brand-new series—Ecstasy Supremes! Now you can enjoy a romance series unlike all the others—longer and more exciting, filled with more passion, adventure, and intrigue—the stories you've been waiting for.

In months to come we look forward to presenting books by many of your favorite authors and the very finest work from new authors of romantic fiction as well. As always, we are striving to present the unique, absorbing love stories that you enjoy most—the very best love has to offer.

Breathtaking and unforgettable, Ecstasy Supremes will follow in the great romantic tradition you've come to expect *only* from Candlelight Ecstasy.

Your suggestions and comments are always welcome. Please let us hear from you.

Sincerely,

The Editors
Candlelight Romances
1 Dag Hammarskjold Plaza
New York, New York 10017

CHAPTER ONE

Captain Kurt Garisen would soon be forty-three years
old and it bothered him to be almost halfway to
ninety. Tall, muscular, and strikingly handsome, he
had the features expected of a captain commanding a
world cruise liner. His lips were full and sensuous,
his pale blue irises the color of his father's Swedish
skies, his dark chestnut hair, a gift from his Italian
mother, was now lightened with shiny silver threads
growing more numerous with each passing day.

He was fair game for every female passenger on
board the *Royal Princess Star,* a fact which in the
beginning had astonished him, but after eighteen
years it was something he had grown to accept as
merely part of his job. He had never married, and
following that first world cruise, decided that he
most likely never would.

It was a warm day in New York. At nine o'clock
in the morning the sidewalks looked as though an
army of two-legged umbrella-and-briefcase-carrying
ants had flooded the city, hurrying and scurrying
in all directions. He was glad he wasn't a part
of it. He could never fit into the gray polyester

life-style. He was a sailor. His home was the ocean—any ocean.

Those commuters. They knew their business with the umbrellas, for by the time the taxi pulled up in front of the building a heavy rain was pelting Manhattan. He found himself to be the only person on the entire block who didn't have an umbrella. He dashed from the taxi into the building, feeling the back of his short-sleeve cotton shirt becoming drenched.

Shaking himself in the entrance lobby, he hurried for the elevator and exited on the fourteenth floor. Rubbing the remaining drops from his arms, he went directly into the managing director's suite of offices, giving a quick wave to Julia Conrad, the receptionist who sat talking on the phone.

She waved toward the closed door and mouthed, "He's waiting for you."

When he peered inside the office door, Nils Malaney motioned to him with a cigar. "Come in, Kurt."

Kurt crossed the enormous office and landed in a chair beside the desk. "Morning, Nils. Sorry I'm late, but it took a while to get through the traffic. It's wild out there."

Nils gave a quick hint of a smile. "That's okay, Kurt. The news is limited. We have met your request for a new medical officer, but beyond that just the usual resignations and replacements." He pursed his lips thoughtfully. "Want a cup of coffee?"

"No, thanks," Kurt answered, looking down at the clean-topped desk made especially for this office, a desk so large it would have to be disassembled to be moved. He glanced up at the bookshelves behind the director and knew every book on ships ever published had found a home on those shelves. Nils Malaney was a genius of some kind, he supposed, but for some reason he could never like the dwarf-size company wizard. Kurt finally raised his brows and commented. "It's a relief to know a new medical officer is coming aboard. I damn sure didn't plan on lifting anchor with that alcoholic of a sawbones on ship. The entire staff almost developed ulcers, including myself." He shook his head. "I promise you, he did not draw one sober breath on the last voyage. We were just plain lucky no one became acutely ill. And we're also lucky to have the staff we have. They were life savers, literally."

Nils puffed the cigar, flooding the area with choking thick smoke before answering, "I know. Mark Payton filled me in. I'm sorry, Kurt," he shrugged and offered earnestly, "that's all I can say." Slowly his shoulders leveled, his eyes narrowed and probed. "However, it should make you feel better to know your new crew member is a highly qualified sincere young physician. I don't foresee any problems at all."

Both men were silent a moment before Kurt Garisen nodded his head once. "I'll admit that bit of news does make me feel better." Then he sighed softly. "If someone in Personnel had given a bit more scrutiny to the last ship's doctor, that person should have uncovered the fact he was an alcoholic. I mean," he continued harshly, "any man who consumes two gallons of Jim Beam daily on ship is bound to drink at least a quart or so daily on land. Somebody screwed up, and royally at that."

Nils gestured with the cigar. "Well, you don't have a worry with this one. I personally checked

9

references, schools, hospitals. The works. This woman is qualified, smart as a whip. She came through training without a hitch. She's sea ready and sea-worthy." Again the quick fleeting smile.

Startled eyes widened with disbelief as Kurt slapped his open palm down hard on the corner of the desk. "Woman! Now, look here, Nils, I thought we were talking about the doctor, the ship's medical officer," he shot back heatedly.

"We are, Kurt." Nils's voice became unusually low. "Bring your rear end into the twentieth century. Your new medical officer is a woman."

Kurt raised the hand on the desk six inches or so then brought it down with another hard slam. "I'll be damned if I sail out of this harbor with a female physician on my ship! My ship's hospital has been plagued with problems for the past two years, and I'm ready for it to stop!" His voice radiated and the veins in his neck protruded. "I want to know who's responsible for this! Tell me!"

"You're talking to him," came the response tinged with light sarcasm. "I'm responsible."

Kurt Garisen's eyes flashed as his own voice grew dangerously soft. "Why? With all the applications you must have received, why? Answer me that one question."

Nils ground the cigar into a white cut-crystal ashtray and answered equally as softly. "She was, and is, the most qualified of the applicants. And that's your answer, Captain." He continued speaking quietly but emphatically. "She's very sharp. The only thing questionable in her background is the breakup of a part-nership in Baton Rouge, Louisiana, but after a thorough investigation, and I do mean thorough, I believe she was more than justified to leave the partnership. Her skills are above reproach. It is our belief that she will be an asset to your ship and to this company."

Kurt stared at Nils, the expression of disbelief still foremost on his face. "Then I have no say-so in this?"

Nils gave a slight shake of his head. "No, Captain. The board has approved her unanimously, and when you leave port three days from now she will be your new ship's doctor. Her name is—"

"Damn her name! Damn you and the board!" Kurt countered, losing a measure of self-control. "There isn't a vessel on any ocean sailing with a woman as ship's doctor, and now, after putting up with the likes of that last one, I'm now being saddled with a woman. Are you guys trying to tell me something?"

"No, calm down, Kurt." He leaned forward a bit and said somewhat apologetically, "I'm sorry that you're upset, but we do have to consider what's in the passengers' best interest, and this young woman is the finest physician we interviewed." Without waiting for a rebuttal he went on. "I don't foresee any problems with the medical staff. After all, a doctor is a doctor. That certainly should end any confrontations that might arise among the ship's nurses or auxiliary medical workers."

Kurt gave a half-laugh and brought his fingers through his unruly hair. "I wouldn't venture a ruling on that statement."

"Well, Captain, I would say it's your job to see that mutiny doesn't occur within the ship's hospital. Wouldn't you agree?"

Kurt drummed his fingers against the surface of the desk and shot the director a threatening glance.

11

"I don't need anyone, not even you, to tell me my job." He got suddenly to his feet. "You hired a woman doctor for my ship, well, she's yours as long as we're in this harbor, but three days from now she'll be mine, all mine." He stared stonily at the director. "And I'll give you ten to one odds she'll not last more than one voyage."

"I'll take those odds, Captain. I'll wager one hundred dollars, and if I win, you'll owe me a thousand. Right?" Without waiting for an answer he continued. "And that goes without saying that she will receive the same professional treatment from you as any ship's doctor. Right?"

"You got yourself a bet, Nils. I'll come by for my hundred in three weeks."

Nils smiled warmly. "Or bring me my thousand, Captain. Either way, I look forward to seeing you in three weeks. Have a good voyage."

A triumphant glint shone in the light blue eyes of Kurt Garisen. "I plan to. Thanks." Not looking back, he nodded briefly and left.

Outside the office he paused and rubbed his chin thoughtfully. Then he approached Julia Conrad's desk, a suddenly twinkle in his eyes. "Julia, sweetheart, I need you to fill me in on a certain matter." He winked at the aging receptionist, who had been with the company for thirty-five years.

As Julia acknowledged his request with a lift of her head, he caught her hand and held it tightly in his for a moment. "Have you meet the new ship's doctor for the *Princess*?" he asked, his smiling gaze searching her face.

Julia's eyes widened and thin lips broke into a

broad smile. "Yes, twice, in fact. She seemed to be quite a lovely young woman. I liked her."

Julia's words impaired his preconceived idea of easily winning the bet with Nils. For some reason he had counted on Julia being more objective in her evaluation of the company's first female ship's doctor, but women usually had a way of sticking together on some issues, and this was probably one of those. But he knew the next woman he asked for an opinion of the ship's doctor being a woman wouldn't be nearly so appreciative of the fact. The ship's head nurse— Rachel Lawrence.

That night as they enjoyed a drink in Rachel's hotel room, he lowered himself beside her on the sofa and draped his arm subtly around her shoulder, his right hand bringing his glass to his lips. His fingers toyed with the dainty black strap of her dress. Rachel was serenely pretty and a poised professional. He had always admired her, even from that initial voyage when she had been a wide-eyed new graduate from West Virginia seeking the glamorous side of her profession. Her rich dark hair, always perfectly coiffed, was parted in the center and hung loosely just above the silky smooth skin of her shoulders.

He looked down at her perfectly rounded breasts that rose and fell enticingly with her breathing. After a moment of silence he leaned forward and brushed his lips across the cleavage exposed by her low neckline, then he straightened. Taking his finger, he stirred the ice in his glass while his eyes narrowed into tiny slits. "We have a new ship's doctor," he announced calmly and with an even smile.

"Oh. I can't say I'm surprised. It seemed inevitable to me that we would. Have you met him?"

He blew out his cheeks and looked back at his glass. "Nope. I haven't met *her*."

"Her! A woman! Don't tell me we have a female chief!"

He rose to his feet and moved silently across to the table where the ice bucket and bottle of Chivas Regal sat. He refilled his glass. "Want another?" He looked around, watching her expected reaction, the smile tugging at one corner of his mouth.

"No," she snapped. "I want to know about the new doctor. I can't believe it!" She shook her head. "Not a woman. I never met a woman doctor who knew her nostrils from two holes in the ground. What in the world is wrong with those people in the front office? I'll bet this is some of that sawed-off runt Nils Malaney's doings!" She looked at him with disbelief in her liquid green eyes, her chin fast becoming set in a determined look. "It'll never work, Kurt." She began turning her head slowly from side to side. "And I'm being optimistic to say *never*."

Kurt shrugged and mumbled, "Maybe, maybe not. Time will certainly tell."

"Are you just going to take it?" Rachel exclaimed loudly, her green eyes flashing at him. "You're the captain."

Impatiently, he shook his glass, stirring the contents. "And Malaney in the managing director. He outranks me."

Biting her lip, she looked down at her feet. "I am not working for any griping woman doctor. I had my fill of them in school. There's something wrong with every damn one of them! God, they're such know-it-

14

alls! I am not working with her, and neither will Sara Lynn."

"Yes, you will," he said with mock sternness, followed by a soft sigh. "Both of you will be the good little nurses you have always been, and that's an order, my dear."

Settling deeper into the sofa, she searched his face. "Have you seen her?"

He pursed his lips. "No, I've not had that pleasure yet. But I will, tomorrow to be exact." He raised his glass directly in front of his eyes. "She reports on ship tomorrow."

She waved her hand in midair at him. "Well, get prepared. She won't have any breasts, no butt, she'll either be wide as a barn or skinny as a rail, but"— she paused dramatically—"her brain is guaranteed to be hanging out both ears. Believe me, Kurt, I know the type."

"I am prepared for the meeting." He drained his glass again. "Now, shall we go to dinner," he said, eyeing her mischievously.

A soft chuckle escaped her lips. "Nothing bothers you, does it, Kurt?"

He grinned. "Only hurricanes, typhoons, and squalls," he replied with tranquility. "Not women doctors."

Erin Barclay, dressed in a striking two-piece light blue linen suit, stood and tried to bring the entire ship into her focus. For a brief moment when she looked up and realized the size of the *Royal Princess Star* her senses abandoned her completely.

"Oh, my goodness," she breathed aloud when her eyes traveled the length of the vessel that exceeded a thousand feet. Then she looked upward over a hundred feet to the top deck, and clasping her hand over her mouth, she for some strange reason felt like laughing.

Placing her briefcase on the concrete beside her feet, she clasped both hands tightly to her hips, her eyes not moving from the monstrous liner snuggled cozily in the harbor. The rush and upheaval of the past few weeks had almost given her a coronary, and looking up at the sleek monster of a ship she quickly realized the past few weeks had been only mild exercise for the heart. Looking at the *Royal Princess Star* was really putting it to the test.

Annoyed with herself for the anxiety she felt building up, she took a couple of quick steps forward, then glared again at the ship, licking her lips nervously. Pictures were deceiving. The pictures Nils Malaney had shown her in the office failed to relay the enormity of this vessel. But then, she was so eager to accept the position on this liner and enter her training, she might have failed to notice its size as well as she would have under different circumstances. But she had arrived at port and there was little doubt now that this ship definitely was not the cozy little ocean liner she envisioned it to be. It looked as if it would take an hour merely to walk from one end to the other.

She scanned it again, then turned to pick up her briefcase, and to her amazement saw a uniformed young man, tall and blond, with a casual smile and bronze skin, standing directly behind her. "Could I help you, ma'am?" he asked politely.

She looked up from strong tanned arms showing below the white short sleeves of the uniform shirt to his broad shoulders, then to expressive brown eyes smiling warmly at her. "No, thank you," she replied softly. "I was just looking at the ship."

He cleared his throat. "I'm sorry, but this is an area restricted to ship personnel. Would you mind telling me how you got here?"

She pointed to the port office building. "I came through there. I'm the physician."

He shifted in surprise. "Ma'am?" His dark blond brows knitted together.

"I'm Erin Barclay," she explained further, then pointed to the liner, "this ship's medical officer."

The new expression on his face revealed absolutely nothing. A total blankness traveled down the elongated sides of the young face with the prominent cheekbones, coming to rest momentarily before another one of wide-eyed surprise traveled the same route. "Oh," he finally managed. He hesitated, staring at her another moment, then said, "I'm sorry, I can't hide my surprise. I had no idea our new doctor would be so lovely. Your predecessors were all quite plain, some damn ugly, but then"—he gave a short laugh—"they were all men. I've never sailed with a female medical officer, Doctor."

A quick smile showed around her eyes. "And I've never sailed—period. It will be a new experience for us both." She raised her brows at the engraved name plate above his pocket.

"Mark Payton. I'm the staff captain."

"Oh," she replied with an implusive smile. "You're the captain. I never imagined the captain would be so young."

"Staff captain," he corrected, "not the captain of

the ship. The commander is Kurt Garisen. I'm his assistant, second in command," he concluded proudly.

She nodded, saying, "Yes, I remember now. Mr. Malaney told me that Captain Garisen would be in charge."

He caught her arm in a friendly gesture. "Are you telling me you've never been on a liner before?" With one eyebrow up he stared at her.

"Exactly," she replied, then added with a joking tone in her voice. "When I was a child I played with boats in my bath water, and those experiences comprise my entire background with floating vessels."

Mark Payton wasn't what she would call handsome, but she thought most women would classify his looks as cute. Cute in his starched white uniform and his bottle-blond hair. And, she concluded standing there, she liked him. He made a good first impression.

"I'll be glad to assist you in learning whatever you need to know about the ship—operations, responsibilities," he offered with a generous smile and a soft squeeze of her arm. "There's quite a lot to learn."

"Thank you, Mark," she replied pleasantly, removing her arm from his touch. Once more reaching down for her briefcase, she glanced up at him. "But for now I suppose I should find Captain Garisen. I was told to report to him this morning at ten." She straightened and pushed her sunglasses back in place. "Could you tell me where I might find him? No one in the office seemed to know."

"He was on the bridge the last time I saw him, which was some fifteen minutes ago."

Her eyes shifted skyward. "And I suppose the bridge is the highest deck?" Looking back at him, she smiled and winked. "I did pick up a few things during my training."

"Right. When you get on the ship, go to the elevators and press the bridge deck button. It opens right out onto the bridge. I would accompany you, but I'm tied up here presently. Are you here to stay?"

She nodded. "Yes. My luggage is in the office."

He nodded. "Good. I'll have someone take it on board for you, and I'll catch you later."

A few minutes later Erin walked off the elevator onto the bridge deck. She could not believe the beautiful elegance of the *Royal Princess Star*. Everything was so spotless.

Clutching her briefcase tightly in her hand, she made her way from the elevator, and following the gold-tone signs on the wall, stepped out onto the ship's bridge. Several men stopped their conversations and looked at her questioningly. "I'm looking for Captain Garisen," she explained in a voice that seemed to echo in her own ears.

Her eyes followed the same direction the men's took. Next to the bridge wall stood the man she quickly assumed to be the captain—an extraordinarily good-looking man. Too handsome for his own good, no doubt.

"I'm Captain Garisen," he said, his voice deep and smooth, but slightly barbed. "What can I do for you?" he asked briskly in the same tone.

She moistened sudden dry lips. "I'm Erin Barclay . . . Dr. Barclay." Not only could she feel the gasps from the other men nearby, she could actually hear one or two. The captain gave no visible change in expression.

19

He looked deliberately around at the men before saying to her, "The hospital is on lower promenade deck to the left of the elevators, Dr. Barclay. I'll meet you there shortly. Now, if you will excuse me, I have other matters pressing at the moment." He eyed her with reptilian blue eyes and turned back to the man standing closest to him.

Dumbfounded, she stood there a moment before slowly turning to move back in the direction of the elevator. She was unable to understand what had just happened on the bridge. Thunderstruck by his aloofness and impertinence, a quick fury boiled up and put her in an angry trance as she walked from the elevator on the lower promenade deck and pushed through the swinging glass doors marked HOSPITAL.

She was appalled. Introductions like that one just didn't take place between two people who would be as important to each other as Nils Malaney had predicted she and the captain would be in the days to come. She was too shocked to feel anything but fury. It was quite obvious to her the good captain resented the fact that she was a woman. If a male doctor had emerged from those elevator doors onto the bridge, the greeting would have been quite different. No doubt it would have been two "good ol' boys" getting together.

Erin resented the hell out of what had just happened, and with her resentment showing plain on her face she walked aimlessly about in the clean, disinfected unit, failing to see anything in her path of vision. For the longest time she couldn't even find her voice, and when she did the words, "That big pompous devil," emerged under her breath.

Pausing beside a bed, she reached out and touched

20

the pressed white spread with her fingertips. At that precise moment the doors flung open and he strode inside. "Well, Doctor, I see you found it without too much difficulty," Kurt Garisen spoke brusquely.

She spun around, eyeing him coldly. "Yes, I found it," she retorted indignantly.

He cut his eyes at the briefcase on the floor. "Has the briefcase now taken the place of the little black bag?" he asked with a trace of sarcasm as he walked closer to where she stood.

Staring unblinkingly at him, she answered smartly, "For carrying papers, diplomas, and the like, I find it to be more serviceable than my little black bag. They get a bit wrinkled when thrown in with my medical supplies."

She felt her face flush as she glared intensely at him. His face was too handsome—a broad brow, an aquiline nose, stabbing blue eyes, dark hair glistening with strands of white, and a tiny mole on his right cheek. Oh, yes indeed, he was Mr. Gorgeous, a magnificent specimen and a great gift to her sex all wrapped up neatly in a gold and white uniform. The captain of the Good Ship *Lollipop*. Well, he could sail right up his own rear end for all she cared. And he could kiss hers en route, because if he thought she would put up with him for one instant, did he forevermore have something to learn about her! The reason she was on this ship in the first place was to remove herself from the clutches of two overbearing, egotistical men who had nearly worked her to death and destroyed her good mind. She had come away something of an expert on the male species of which she was now staring at a prime specimen.

Neither smiling, they continued to stare coolly at

each other. Finally, at the apparent lack of anything else to say, her captain announced curtly, "I expect my sick list at seven promptly."

Looking at him, at the scowl on his gorgeous face, she could have prepared him her first sick list at that precise moment, but it would have only one name on it—hers.

CHAPTER TWO

Erin sat in her office reading the medical files of the passengers who could possibly pose medical problems on the forthcoming voyage. This had been a day she would not soon forget. She had met her staff, which consisted of two women and two men. Two nurses and two auxiliary workers. The introductions had been brief and friendly for the most part. She had not formed any opinions about her staff, except for one, that of the head nurse. Rachel Lawrence would be trouble. That particular expression on that nurse's pretty face meant trouble. But Erin was prepared to deal with the captain of this ship, and she certainly was capable of dealing with the head nurse.

It seemed that for years she had met with nothing but resistance in her life and the battles had worn her down. And now with a move she had with optimism believed might rid some of the uncertainties from her life, she found herself in less than one single day wondering if she was not soon to face her greatest resistance yet. She felt like a walking, breathing test pattern.

She dropped the folder on top of her desk and

rubbed her face vigorously with both hands. She had met so many people in the past twelve hours that faces and names were running together inside her head. Slumping back in her chair, she reached into her lab coat pocket and pulled out a red leather cigarette case. Not exactly a healthy habit, but one she couldn't seem to shake since med school. She lit a cigarette, then again turned her eyes to the folder on her desk. Of the fifteen hundred passengers that would travel the twenty-one-day cruise, she had before her medical histories on ten diabetics, two cancer patients in the advanced last-chance-to-see-the-world category, one postoperative triple bypass coronary, one pregnancy of six months. A total of fifteen. One percent of the passengers. Certainly a lesser ratio than she had anticipated. But then, she had to consider the others coming aboard who had not complied with the simple request that medical background history accompany those passengers with known illnesses, and in addition those who would bring their charts with them and personally drop the information by the hospital.

She remained at the desk until she finished her cigarette, and as she ground the butt into the ashtray on the desk, she rose to her feet. She had not gone up on deck to watch the ship leave port. Her mood was not that festive at the moment.

Walking from her office she entered the bay of the hospital, where seven beds were neatly aligned. Beyond the room were three isolation rooms, an operating room, a treatment room, and an x ray cubicle. She had spent the afternoon checking cabinets and shelves for supplies and had been surprised to find the facility so very well stocked with every imaginable supply. She had learned from personnel records that the nurse, Sara Lynn Brenner, called S.L. by her coworkers, was also a certified registered nurse-anesthetist. Johnny Manning, the black orderly, also doubled as x ray technician. And Hal Haywood, the curly red-haired orderly, served as lab technician. The ship had a pharmacy, and a pharmacist she had not yet met, also a dentist would be available on the world cruise which would begin in January. She turned back to her office, thinking January seemed a lifetime away.

Her thoughts were suddenly interrupted by a soft tapping on the glass entrance door. Looking around, her face lit up when she saw Mark Payton standing outside in his white dress uniform. Opening the door, she smiled. "Hello."

He stepped inside and reached out for her hands. "Ah-ha, I found you," he said lightly.

"Was I lost?" she returned in the same lightness, quickly retrieving her hands from his.

"Aren't you coming up to the captain's welcome-aboard party?" he asked.

"I hadn't planned to," she returned without hesitation.

"Well, Madam Doctor, I have arrived to change your plans." He grinned "The captain requests your presence"—he motioned upward with his head in tiny jerks—"upstairs."

She lifted her brows suspiciously. "Which captain?"

"Both. Captain of the ship, and also captain of the staff. It's an order, ship protocol and all that."

She paused for a moment and looked down at her clothes—a navy blue skirt and a white blouse covered with a lab jacket. "I don't think I'm dressed for a party," she argued.

His habitual grin appeared easily and with much confidence, he offered, "Then I'll escort you safely across the hall to your stateroom so you may treat that ill in record time." He grabbed her hand again. "Come on, I'll wait while you change."

Minutes later, as she slipped into a soft pink lace and silk dress and pulled on a matching lace dinner jacket, it occurred to her that Mark Payton had most likely just lied to her. She could not envision Captain Kurt Garisen requesting her presence at any function, unless it was strictly ship protocol.

"Are you sure you're telling me the truth, Mark?" she called out, sliding onto her vanity stool and reaching inside her jewelry case for a pair of earrings. Her deep brown eyes moved slowly across the mirror as she put on the earrings, pushing them up under her freshly brushed ash-blond hair which had been freed from the knot at the nape of her neck.

"Would I lie?" he shot back from the separate sitting room area of the deluxe cabin assigned the medical officer of the ship. Clearing his throat sharply, he asked, "Have you had dinner?"

"No," she called back, giving her reflection one last review. She didn't expect much of the evening ahead and she was quite certain her expectations would be realized. Slowly, she rose from the stool and removed her cigarettes from the lab jacket pocket and slid them into her small clutch purse.

The expression on Mark's face confirmed the effect she had hoped for while dressing. He rose quickly, his eyes flicking up at her, and said with a visible warmth in his expression, "That was some transformation."

"Thank you, Captain Payton," she returned with a brief smile. "I suppose I'm ready."

Walking from her suite to the elevator clutching his right arm, she felt a slight apprehension about what she would find upstairs in the *Princess*'s dining room, where the welcome-aboard festivities were taking place.

Inside the elevator she removed her hand from Mark's arm and allowed it to fall inconspicuously to her side. Mark chuckled genially, saying, "If you sail the seas long enough, you can encounter anything."

"Oh?"

"I would never have imagined that I would be escorting the ship's doctor, and loving every minute of it, I might add." His white teeth flashed at her. "As a matter of fact, I feel my health taking a sudden turn for the worse. I may need some personal attention."

Smiling across at him, she made no comment.

She would never have believed the number of people packed inside the super-sophisticated dining room. She knew the capacity of the luxurious room could not be more than five hundred at a time, but there seemed to be at least double that number of people crammed inside. The tables were filled, the dance floor crowded, and it took the two of them several minutes to work their way through the tables to the large round one situated very close to the raised orchestra platform.

Gripping her hand tightly, Mark scouted the path, weaving in and out among the tables, speaking and nodding to various persons, until they reached the edge of the dance floor. Taking her in his arms, he said softly, "We might as well dance the remainder of the way."

The smile on her lips froze as she felt herself being crushed in his arms. There were too many people crammed together for even the most innocent of dances not to become an intimate merging of bodies. She hadn't realized how tall he was until her eyes riveted on his chin as she tried to maintain a desired distance from him. She stood over five ten in heels, so he had to be well over six feet, maybe six three or six four. He was broad-shouldered and very personable.

His arms tightened around her waist and she breathed an audible sigh of relief that the orchestra elected that precise moment to conclude the song. Rather uncomfortable, she pulled away from him and said, "I suppose now is the ideal time to find the table."

His eyes focused on her face a moment, as if he were about to speak, but then changed his mind. Clutching her arm, he guided her to the large table, where the first person she saw was the captain of the ship, Kurt Garisen.

He was decked out in his finest white dress uniform, and his thick and previously unruly hair was neatly combed, with only a misplaced strand or two loose and touching his forehead. He was talking and all attention at the table was directed toward him. Erin could tell he was so damn sure of himself, with his compelling looks and smooth deep voice, that he expected no less than every eye to be fastened on him as though he were some kind of wonderful god come to life to mingle with the peasants.

A few heads turned to glance her way while she and Mark quietly seated themselves directly across the table from him. The heavy round table was arranged so that from where Erin sat she had the enviable view of the man of the hour. She could not look up without seeing his face, so she chose to keep her head down or turned to the side where Mark sat. She was dismayed to find Mark eyeing his superior with an almost childlike adoration in his light brown eyes.

Momentarily, the waiter appeared and Mark ordered the previously agreed upon before-dinner cocktails and requested a menu for her. She shook her head, stating softly that she had decided not to eat dinner after all.

"I thought you hadn't had dinner," he leaned over and said in a whisper.

"I haven't, but I just realized I'm not hungry."

"Oh, Well, if you change your mind, we'll order later."

She nodded agreeably. She didn't plan on being here later. One drink and she intended to excuse herself to her room for the remainder of the night. Tomorrow would be a busy day for her, a challenging day, and she planned to be both mentally and physically prepared to greet it.

Suddenly, her head turned and her eyes locked on the green eyes of a dark-haired woman. Approaching the table and taking her seat, Erin had failed to notice that the woman was seated to the left of Kurt Garisen. She had failed to notice that it was Rachel Lawrence, so different did the nurse look in evening clothes. She had her shoulder-length black hair styled in an array of curls and wore a shiny green evening gown set off by a single gold chain.

Quickly, Erin's eyes scanned the other guests at the table, not at all surprised to find that neither S.L. nor the two young men in her charge were included in the elite gathering. With tongue in cheek she picked up her glass by the stem and sipped slowly as she imagined the relationship that existed between her head nurse and the ship's captain. *Well, I'll be damned*, she thought. *They're lovers*. She brushed her fingers lightly across her lips as she watched Rachel exchange private glances with Kurt Garisen. This definitely was a complication she had not imagined encountering.

After they had been at the table long enough for some of the party to have a second drink served, the captain acknowledged her presence by pressing forward a bit and generously tossing the following remark to her, "Dr. Barton, we're happy you could find the time to join us." His brows arched upward and his lips curved in a charming smile.

"Please call me Barclay, Captain, since that happens to be my name," she replied coolly, but with a smile and a tilt of dark brows.

Quickly fighting back momentary embarrassment, Kurt Garisen looked abruptly to Mark and instructed him. "Would you make the doctor's introductions, Captain Payton. I seem ill-prepared to do so."

"Of course," Mark answered with a flush and leaned forward a bit more. "It is my pleasure to present Erin Barclay, ship's medical officer." He went around the table with the introductions, skipping only the captain and the nurse sitting beside him.

Erin acknowledged each name with a brief smile

and a cordial nod. There was no way she could remember the dozen names. After the introductions, several of the guests left for the dance floor and conversation grouped off among those remaining.

Mark turned to her and spoke. "I just realized something," he said. "You don't like the captain."

"I have no feelings either way, like or dislike," she interjected quickly, her tone lower than his. "He's the captain and I respect his position and responsibility."

He lifted her hand and began to play with her fingertips. "Of course, it's none of my business how you handle your affairs, but to embarrass him at his table is not the wisest approach."

"There is no excuse for his error, Mark. If he didn't know my name, he should have kept his mouth shut. I was not going to allow him to introduce me as Dr. Barton. It happens not to be my name."

Mark shrugged slightly and grimaced. As he started to speak, a clearing of the throat behind his chair halted his words. Both he and Erin looked around.

Kurt Garisen stared coldly down at her. "Doctor, would you honor me with this dance?" he said more as a command than a mere request.

Erin withdrew her hand from Mark's and cautiously rose to her feet. "Of course, Captain."

Seconds later, stepping onto the dance floor, he stiffly extended one arm to her waist and clutched her right hand in his. She was amazed that his hand swallowed hers in its entirety and put an unwelcome strained sensation in the base of her stomach.

Holding her more than an adequate distance from him, he glared into her eyes. "Doctor," he said quietly, almost threatening, "do you know what an albatross is?"

31

"Yes," she replied without hesitation. "A bad-luck bird."

"Don't become mine," he said, his voice as stiff as his arms.

Before she could offer a comment in return, someone behind her pushed against her back, shoving her against the shoulder of his resplendent uniform. Her chin and cheek brushed the fabric harshly, and when she was able to straighten again she saw the dark blotch of makeup left on the white coat.

He glared down at his shoulder. He looked at her, then again to his shoulder.

"I'm sorry," she offered, her eyes shifting curiously toward his determined features. "It was an accident."

He rolled blue eyes upward and immediately released her. "I would hope that makes us even, Doctor."

She smiled a noncommittal smile at him. "If you want to keep score, I suppose."

"Thank you. Now, if you would be so kind as to make my apologies at the table, I will rejoin you again when I am attired properly." Giving her a brief nod, he walked from the dance area as she stood watching him leave, shaking her head slowly. Then she grinned, an open, honest grin. That was his reward for comparing her to an albatross.

She looked at him until he vanished from sight, then returned to the table, where she informed Mark that she was ready to leave the festivities, and without waiting for him to join her she walked out of the ballroom. Instead of taking the elevator, she descended the one flight of stairs down to her deck.

To her surprise, when she rounded the corner she

saw Mark Payton coming down the hall toward her door, a bottle of wine under one arm and two glasses in his other hand. Wearing a solemn expression, she approached him slowly and began to firmly shake her head. "No nightcap, Mark."

"Ah, come on, Erin," he coaxed. "Let's have one more for the sea, that's all. One friendly drink between shipmates."

She deliberated a moment. "One," she replied, walking past him and sliding her key into the lock. "Just one," she repeated, opening the door and glancing back over her shoulder at him.

He followed her inside and sank down on the colorful sofa, looking up at her while removing the cork from the bottle. After the pop he poured. "Are you unpacked," he asked cheerfully.

Nodding, she slipped into the aqua easy chair across the table from him. Drawing her feet up under her, she reached for her glass.

"What happened on the dance floor?" he asked after taking a sip of wine.

"I got a smudge of makeup on the captain's jacket," she answered, lifting the glass to her lips.

Mark chuckled.

"I assure you he didn't see the humor in it."

His tanned face grew brighter. "Well, there's humor there. First, the name screwup, then you mess up his jacket." He laughed. "I have been waiting ten years to meet the woman who doesn't fall all over him, and I think I may be looking at her."

"I noticed one of my nurses has managed to earn herself quite a good chair at his table," Erin said matter-of-factly.

"Rachel?" He lifted his brows slightly. "That's nothing new. The captain and Rachel have been good friends for years, both on ship and on land. But," he went on, "it's obviously nothing serious. Just good friends."

Taking another drink, she lowered her glass to the table, holding the stem a moment, then releasing it and folding both hands in her lap. She felt her throat constrict slightly. "I would hope such a situation will not create a problem in the hospital."

"It won't. It never has."

Erin lapsed into a thoughtful silence. She didn't like it. The charge nurse being such a good friend to the ship's captain. She didn't like it at all. She wouldn't allow their friendship to interfere with her job or with the smooth operation of the hospital. Still, it could turn out to be a very sticky situation.

Lost in her thoughts of the dilemma, she did not see Mark's movements until she felt his hands lift hers from her lap. Without a word he pulled her up from the chair and into his arms. For an absurd moment she merely looked at him, then began to free herself by firmly grasping his arms, which held her tightly around the lower part of her back. "Mark . . ." Their eyes met.

Without any shyness, he said, "I find you to be delectable, beautiful, and desirable."

She felt his arms tighten as he bent his head to hers and kissed her. Her nails buried into the fabric of his uniform shoulders and she shook her head with a sudden vehemence, freeing her mouth from his. "No . . . no," she said, and immediately wrenched free of his embrace, backing quickly away from him. She folded both arms across her chest. "No, Mark," she said emphatically. "No."

34

"What is it, Erin?" His question was barely audible.

"I really don't know how to put this any other way," she began in a soft, but firm tone, "but I am not looking for involvement at this particular time in my life."

"Do you know what you're saying, Erin? Involvement is what makes the world go round," he argued, maintaining a lightness in his tone and a sparkle in his eyes.

"Or stops it dead on its axis," she concluded quickly.

He hesitated a moment before speaking again. "And is your world not turning, Erin?"

"At the present time, no," she said in reply. There came a long silence and she forced herself to look away from him. Uncomfortable with the conversation taking place, she felt the need to end it. She didn't want to deal with memories, not now. Now all she wanted was to lose herself to this new world, this new life. Giving a heavy sigh, she touched her neck and her fingers spread out above her breasts.

"Erin?" He said the single word, then started toward her again, studying her face intently. "Erin," he repeated.

At his first step, much to her amazement and his, the telephone rang sharply, the shrill cry piercing the tension-filled air of the room.

Quickly pulling herself back together, Erin reached for the receiver and brought it shakingly to her ear. "Dr. Barclay," she answered in little above a whisper.

"Doctor, this is S.L. We have a patient here vomiting her head off."

"I'll be right there." Dropping the phone loudly, she turned to Mark. "Duty calls," she said, not able to keep the relief from her voice.

35

Stepping inside the bedroom, she lifted her lab coat from the foot of the bed and slipped it on. Walking back into the sitting room, she glanced at Mark, who sat with his head slightly bent, eyeing the phone with dismay. "Mark, I want you to know that the phone didn't intrude on anything. If you and I are going to be involved, it will be as friends . . . from the neck upward." Surprisingly, her voice seemed brighter, even to her own ears.

He blew out a long breath, his brown eyes sparkling devilishly. "And what if I prefer to be enemies . . . from the neck down?" He grinned.

"Then we'll have to compromise, and both of us will most likely be sorely disappointed." She reached for the door and opened it.

He followed close behind her, breathing over her shoulder. "This is just the first night, Erin," he whispered. "Let's don't place heavy restrictions on such lovely possibilities."

Closing her door and locking it, she said softly, "Good night, Captain Payton."

"See you," he returned with a smile, and when she walked through the hospital doors, he went over to press for the elevator.

Swift steps carried her past the ward of beds and into the treatment room, where a young woman lay in the fetal position on the examining table, clutching her stomach. Erin spoke first to the nurse. "Good evening, Miss Brenner."

The nurse returned an awkward smile of greeting as she passed Erin the chart.

Erin cringed as she approached the patient, who lay semiconscious, her body jerking with dry heaves. Apparently the violently ill young woman had drunk her weight in evil spirits. Glancing at the name on the chart, Erin said, "Miss Woodson, I'm Dr. Barclay."

The young woman moaned, pulling her knees closer to her body.

"She came in here alone," S.L. volunteered.

"I'm sure we have a case of overindulgence, but to make certain let's do an abdominal check."

S.L. nodded, then spoke to the young woman in a firm voice. "You need to lie on your back so the doctor can check your stomach." She placed her hands on the woman's shoulders and assisted her in turning over into a supine position.

Placing the tips of the stethoscope in her ears, Erin moved the round apparatus at slow intervals across the woman's abdomen. Sighing, she cut her eyes up to S.L. and said, "Bowel sounds are very prominent." She listened to the woman's chest for lung expansion, then removed the stethoscope from her ears. Using the palmar surface of the fingers of her right hand, she began to palpate the upper quadrant of the abdominal region. Sliding the sheet back, she checked the lower abdomen for tenderness or rebound. Nothing was revealed by the examination. "Looks like a simple case of upset stomach."

"I thought so," S.L. agreed with a nod.

Erin walked to the head of the table and looked closely at the patient's face. For the first time since entering the treatment room, she realized how very young Miss Woodson was, not over twenty, or twenty-one at the most. "Are you traveling alone, Miss Woodson?" she inquired.

The girl shook her head one brief time. "No." She added nothing more to the single word.

"Are you with your family?"

Red-streaked eyes opened and peered up questioningly at the physician. "No." She inhaled. "I'm with a friend. He's gone up to the welcome-aboard party. Otherwise he'd be here with me."

"I see." Erin caught her nose across the bridge and rubbed downward. "Uh—you've had quite a bit to drink tonight, haven't you?"

"Only a few bourbon and Cokes and one or two margaritas. That's all."

Erin pursed her lips. "Well, as far as I can tell your discomfort at the moment is probably caused from drinking. We'll give you an injection for your nausea and by tomorrow you should be feeling somewhat better. For the next day or so I would suggest that you stick to liquids, mainly tea and soup." Erin turned to S.L. "Why don't you give her twenty-five milligrams of vistaril i.m., Miss Brenner, then in thirty minutes or so we'll have someone take her back to her cabin. I don't think she'll need overnight observation." She reached down and checked the turgor of the patient's skin and changed her mind. "I don't know, maybe she needs a bottle of fluid. She's pretty dehydrated. I suppose a thousand cc's of Ringer's to replace some of the lost electrolytes." She blew out a long breath. "Perhaps we should keep her here until morning." She rubbed her left eye thoughtfully. "After you give her the injection I'll help you move her out into the ward, then you can start the IV, or I can start it if you like. Her veins look somewhat elusive."

"I'll start it," S.L. said with confidence. "And I can get her to bed by myself. There's the chart, and there's coffee in the lounge if you want a cup."

Erin nodded, picked up the chart, and walked into the lounge, where she poured herself a cup of the freshly brewed coffee. Placing the cup on the table beside the chocolate-colored leather sofa, she sat down and opened the plastic chart. Suddenly, the thought struck her. God. This was the first chart she'd touched since the one she slung at her former partner's feet months ago in Baton Rouge.

She lit a cigarette and blew a mouthful of smoke toward the ceiling before placing the cigarette in the ashtray. She looked back at the chart, then turned her attention to the treatment room and watched the nurse assist the young patient from the examining table. She realized right at that moment that Sara Lynn Brenner would be an asset to her on this voyage.

Clutching her head, she was suddenly gripped by the most overwhelming fear. What did she know about ship personnel? What did she know about ships? What was she even doing here?

Giving her head a quick toss to rid herself of the bothersome questions, she removed a pen from her coat pocket and bit the top off, holding it between her teeth while she wrote the necessary entries on the chart. After a few minutes she closed the chart and placed it flat on the table before picking up the cup of coffee.

S.L. appeared in the doorway. "The IV's infusing at sixty drops per minute. She's already asleep." She shrugged. "Or passed out."

Erin looked up at her. "Good. Rest is the best remedy for what ails her."

The young nurse looked fresh and bright in the white pants uniform; she was not a beautiful girl, but certainly attractive. A thin girl with short brown hair and almost no curves to her petite figure, she was quite the opposite of the femme-fatale head nurse enjoying the party upstairs. S.L.'s face was completely devoid of makeup, but then, she had little need for it, with her flawless olive complexion and dark blue eyes which revealed no emotion.

"How did you happen to be here when Miss Woodson came in?" Erin questioned softly, motioning the nurse inside the lounge.

"I'm on call," S.L. replied. "That's how we work it. When the unit is empty, one of us is on call at all times to cover any admissions or emergencies. The radio officer paged me." She pointed to the Pagemaster on the coffee table. "I didn't know if you wanted to be disturbed for something as minor as this. We usually handle cases like this on our own, but you didn't say at the meeting, so I thought it best to call you."

"Am I responsible for these patients?"

S.L. looked blank. "Yes, of course."

"Then I certainly want to be called for each and every one."

"I thought you might. That's why I called."

Erin watched as the nurse poured herself a cup of coffee, then seated herself in the single chair in the lounge. "I suppose this is the usual type case," Erin commented softly.

"Sort of, but each case has its own uniqueness."

"What do you mean?" Erin asked, puzzled. "Didn't she merely have too much to drink?"

S.L.'s brows creased in a perplexing frown. "Well, I suppose so, but we get a lot of this when we're sailing. Sometimes it's too much celebrating, and then there is the seasickness. We get a lot of that from first-time passengers."

Erin's eyes rolled upward. "On a ship this size? Seasickness?" Her eyes searched the nurse's face. "I thought this was a traveling city sort of thing." Her training period had not emphasized seasickness. It had been discussed, but somehow she had gotten the idea that it was not a common occurrence on a ship this size. Thus far in the cruise she could hardly tell the ship had left port.

S.L. grinned. "Well, the brochures don't usually include the rolling or the rocking. Even this ship gets tossed around in bad weather or rough seas. That's when we really fill up, and make cabin calls at all hours of the day and night."

There was no talk for a few seconds as a thoughtful silence hung between the two women. S.L. studied her plastic foam coffee cup, which she held out in front of her at eye level. Then she looked past it and at Erin. "What are you doing here, Dr. Barclay?" she asked innocently, looking at Erin over the top of the white cup.

Erin's face became a mask that hid all her emotions. She smiled briefly before saying, "Oh, I suppose I needed the time away, a time—oh, I don't know." Then on impulse she returned the question. "What are you doing here?" Strangely, formality had vanished, had completely disappeared between them.

S.L. stared at Erin gravely, then answered with a dreamy softness. "I'm here because I love it. I love the ocean. I love traveling, seeing the world. I don't think I can ever see enough of it, or even see it all. This is my third year with the line."

"Three years? You look so young."

"I'll be twenty-five in August. This was my first job after finishing anesthesia school."

Puzzled, Erin stared at her. "Why did you go to the trouble of studying anesthesia if you didn't intend to work in an operating room?"

S.L. smiled shyly. "Probably for the same reason you became a surgeon and now find yourself to be a ship's doctor." Her eyes slipped away from Erin's. She raised the cup to her lips, turned it up, and quickly finished the coffee, then dropped the cup into the wastebasket. "I'll finish up here," she volunteered and stood, then walked over and reached for the chart. "I'll make the usual charges when she's discharged in the morning."

"Will you stay all night?" Erin inquired.

"Oh, yes. As long as a bed is occupied, one of the staff is required to be present in the unit. Do you want to see her before she's discharged in the morning?"

"Yes," Erin said, rising. "I'll come by early."

S.L. nodded, fingering the chart. "Good night, Dr. Barclay."

"Good night, S.L." Walking through the bay, she looked over at the pale, sedated figure on the bed, and shaking her head, left the unit.

Outside the door she met Captain Garisen as he stepped from the elevator. "I understand you have an admission, Doctor," he stated bluntly. "Anything serious?"

Their eyes met and held as Erin answered, "No, nothing serious. A young woman who had a little too much to drink."

Immediately, he sported an aggressive look of disapproval. "And you admitted her to the hospital?"

42

"Yes, I did."

"Well, Doctor, I might advise you now that if you choose to admit everyone who drinks a bit too much on this ship, you won't have enough beds to hold them all, particularly these first couple of days. You will be required to exercise exceptional judgment on admissions. Most illnesses can safely be returned to their cabins."

Erin stared at him, then snatched her eyes from his face. "Captain, I promise I won't tell you how to navigate your ship if you won't tell me how to practice medicine. Your sick list will be delivered to you promptly at seven."

She started to walk away from him in the direction of her cabin, expecting him to say something more or to call after her. She was surprised when he didn't, and maybe even a bit disappointed.

That night after she retired she thought of him, of the virile physique, the powerful structure of his body, the intense, handsome face. Then she grew dismayed with herself, wondering why she was thinking of him at all. With so much facing her in the second day of this new life she had chosen for herself, it seemed a total waste of time to be consciously thinking about a man she was sure would try to throw her overboard the first chance he had.

CHAPTER THREE

It was well past midnight when Captain Kurt Garisen excused himself from the festivities taking place in the dining room. A buffet had been served and he picked up a single boiled shrimp and placed it in his mouth as he left the still packed room. Still chewing, he climbed the inner steps of the companionway up to the bridge, the ship's command center, his thoughts on the woman who had said only a few biting words to him since coming aboard the *Royal Princess Star*. And those few words were not as pleasant as he might expect from one of his staff members. He had been quick to notice she was quite lovely to look at, a woman who appeared, in his shrewd opinion, to be in a perpetually agitated state within.

There was a mystery about her. The very fact that she now sailed on his ship intrigued him. She was not at all what he expected her to be and he wasn't sure whether that fact pleased or displeased him. Although he had seen attractive women by the thousands, there was nevertheless something about this woman, some undefinable quality that made her different from all others, and he couldn't keep himself from wondering about her.

Stepping onto the bridge, located above and forward of the passenger area of the ship, he glimpsed his staff captain, Mark Payton, embroiled in a heated argument with Samuel Tondi, the cruise director. Without wasting a moment of time, Kurt called out, "What's going on here?"

The tone of his voice immediately brought a veil of silence to the bridge. Mark Payton, his eyes still bright with anger, turned abruptly and said, "Nothing, sir."

Kurt Garisen pursed his lips thoughtfully, moving in slow footsteps toward the two men. "Then I would suggest you do your 'nothings' somewhere other than on the bridge of this ship." He paused before adding, "As a matter of fact, I would suggest that for the remainder of the voyage you postpone your 'nothings.' I am tired of the bickering between the two of you, and I will not tolerate it another single minute. Do I make myself clear, gentlemen?"

Both Mark Payton and Samuel Tondi gave a single nod of their heads in a simultaneous move.

"Good," Kurt went on softly. "Now, Mr. Tondi, you may be excused to your duties at hand, and Mr. Payton, I would like a word with you."

After Samuel Tondi left the bridge, Kurt's scowl softened somewhat as he looked disparagingly at the man standing opposite him. "Mark," he said with a sigh, "I want this to stop between you and Tondi. Now."

Mark blew out a long breath. "All right, Kurt."

Walking past him to the panel of instruments that greatly resembled the cockpit of a large jet, Kurt looked back. "What was it all about anyway? Or do the two of you need no excuse to argue?"

Mark shrugged slightly. "If you don't mind, Kurt, I'd rather not say."

Kurt's brows rose. "But I do mind, Mark. When key members of my staff are at each other's throats the first night out of port, it's time for me to mind. I'm aware, and have been for the past two years, of the fact that you and Tondi don't exactly like each other." Pausing to study Mark's bland expression for a brief moment, he continued. "But from what I could hear taking place tonight, I recognized the difference from your usual banter. I want to know what sparked it. What was it about?"

"Kurt, you don't really want to know," Mark half-moaned.

"Let me be the judge of that."

Solemn-faced, Mark moistened his lips. "Well," he inhaled deeply, then continued, "we were discussing Dr. Barclay."

"You were *what*?" Completely surprised at Mark's answer, he raised one hand and stroked the side of his head.

Mark threw out one hand. "Skipper, you know what a son of a bitch Tondi is about women in general. You've seen him in action. Well, he made an off-color remark about Erin."

Kurt's brows rose higher. "Erin?"

"Uh." Mark cleared his throat. "Dr. Barclay."

"What exactly did he say?" Kurt urged his junior officer on.

"He said he'd never had a *surgeon* and I told him it seemed highly unlikely he ever would if he was

46

setting his sights on—er—Dr. Barclay." Shrugging, he finished, "That's what sparked it all."

Kurt blinked with disbelief, looking directly into Mark Payton's eyes. "Are you telling me you two grown men, responsible members of my crew, were up here on this bridge arguing about a woman who's been aboard this vessel only a few hours?"

"Well, I just wanted him to know it was hopeless from the beginning. I know firsthand that she's not on board thinking this is *The Love Boat.*"

Without a word Kurt started in the direction of the door. Reaching the exit, he turned back to Mark, drawing in a deep breath before saying, "Firsthand knowledge usually comes from being there. Right? Have you made a move on her, Mark?" he chided under his breath.

Mark flushed a bright red.

Releasing a long sigh, Kurt walked away from Mark, again shaking his head slowly from side to side. He looked past what had just taken place on the bridge to the days ahead. Twisting his lips, he stepped in thoughtful silence to his cabin, recalling Rachel's description of the woman doctor. It was for damned sure the head nurse had not accurately described the medical officer of the *Royal Princess Star*. He had known that the moment he turned around and saw her standing on the bridge. With no embellishment she had been as attractive at first glance as any woman he had ever seen, but in the lace dress tonight, without exception she had been the most beautiful woman in the room. His crew was already arguing over her like a bunch of prowling tomcats, and he was pacing the hallway, his own mind possessed with thoughts of her.

47

Muttering under his breath, he admitted, "Probably all concerned would have been better off if Rachel's description had fit. If she had to be female, why couldn't she have been ugly?"

Erin spent the next morning in the hospital unit studying the additional records brought on board by the passengers. The lone patient had been discharged from the ward earlier, the sick list sent up to the captain by Hal Haywood at seven prompt.

Around noon S.L. knocked on the door, then stuck her head in and asked, "How are you making it?"

"Fine," Erin replied and smiled. "I feel as if I've hardly left land."

S.L. laughed. "Better hold off on any final conclusions. We're due to hit some rough seas this afternoon, I heard Mark Payton saying at breakfast."

Erin's eyes widened. "But it's so beautiful outside. Are you sure you heard him correctly?"

S.L. grinned and tilted her head. "When Mark Payton speaks, S.L. listens." She laughed, then said, "You want to go for lunch?"

Smiling, Erin declined with a shake of her head. "Thanks, but I'm not really hungry. I don't have my sea appetite as of yet."

S.L. lingered in the doorway a moment before saying, "I'm not trying to tell you what to do, but it's best to keep a full stomach. Did you have breakfast?"

"Only a cup of coffee. I'll get something when I finish reading over these last records."

Slowly the door closed and Erin again turned her eyes back to the newly acquired information. Almost immediately the door opened again, but this time without a knock of warning. She glanced up to see

Captain Garisen's tall body leaning forward in the doorway. She eyed him suspiciously an instant before saying, "Yes, Captain?"

Holding lightly to the doorframe with both hands, he said factually, "Thought I'd drop by and warn you we're in for some thunderstorm activity a little later on. Radar's picking up a line about forty or fifty miles east coming at us. We'll probably have a moderate amount of pitching and rolling, but it shouldn't last for any extended time." He grinned. "You might want to get out the Dramamine."

Eyeing him, she said professionally, "Thank you for the warning." She turned her gaze from him, not at all comfortable with the way he was looking at her—as if she were transparent, or naked. Nor did she particularly care for the zigzagged grin on his lips.

To her surprise, and without invitation, he fully entered her office, closing the door softly behind him. "I couldn't help but notice when I returned to the party last night you were gone. Was it because of your patient," he asked.

"That, along with the fact I was tired," she said, only half-glancing at him standing close to the back of her chair. She bit her lip, trying in vain to ignore his presence, and only half-succeeding. Drawing in a deep breath, she turned, then asked, "Is there something else, Captain?"

His eyes moved from her face to the desktop, then back again. "Oh, I was wondering," he said with a teasing smile, "what inspires a surgeon to become a medical officer on a cruise ship?"

"Just a surgeon, Captain, or a woman surgeon?"

He laughed, a twinkle appearing in the deepest,

bluest eyes she had ever seen. "Perhaps both. I don't know what would bring a surgeon to your present position. I'm sure you know there're not too many operations on a liner. Why did you become a surgeon in the first place if you're accepting this kind of assignment? Aren't you afraid you'll get rusty, or lose your skill?"

"If I should, I'll take a refresher course before I return to active practice ashore," she said, looking straight into his cool blue eyes. "I'm really not worried about my skill." She didn't indulge herself with the reasons behind her choice of career and she most assuredly wasn't about to indulge him.

He stared at her, at the dark brown eyes flecked with amber. "Why are you on my ship?" he asked almost inaudibly.

She smiled. "Because it was your ship that needed a medical officer." She forced her tone to remain light.

Tearing his eyes from her face, and without another word, he opened the door and exited.

After he had gone she turned back to her desk, realizing her body had warmed in his presence. Biting her lip, she held her breath a long minute before exhaling slowly, warning her subconscious to behave itself.

The thunderstorms came as predicted. By midafternoon the swell of the sea and the strong winds had put the huge liner in a noticeable pitch, rising and falling as it drove through the open water. A slightly uncomfortable feeling took root in the pit of Erin's stomach. By dusk thirty-six passengers had taken advantage of the clinic, and with each treatment her own discomfort grew.

A small outbreak of perspiration across her forehead brought a new determination to her struggling mind. *I'll think it away,* she told herself, and every few minutes she would excuse herself to her office, where she commenced deep-breathing exercises to fight back the rising nausea.

All four of the staff were hard at work without apparent difficulties of their own. Injections were being given to those passengers who were advanced to the body-wracking dry heaves.

As Erin emerged from her office following a deep breathing exercise Rachel Lawrence cut her a quick glance and grinned slowly as she said, "Why, Dr. Barclay, you're beginning to look a bit peaked yourself."

Erin didn't reply; she couldn't. Instead, she walked past the grinning nurse to where S.L. was busily giving a departing passenger brief instructions and stood holding on to the treatment table, waiting for the passenger to leave. After the woman had gone Erin leaned forward and whispered into S.L.'s ear, "I'll be in my room for a few minutes."

S.L. raised sympathetic eyes at her. "Do you need an injection?" she whispered back.

Erin smiled weakly. "Oh, no." Turning quickly, she exited the hospital and dashed to her stateroom, where she flung herself onto the bed facedown. She knew she was beyond the help of injections. She was so sick she just plain wanted to die. She had not considered spending eternity keeping Davy Jones company, but at that moment she didn't care. Burial in the drink suited her just fine.

51

The liner pitched through her choppy sea and Erin's condition regressed. Ten minutes inside her room and she could not even raise her head from the pillow. No doubt existed she was done for, and in less than twenty-four hours at sea. That fact should raise Captain Garisen's spirits.

Twenty minutes after she had left the ship's hospital, a soft knock sounded at her door. Erin tried to rise but couldn't.

"Dr. Barclay," came S.L.'s voice through the door, "are you all right?"

Thankful it wasn't the captain, Erin mumbled, "I'm growing my sea legs."

The latch clicked and S.L. slid quickly inside, looked at the lifeless blob on the bed, and said, "Oh, my Lord."

"My exact sentiments," Erin groaned, then added, "I'm dying."

"No, you're not," S.L. contradicted. "This happens to all of us at some time or other." She moved back toward the door and said, "I'll get you something. It'll help."

A few seconds later she returned with an IV pole, a bag of fluid, and a syringe. "This will give you some strength and settle your stomach," she said as she worked. Securing the IV pole to the bed with a band of wide tape, she talked as she proceeded smoothly with her treatment. "If anyone should ask, I'll cover for you. I'll say you're out making cabin calls. No one will be the wiser."

"And when I die, what will you tell them then?" Erin muttered.

S.L. smiled warmly. "That's one consolation; we've never lost a passenger to seasickness—or a doctor."

"Then I think fate is about to permit me to be first."

S.L. laughed. "It isn't funny, but at least you're keeping a sense of humor." She popped the needle into Erin's hip, then said, "Roll over and let me start the fluid."

Erin obeyed and seconds later was rigged up to a fast-flowing bag of D5W.

"I've added some vitamins and potassium to the dextrose," S.L. said, placing the last strip of tape over the infusion site. "Maybe tonight you can take some liquids by mouth."

"Oooh, don't mention it," Erin groaned, shaking her head against the pillow.

S.L. straightened. "Believe me, Dr. Barclay, it'll pass." She brushed her hands together. "Now I've got to get back to the hospital before we're both missed." Hurrying to the door, she looked back. "I'll check on you later."

Within minutes Erin drifted off into a rolling, sedated sleep.

Kurt Garisen entered the hospital unit, looked around, and inquired grimly, "How's it going in here?"

The beehive of activity within the unit had slowed along with the swells of the ocean and the dying down of the wind.

Rachel Lawrence smiled over at him. "The worst has passed."

S.L. and the two orderlies nodded in agreement.

Again his eyes scanned the unit, resting momentarily on the open door to Erin's office. "Where's the doctor?" he asked.

53

There was a moment of silence and S.L.'s eyes flew from the captain's face to Rachel's.

Rachel gave a noncommittal shrug. "Haven't seen her in the last couple of hours."

His eyes fastened on S.L. "Do you know where she is?"

Clearing her throat, S.L. declared, "I believe she went out to make a cabin call."

Apparently satisfied with S.L.'s answer, he turned to leave. Just as his hand reached out to touch the door, Rachel threw out tonelessly, "You might check *her* cabin. When she left here she wasn't exactly the picture of health herself."

When he left S.L. turned immediately to Rachel and asked quietly, "Why did you do that?"

Rachel replied flatly, unemotionally. "And just what will he find if he checks her cabin?"

"You know damned well what he'll find," she said, exasperated.

"So"—Rachel lifted one eyebrow—"let him find it, or should I say, her?"

S.L. rushed to the door and peered out in time to see Kurt turn down the hallway leading to Erin's cabin. Clutching the top of her head, she stood there slowly shaking it from side to side.

Kurt Garisen rapped lightly on her door, and when he heard the moan, a puzzled expression covered his face. He stood unmoving for more than a minute before he hesitantly pushed open the door and stuck only his head inside.

There were no sounds now as he looked at the pale, sleeping face, the tousled ash-blond strands falling loose on the pillow. Lying atop the bed, flat on her back, the contours of her body were outlined against the pastel bedspread, and he watched her chest rise and fall in even, sedated breathing.

For the longest time he stood there, his clenched jaw relaxing as one side of his mouth curled up in a near smile. Softly closing the door, he turned back in the direction of the hospital, muttering to himself, "You're not half-bad when you're unconscious, pretty doctor."

Straight-backed, he reentered the hospital unit and motioned S.L. over to the door with a crooked finger.

Hesitantly, she obeyed, and when she was out of earshot from the other members of the staff, he crossed his arms across his chest and whispered, eyeing her firmly, "The medical officer's IV is about empty."

"Yes, Captain," she breathed. "I'll see to it."

Eyeing her grimly, he again turned and left the unit, this time crossing over to the elevator. Pressing the Up button, a little smile began to play along his lips. Remembering how Erin Barclay had just looked, he couldn't deny there was something very special about the sight.

Clasping his hands behind him, he stepped into the elevator.

CHAPTER FOUR

Erin's eyes scanned the hospital bay, where curtains were drawn around the last two remaining patients from yesterday's storm. She had bounced back from her own ill health to the extent she could work without her knees buckling beneath her weight, but she was not one hundred percent cured. The experience had given her a new appreciation for the word *seasickness*.

Crossing the room toward her office, she suddenly remembered her grandfather's aversion to flying. Years ago during a summer vacation she had sat on the porch of his country home with him outside Atlanta and he would grumble at the planes. "If God meant man to fly, he would have given him wings instead of arms, and beaks instead of noses."

"But that would make us birds, too, Grandpa," she had said.

Glancing at Rachel Lawrence coming out from behind one curtain, Erin gave a stiff smile, turned, and hurried on into her office, where she closed the door. Her thoughts half-lingered in the past with her outspoken grandfather. If he had been on board the

Royal Princess Star yesterday, she imagined he would have said something appropriate, as, If God had meant for man to cross the oceans, he would have given him fins and a fondness for worms.

She sat down at her desk, a vague smile on her lips. After picking up the sick list her eyes widened at seeing her own name scrolled in large black flamboyant letters near the bottom of the second page. Staring at the entry, she frowned and muttered, "Thanks, Rachel." For an anxious moment she wondered how the great captain would react at seeing the medical officer's name on the list, then with a sigh signed the pages, folded them, and slid them into an envelope.

Rising from her chair, she picked up the envelope and walked back out into the ward. She stared over to Rachel. "Are you here alone, Miss Lawrence?" she asked coolly.

"Aye, sir," Rachel replied, widening her large eyes.

Erin stood patiently, fighting back the sudden flare of irritation. With aggressive coolness she finally said, "It isn't necessary to call me sir, Miss Lawrence." She moved quickly to the worktable beside Rachel and dropped the envelope, then said with a fleeting smile, "But you may deliver this to the captain if you don't mind. Then if you're so inclined you may use the word *sir* in its proper context."

"What about the patients—" Rachel began, only to find her words severed.

"I am perfectly capable of looking after the patients, Miss Lawrence," she replied tightly. "Now go, have your fun."

Nodding curtly, Rachel picked up the sick list and twisted from the unit.

Watching the doors swing shut behind the nurse, Erin touched one temple reflectively. She had never fully understood the resistance of some nurses to women doctors. But there had always been one on some unit of some floor for as far back as she could remember.

After checking the two patients she reentered her office and left the door open, which enabled her to roll back from her desk and peer out into the bay area. Her battle for acceptance had gone on for years. She had come from a medically oriented family, an only child of a beautiful psychiatrist and a talented surgeon. She had been exposed to the ills of mankind at the breakfast table and at the dinner table from the time she was a toddler until the day she left for college. Only her grandfather had balked at her announcement of becoming a doctor. That last summer he had been alive she spent a week with him before entering her freshman year at Tulane University. That week had been one of the most memorable of her life. Perhaps he had sensed that the time they shared would be their last together, for he had been so different. Previously, he had always been the marvelous comedian, the entertainer. But not that summer.

He had picked her up at the airport with an absolute seriousness on his face. "Your mother tells me your intentions are to enter medical school, Erin," he said solemnly as he left the Interstate and turned onto the narrow two-lane road to his home.

"Yes, Grandpa," she answered with a broad smile. "I've decided to become a surgeon." At least she had participated in the decision concerning her career, or so she thought at that time.

"Like your daddy, I suppose," he grumped.

"I only hope I'm half as good as Daddy," she answered with pride.

The subject was dropped and not picked up again until the next morning over a plate of his fluffy homemade biscuits. "Why a surgeon, Erin?" he asked abruptly, passing her the butter.

"There's just a challenge associated with being a surgeon that isn't present in other fields of medicine, Grandpa." She had decided to become a surgeon when every other choice she had discussed had been scratched by both parents. Their determination that she select a career in medicine had been awesome.

Watching her, he hesitated, seemingly in search of words. "Challenge? Erin, there's challenge in giving birth to a child, not in cutting another human being. There's challenge in loving and being loved, not in removing a diseased gallbladder. My dear girl, a career is not as important as happiness. A career will not warm your feet on a cold night or cradle you in its arms."

"But I'll be happy, Grandpa. Dad's happy. Mother's happy. And look at them; they've had careers all their lives." It had to be medicine. Didn't he understand?

Pushing back from the table, he touched a frayed spot on the tablecloth near his plate. "Ever since the day man realized he had arms he has reached for the stars. A little ambition is a good thing; it adds flavor to our lives. But too much ambition, Erin, is like too much salt, instead of flavoring, it becomes our poison. That's why men have thirsted to death in the middle of an ocean. Too much ambition, too much salt. The one common trait we share around the world is our discontent, our inability to be happy. But I want you to understand, Erin, we choose our unhappiness. No one else chooses it for us. Happiness is here within our grasp. Don't reach too high or stretch too far, or you'll miss it. I want you to always remember the stars were deliberately placed beyond our reach. Now, butter your biscuit."

He died that September without ever understanding her reasons for entering medicine. Or maybe he understood and she didn't.

She was still thinking about him when she felt eyes fastened upon her, a silent glare bringing her back to the present. She looked up in surprise at the handsome features of the tall, lean captain. He stood slouched against the doorframe with his hands deep inside the pockets of his white trousers. She had no idea how long he had been standing there watching her. Feeling a momentary unease, she flushed and said, " 'Morning."

He grinned. "Feeling better?" he inquired, then touched his top lip with the tip of his tongue.

"Yes, thank you," she replied, taking immediate offense at his sneaky grin. "I had a mild touch of virus, nothing serious," she added sharply.

He chuckled. "Yes. You and thirty-eight others. Same virus, the sea bug."

Her creamy skin turned a shade darker. Directly returning his gaze, she kept her face impassive. She had never laughed at another's illness and did not take kindly to him laughing at hers. But then, she suspected his sense of humor was a bit warped by the pressures of his inflated self-image.

When he pushed back from the doorway and disappeared from her line of vision, she thought he was gone, so she turned her head back to her desk. At that instant he was back, this time holding two cups of coffee. Handing her one, he said under his breath, "It's a beautiful day outside." He lowered himself into the chair beside her desk and smiled over to her.

She merely looked at him, blinking. For some reason she didn't expect a man of his great gifts to begin a conversation with a remark about the weather. A smug half-smile touched her mouth.

His eyes dwelled on her face, then strayed casually to her neck, her shoulders, before rising back to lock eyes with her. Then he took a sip of his coffee and looked to the floor. Without raising his eyes he began to speak deliberately. "You're very young to be a doctor, aren't you? Particularly a surgeon."

"I didn't cut any corners," she replied, "or any classes." She smiled.

"Were you a good surgeon?" he went on boldly, his eyes sliding to glimpse her expression.

One eyebrow rose. "I was competent."

"What does that mean?"

"Competent means—"

Lifting the cup of coffee, he interrupted, "I know what competent means, Doctor." His pale blue eyes twinkled directly at her, and realizing his line of questioning was leading nowhere, he suddenly grinned broadly. "Tell me, how did you do it?"

"Do what?"

"Cut on someone," he remarked calmly, still wearing the grin. "How did you make that first incision across human flesh?"

Momentarily taken aback, she was slow in smiling.

But as the curve in her lips widened, she answered, "With my eyes closed, of course."

He laughed. "Welcome back, Doctor. I see you're cured," he said, rising from his chair and peering down at her with the first hint of admiration shining in his perfect blue eyes.

Without another word he left, and when he was gone she sat looking at the empty doorway. Her lips parted with a sigh. Matching wits with that handsome man would certainly keep her on her toes. Then suddenly a look of concern flooded her face, and shaking her head, she rose and went out into the ward.

The golden noon sun warmed the terrace around the pool. A quick dip and Erin stepped out to claim one of the numerous deck chairs vacated by lunchgoers. She and S.L. had eaten the noon meal earlier with the chief purser. Following the light luncheon buffet at the pool, S.L. had returned to the ship's hospital for afternoon duty with the one remaining casualty from yesterday, and Erin had changed into her swimsuit and coverup to take advantage of the magnificent veil of sunrays.

She hardly noticed the few remaining sunbathers as she slowly stretched and relaxed to drink in the warmth through her pores. She turned her head to the sound of low voices and her eyes widened at seeing the youthful Miss Woodson in the company of an attractive elderly gentleman. Her eyes widened farther when she realized that same elderly man had been one of the first to enter the hospital yesterday afternoon at the onset of the storm, not to seek aid for himself, but for his elderly little wife. He had doted over her, pouring out concern and calling her "darling." And now here he was beside the pool with his hand resting comfortably above Miss Woodson's knee. *Why you old goat*, came the first fleeting thought across her mind. Then she turned her gaze away from the couple and closed her eyes behind fashionable sunglasses.

We're all fools, she sighed inwardly. *Young and old alike, we're all fools*. She folded her hands behind her head and took a deep breath to fight back one of the loneliest moments of her life. Suddenly, she found herself being smothered by an avalanche of memories. She lay very still, her eyes tightly closed, but staring clearly into the past. *It's all down the tube*, she thought forlornly. Marriage, career, both over. Gone.

In the beginning she had played by all the rules. Acceptance had been terribly important to her. Important enough to cast shadows on her values and to dance to the tune played by hospital bureaucracy. Then she had gained a gigantic career boost when she became the practicing associate of a big-time surgeon in the Louisiana capital city. With success brushing at her fingertips, she pulled out all the stops. She finally married golf professional Bill Roberts, the man she had loved for two years. Their union should have turned out to be the perfect marriage. They never saw each other. Erin had been thirty, Bill thirty-six. Before their marriage, the fact that she was a surgeon had not bothered him in the least. Then suddenly, before the honeymoon expenses had been paid, Bill began his one-man crusade against women in medicine. At first she smiled away his complaints.

"Erin, how come we never have dinner together?"

"Darling, can you imagine leaving a patient half-sewn-up on the table with the excuse, sorry, but I have to go make dinner now." The initial questions from his corner were smoothed with a kiss, but in coming months their home life became a deadly skirmish.

Suddenly, the two most important men in her life became the heavies; her husband, Bill, and her partner, Raymond Morrow. The partnerships that should have lasted a lifetime began to destroy her. She found herself being pulled in five directions. Bill left the tour to become the club pro and immediately put in his order for a baby—a son to be exact. That same summer Raymond decided to join a group of surgeons on a two-month hiatus in South Africa. She was supposed to get pregnant and operate twenty-four hours a day at the same time.

Somehow word leaked out that she was a sucker for those who were down-and-out and the office walls bulged with people without a dime to their names. She had on her hands Raymond's wealthy patients, her own penniless brood with every known ailment in medical manuals, a hostile, frustrated husband lying in an empty bed waiting to make her pregnant, and a partner living it up on the Gold Coast.

Finally, when Raymond returned the last part of August, she took a week off to regroup her priorities and reassess her ambitions. Her marriage had suffered terribly. As Bill had so eloquently put it; "Erin, any man married to you should be a eunuch."

She had countered with; "Bill, would you like a separation?"

He sneered before slamming out the door. "Hell,

a separation! That's all we've had! What I would like is a marriage!"

In her anguish, the situation on both fronts of course worsened. The fact that nothing was turning out as she had planned brought the most excruciating pain she had known. Her life had become a waking nightmare.

Her thoughts, chained to the past, suddenly broke and she shook her head and opened her eyes to see the sun overhead and hear the sound of strangers all around her. Three years of struggling with both Bill and Raymond, trying to save her marriage and partnership, had put her only one step ahead of a complete breakdown. She had realized her limit. Now, here alone in the midst of strangers, she could think about that last fateful night six months ago. Feeling the lines of her face tighten, she could see the dark stormy night in Baton Rouge.

It had been fifteen minutes before midnight when she, tense and tired from two hours in the operating room, fell in a slump onto the sofa in the doctor's lounge of the Chandler Medical Center and removed a wrinkled cigarette pack from her lab coat pocket. She ran her finger inside the pack and groaned when she found it empty. Balling the pack tightly in her hand, she threw it across the room at the wastebasket. She groaned again and closed her eyes, letting her head fall back against the sofa. Across her knees lay a plastic chart, and when it slid onto the floor, she did not open her eyes nor reach to retrieve it. Nor did she open them a few moments later when the door to the lounge opened and a voice from the doorway said somewhat breathlessly: "Sorry, Erin. I got here as fast as I could. My beeper was out. I told you we'd be at the cabin, and that's eighteen miles." The door closed behind the tall thin man and he stepped closer to the sofa. "Sorry, hon."

"Have you got a cigarette?" Still, her eyes remained closed.

"No, all I have are cigars."

She extended her opened palm. "Well, give me one of those."

He deliberated momentarily, then passed her one. Leaning against the wall, he stared at her while she removed the cellophane, placed the cigar in her mouth, and lit it, opening her eyes only when she started to strike the match.

She looked up at him sharply and drew in a mouthful of smoke. Slowly, she blew it out without inhaling. "You will never do this to me again, Raymond Morrow! This was the last time, *partner!*"

"Now, Erin." He began stiffening away from the wall. "You're tired. Don't say anything tonight you'll be sorry about tomorrow." His shoulders pulled back, he took a step toward the sofa. Distinguished, in his early forties, his hazel eyes pierced hers. "Don't say anything more. Just finish your post-op orders and go on home. Okay?"

· With a sudden swift kick of her foot, the chart glided across the floor and came to rest on top of one of his shiny leather shoes. "You finish the orders, *Doctor!* He is still your patient! You admitted him this afternoon! You finish the orders! I only saved his life, but he's your patient! I'm just good old Erin to the rescue! You thought enough of his life to leave him drowning in his own blood. But he's still yours, just like all the others!"

An angry expression marred the thin face of Raymond Morrow. He looked down at the chart, then across at her.

She stretched out her long legs, her ash-blond hair knotted atop her head with loose strands falling down along the sides of her face. The deep brown eyes were filled with molten fire aimed straight at him, the dark brows lifted high. She drew again on the cigar, not blinking.

"You look ridiculous smoking that thing."

"I am ridiculous," she said with a disgusted toss of her head. "Damned ridiculous. Three years of being ridiculous. But"—she paused dramatically—"I'm finished being ridiculous, and that's a fact. To be perfectly clear, I'm finished, period."

"What are you talking about?" he retorted angrily. "You're not starting that old I'm-doing-most-of-the-work argument again, are you? If you are, you'd better realize I'm getting pretty tired of hearing it myself. It seems you have a short memory, Erin. You didn't specialize in women's fields, remember? No, you had to cross into men's specialty—surgery. You could have been anything you chose—allergist, pediatrician, obstetrician, family practitioner, but no, you had to be a surgeon. And even then, not just any surgery, not ophthalmology, or ENT, or plastic, no indeed—general. You had to be able to dabble in a bit of it all. Well, remember me, I'm the one who got you on staff here at Chandler." He pointed to his chest with both hands. "I'm the one who stuck his neck out on a limb for you. I'm the one that took you into partnership, got you privileges at one of the best known hospitals in the south." Again he pointed to his chest. "Me. Raymond Morrow, your partner! Your income topped a hundred thousand last year.

You stepped into a gold mine, and this is gratitude!"
He swooped up the chart.

She took in another draw and held it a long time,
then let it out slowly. The strong smoke was beginning to make her nostrils sting and her throat tickle.
She pointed the thin cigar at him, blind to the ashes
breaking off and drifting down over her clothing.
"Just for our mutual understanding of the word
gratitude, what I stepped into was not a gold mine,
hon," she threw in sarcastically, "but rather a pile of
crap. And a hundred thousand dollars can't make
crap gold. Nor could a million. You're not a good
surgeon; you're not even a good doctor. I don't know
what you are, Raymond! You couldn't care less that
your patient lying out there in the recovery room
almost bled to death before we could get him open
and stop the hemorrhage. But then, why should you
worry? Good old Erin stepped in just in the nick of
time. Good old Erin laid him open and clamped the
bleeder. Good old stupid, ridiculous, dumb, ignorant,
used-up Erin." She stretched her long, sinuous neck
toward him. "Well, good old Erin is leaving! Good
old Erin has had it!"

Raymond Morrow looked down at the chart in his
hands. Two fingers of his right hand tapped against
the plastic. He swallowed hard, then said with a
tinge of a threat, "I don't believe you want to do
that, Doctor. Not if you plan to continue practicing
medicine in this part of the country."

"Raymond," she said mockingly, "don't threaten
me. Our contract expired three months ago. I'm free
to go wherever I want, whenever I want." Her eyes
narrowed. "But I've been waiting for just the right
moment—and that moment has arrived. I have an-

other position waiting for me. I'm packed. My patients have been transferred to other physicians, not to you." She rose slowly from the sofa and moved in the direction of the door. "Good-bye, Raymond."

He grabbed her arm. "You can't do this! I won't allow it!"

She wrenched free of his touch. Pushing the door open, she stepped into the surgery corridor and gave a quick glance back at him. "Just watch me." Then the door closed behind her and she was gone.

And on those three words three years of a tumultuous partnership ended. The medicine she loved wasn't beautiful. It wasn't wonderful. It wasn't fulfilling. It was a rat race, and if she stayed on she would become just another wealthy, first-class rat. A rodent like Raymond, her elusive partner. She'd rather die first.

The condominium she shared with Bill a half-mile from the medical center became the site of her second battle of the evening. They had signed a lease on the condo with an option to buy, and considering what she had just done and was about to do, she was relieved the lease expired at the end of the month.

A well-groomed lawn fronted the building, with shrubs and trees growing along the low brick wall that extended down the sides of the lawn to the edge of the sidewalk. She turned into the drive and drove to her section, the last in the complex.

A cool summer breeze brushed her face as she opened the door of her Mercedes. She slammed the door and looked up at the light in the bedroom window. "Oh, Bill," she thought half-aloud, "forgive me."

A moment later, as she stepped through the ornately carved wooden door, a voice from upstairs called down. "That you, Erin?"

"Yes." She slung her purse onto the table in the entrance hall and looked up the stairs. Then she went into the kitchen and began to make herself a pot of coffee. She was pouring the water into the Mister Coffee when the masculine voice sounded behind her.

"Hello, darling." Bill walked up and leaned over to kiss her cheek. "What are you doing?"

"What does it look like?" she returned sharply. She watched the first drops fall into the glass receptacle, then turned to face him. He was wearing only white boxer shorts, standing barefoot on the linoleum. She brushed past him and moved to the table where she pulled out a chair and sat down.

He walked to the chrome and glass table and pulled out a plush black leather chair, seated himself, and said, "What happened tonight?"

"Why do you ask?"

"Raymond called and said you had some kind of spell. Apparently he wants me to play a mediator of some type, to try to talk some sense into you." He shrugged. "What's it all about?"

"I'm tired of him. I just walked out, quit." She spoke in a quiet voice.

He rubbed one eye, then paused and looked at her thoughtfully. Finally, he said, "I see."

"I doubt that you do." She rose to her feet and walked again to the coffeepot. She removed one cup from the cabinet and filled it, then moved back to the table.

He shifted in his chair. "I wouldn't care for any, but thanks for asking."

She turned to him. "If you want coffee, you have two legs, get up and get it"

He surveyed her with a growing concern in his dark eyes as she sat quietly drinking the coffee, her eyes on the cup in her hands. He took a deep breath. "I think it's the right thing to do. Hell, I think it calls for a celebration."

Her eyes came up, wide on his face.

"You've finally come to your senses," Bill went on. "Now you can make a home and we can start a family. Don't you see, Erin, you should have done this a long time ago. Think of all the trouble it would have saved us."

She stared at him for a long time, and her brown eyes hardened. He was a stranger. He didn't have the foggiest idea of the pressures she had been facing. And he didn't care. Her resignation would make life easy for him. He'd always felt cheated by her career. She took in his pleased expression and shuddered a bit, a chill running over her entire body. Reaching up, she swept back a lock of hair that had fallen over her forehead. "I'm afraid you don't understand," she said in a whisper.

Bill leaned back in his chair and studied her, his glare unrelenting. "What is there to understand? Huh? You quit, and I'm glad. Now you can be my wife. That's something you've never been." Suddenly, he smiled. "We can make plans. In my opinion, it's the greatest thing that has happened to us."

She tilted her cup to her lips and continued to drink her coffee.

He reached out his hand and touched her arm. "Don't you see what you've done, darling? You've done what any sensible woman would do—think first of her husband and family. And if you're worried about repercussions from the fight at the hospital, I'll help smooth them out. I know Raymond Morrow, remember? I play golf with him and you get to know a man on the greens. He's not a bad sort of guy, just a bit immature, but basically he's okay. He'll understand your decision when he realizes our marriage was at stake, when I explain how your work was destroying us."

She greeted those words with silence.

He continued. "I think the best thing to do is take some time off. We could go up and catch the tour. Canada is nice this time of year. I'd like us to have a bit of time alone. And you could enjoy the company of the other wives when I'm on the course."

She shook her head. "Just don't say any more, Bill," she commanded softly. "Just shut up, please."

He looked at her, puzzled. "Erin, I said I understand." He inhaled a deep breath. "It's been hell on us, but it's over, and we survived." He gave an uneasy half-laugh. "To be honest, there was a time when I wouldn't have given a plug nickel for our marriage, but now I think it's going to be okay."

"I don't want to do this tonight, Bill," she said sharply. "But you're forcing me."

"Do what? You've already done what you needed to do."

"Not all I need to do. You see, I have no intentions of remaining here."

"Say that again."

"That's it, Bill. I'm leaving."

He stiffened. "Sounds like you're leaving more than the partnership. Are you leaving me, Erin."

She nodded. "Yes, Bill, I am."

He was on his feet. "Why!" He shook his head wildly. "Why would you leave me? I'm your husband. My God, I've put up with you when no other man would have!"

"It's very simple, I'm tired of you, too, maybe even more than of Raymond Morrow. Consider my leaving your bonus, Bill. You'll be free of me."

His face twisted as he stood beside her chair, his tanned face flushed and red with frustration. "Free of you? What are you talking about? We've been through a lot together."

Erin looked at him sadly. "No, Bill, we've been through a lot apart."

It had taken her six months to put her life in some kind of order. She had divorced Bill at the same time she had taken a long vacation from medicine. Those actions were the first sane moves she had made since leaving her surgical residency. This year on ship was strictly a time to reflect. To plan. The ill-fated partnership had left her with ambivalent feelings about her career; the ill-fated marriage had done the same for her feelings concerning men at this time in her life. A shipboard romance was one thing she could do without. She wasn't broadminded enough to take part in a meaningless affair or narrow-minded enough to think true love floated out there somewhere atop a wave.

A sudden movement at her side distracted her. She looked up to see the naked chest of Kurt Garisen, the dark hair laced with white glittering in the bright sunlight. She squinted.

His smile challenged her. "How's the sun?"

"Warm," she answered factually, if not pleasantly.

"Have you tested the water?"

"It's warm too," she answered, adjusting one side of her glasses, a tight half-smile finding her lips. If she had been an innocent virgin or a wanton divorcée, the sight of his muscular body so close would have immediately made her aware of an increase in her heartrate. But being the reflective surgeon she was at the moment, she merely allowed the half-smile to linger on her lips as she stared at him. He was the golden man with everything apparently in the right place. A real sea lion.

He dove into the water and swam several laps across the pool. Half-ashamed of her open curiosity, she sat up and watched him swim. Then without another word to her he was out of the water and gone.

She did not see him again until the next morning when he appeared in her office door, cup of coffee in hand. Looking at him in the stiff white uniform, she suddenly remembered how he looked at the pool in the less than modest trunks, displaying his almost perfect nakedness above and below the narrow band of fabric.

He made himself comfortable in a chair and she looked at him closely, at the same time wondering just what kind of game he was playing. He was too cordial, too friendly, completely out of character from the Billy Goat Gruff she had met on the bridge that first day. Whatever he was selling, she wasn't buying. And he'd probably realize that fact before they reached Southampton, England.

CHAPTER FIVE

A sunset in the mountains was one thing, but nothing could compare to the declining ball of fire slipping serenely below the tarnished gold at the ocean's horizon. Kurt Garisen had watched countless sunsets from the bridge of a ship only to find each new one more fascinating than any prior. Water and fire meeting in a crimson glow soon to be followed by the dark. He loved it.

Walking along the deck, his thick hair danced in the wind as he touched his lip thoughtfully with his index finger. Following a forty-eight-hour port call in Southampton, the *Royal Princess Star* had circled the British Isles and was now on the westerly course toward home.

He found himself to be in a strange mood as he walked along, watching the sun go down. Suddenly he turned and went down to his cabin, where he shaved and dressed for dinner. He picked up the list of guests who would be seated at his table, scanned the names, then, brushing the back of his hand across his forehead, sat down and dropped the single sheet of paper beside the lamp. He fought the powerful impulse to do what he had wanted to do since the first night of the voyage. He sat there staring into space, but visualizing the sedated Erin Barclay lying on her bed at the storm's end that first day out. No woman had ever looked so attractive to him. Without another thought he picked up the phone and rang the hospital.

Hal Haywood answered promptly. "Ship's hospital. Haywood speaking."

"Mr. Haywood, Captain Garisen. Is Dr. Barclay there?"

"Yes, sir, she is." Hal cleared his throat. "She's suturing a laceration on Mr. Hudson's hand."

Kurt's eyes rolled upward and at the same time he shook his head. "What's Mr. Hudson done now?"

"He cut his hand, sir, trimming steak. It's not much, Captain, a few stitches will close it."

Kurt could not understand why, but Chef's Assistant Clarence Hudson could not walk down a corridor without tripping on his own feet. Accident-prone. The man was accident-prone. Oversize, terribly shy, and gawky, the man could not scratch his head without poking his finger in his own eye. Everyone on ship tolerated his ineptness for the simple reason he could turn food into art. Kurt grimaced, wondering if Clarence would ever learn knives had a sharp side. But he would keep him on staff until he broke his own neck or cut off his own arm. Then the line would either bury him or retire him, whichever.

"Anything I can do for you, Captain Garisen?"

A slight hesitation, then a half-smile. "Yes, Hal, would you ask the doctor if she would join me for dinner tonight."

"Sure. Be right back." He was gone only moments before announcing, "She said yes, Captain."

"Good. Tell her I'll pick her up at eight o'clock." During the minutes that followed Kurt made several calls. First to Mark Payton with the request that the younger man entertain those dining at the captain's table tonight, then to the ship's galley with his selection of the meal to be sent to his room at nine o'clock. That would give them an hour to have a drink and relax before the meal arrived.

Rubbing his hands together, his lips stretched into a narrow line. He was nervous. He looked at his watch, then poured himself a drink. He wasn't sure he'd ever felt anything like this before. Telling himself he was being absurd and acting close kin to Clarence Hudson, he inhaled deeply and poured himself another drink. He didn't usually fortify himself with alcohol, but for some unknown reason he felt he needed it this particular night. Patience was not his best virtue. Especially when he was waiting for a woman who might just punch him in the nose when she realized where dinner was being served.

Time dominated Erin's movements. She rushed into her cabin and bathed quickly, then dressed in the one remaining gown she had not yet worn in the main dining room. Seating herself at the dressing table, she lit a cigarette and blew out one long mouthful of smoke before she placed the cigarette on the ashtray. With the thin smoke swirling close to her face, she applied her makeup. She had no idea why she was being honored tonight with a chair at the great table, but there surely had to be a reason for the invitation. She was curious and maybe even a bit

77

flattered. Quite frankly, she still did not have a cut and dried picture of the captain or his motives. His short excursions by the hospital told her nothing except that he liked coffee.

She touched the side of her hair with a sudden distracting thought. Why was he coming by for her? Usually his guests joined him at his glorious table. He didn't normally traipse around the ship gathering them up.

As she put the last touches of mascara to her lashes, it dawned on her that there was something strange about this particular invitation. Were the two of them about to make a grand entrance into the dining room and set all tongues on ship wagging with a magnificent sweep among the tables? She found that thought to be something less than intoxicating. But before she could dwell on it a gentle tap sounded at her door. Snuffing out the cigarette, she slipped from the stool, straightened the skirt of her elegant cream-colored silk dress, and moved to the door.

Standing straight, hands behind his back, legs slightly apart, Kurt stared directly into her face, his own expression somewhat apprehensive. "Good evening, Doctor," he said with only the barest hint of a smile.

"Good evening, Captain." She stared at him a moment, her smile turning to puzzlement.

He gave a bit of a start. "Are you ready?"

She looked at him, only half-believing he had asked such a question. This was the man born to command. This was the lady-killer, the nurse lover, the ship's knight on a jaded horse. And he couldn't even tell when a woman was dressed? So much for ship scuttlebutt. "Unless you want me to change, I'm dressed," she said softly, with more drama than usual.

He shook his head and laughed. "Now that the small talk is out of the way, shall we go?" He reached out and closed the door when she walked out, a grin lingering on his lips.

Then she smelled it. Booze. Hundred-proof breath. Perplexed, she drew back and stared at him. This explained the fondness for coffee at all hours of the morning.

Pulling himself up straighter, he said. "I thought you might enjoy a walk on deck before going into dinner. The night is lovely."

"That's fine," she answered calmly, thinking he could make use of the fresh air. He had an image to maintain. What would the other dinner guests think if old Neptune himself fell face-first into the baked Alaska?

As they reached the elevators, the hospital doors swung open and Rachel Lawrence emerged. She took a step, then stopped dead when she saw the two of them standing in front of the elevators.

Erin watched as Kurt Garisen blushed as beautifully as any woman. Shifting uneasily and clearing his throat, he nodded at Rachel, a thin little smile playing at his mouth.

Slowly and deliberately, Rachel eyed him into a state of fidgety agitation before she turned sharply and flounced back into the unit. Erin's glance dropped innocently to the floor, but from the corner of her eye she could see his long fingers yanking a path between his collar and his neck.

Once they were out on deck the dramatic captain of the ship returned and took charge. With a sure casualness in his step they walked side by side to the railing. "There's nothing quite as beautiful as a starlit night at sea," Kurt said softly, almost in a whisper.

Erin agreed without hesitation. "Yes, it is lovely." Something in his voice, the distant look in his eyes, made her tilt her head at him in wonderment. Her mind signaled her to be careful.

"Has this voyage lived up to your expectations, Erin?" he asked, a smile softening his features.

She glanced upward to the heavens, but said nothing. It was the first time he had called her by her first name and it sounded nice. "I think so," she finally answered his question. She didn't know how the conversation would fare if she admitted she had no real expectations about the cruise other than using the time to reflect on past errors and hopefully plan a future that would be free of the same.

They moved on a few feet before he asked, "Would you like a drink?"

She pondered a moment before, "Yes. Perhaps a glass of sherry."

"A glass of sherry it is." He smiled, then moved away from her.

While he was gone she leaned on the rail and again turned her gaze upward. A cool breeze swept her face and twisted her hair. A mingling of sounds reached her ears—the laughter of others out on deck enjoying the beautiful night, the low conversations filling the air, the swirl of water far below, the rhythmic hum of the engines smoothly plowing a path among the swells for the gigantic liner to pass. Standing there alone, she became filled with a sense of peace, of calmness. Her hand came up and touched her throat as she gazed at the millions of stars glittering brightly from a velvet black sky. She desperately wanted to be content, to be happy. She wanted to regain her great love for her profession, for life itself. And for the first time in months she felt she might have set the right course.

"Your drink," Kurt said from behind.

She turned and smiled. "Thank you," she replied softly, taking the glass from his hand and at the same time noticing that he was holding a glass of something on the rocks for himself. She quickly wondered how many that made. She liked him fine at the moment, but she didn't know how well she would like him drunk.

"Would you like to find a table?" he inquired in a polite voice.

"No, this is fine," she returned quickly, then took a step or two, Kurt following close to her side.

"Tell me," she said abruptly, turning her eyes to his profile, "aren't you being missed in the dining room?"

He chuckled. "I hope so. But I'm sure Mr. Payton is managing admirably in my absence."

Her eyes brightened. "You mean Mark is heading the table?"

Kurt nodded. "He does occasionally." He paused for a moment, then added, "Even the most wonderful thing can get boring if you do it night after night."

Her expression became a bit speculative at that statement, but she allowed it to slide, perhaps because at that moment it occurred to her that his invitation had not been to dine at his famous table with him and a dozen other guests. It had been a one-to-one invitation and here they were on deck, one-to-one. A bit surprised, she said, "Then we aren't dining with the others?"

"No." He smiled. "I thought we might share a meal in privacy. You don't mind, do you?"

She really couldn't answer, not until she knew exactly what his *privacy* meant. And that she soon discovered.

Looking at his watch, he said, "Our meal should be arriving about now." He offered her his arm.

She took her time before touching his sleeve. "Should be arriving? Where?" she asked at the same time her fingers touched the fabric of his jacket.

He gave her a craggy smile, but instead of supplying her with an answer he led the way straight up to his cabin. Looking at his door, she stepped back and said, "I don't believe this. These are your personal quarters." She wondered if he actually thought she was going inside with him.

"It's only dinner," he began. "You'll enjoy it, I promise."

Her lips twisted in a rueful little smile. "Well, Captain, I'd really rather not dine in your cabin. I don't operate in mine, and I don't think I'm going to start taking my meals in yours."

He lifted one hand, the one holding the empty glass. "As I said, Erin, it's only dinner. Have I given you any reason to distrust me or my motives?"

She paused for a moment. Perhaps she was being a tinge prudish. After all, it wasn't as if she couldn't take care of herself. She was more than capable of taking care of the both of them if the need arose. She went inside, thinking it wasn't the smartest thing she'd ever done, but it certainly couldn't be the dumbest either. Not in view of the mile-wide waste she'd left behind in her Louisiana wake. She didn't know how much trust she could place in him or his motives, but she knew exactly how much trust she could place in Erin Barclay. She was virtually a walking Fort Knox of emotions and her intentions were to remain exactly that way.

His deluxe stateroom was double the size of her own compact quarters and, as she expected, emphatically masculine. His inner sanctum no doubt. She looked around the room from the safe distance just inside the door before relaxing at seeing the table at the center, the trays and plates still covered. "Why, Captain, I do believe the food fairy has been here," she offered sweetly as he set about busily placing chairs and removing the silver covers.

With his most obvious charming smile he motioned her over to her appointed seat and remained standing close to her chair while her tall, lithesome figure moved gracefully into place. Then there was a deadly silence before he asked seductively, "Comfortable?" He leaned forward so that his breath could be felt at the top of her head.

She squirmed in her seat and said, "Yes. Thank you." She did not dare turn her head with him lingering over her. He purposely brushed so close to her back that she felt the material of his uniform against her flesh. *Sneaky devil*, she muttered to herself and at the same time turned a tranquil face to watch him take his seat.

Next he filled two crystal goblets with wine and placed one in her hand. With a boyish, vulnerable smile, he said innocently, "Shall we drink to beautiful nights at sea?" He raised his glass.

Her lips curled slightly. "Yes. And also to those

less than beautiful, but memorable in their own special way." She drank slowly and watched the look of puzzlement spread a wrinkle along his brow.

Light blue eyes stared at her intently before he gave his head a tiny shake and peered down at the fresh seafood delicately prepared and daintily presented on the silver serving dish. They ate in silence, then suddenly he lowered his fork onto his plate, raised his head, and looked directly at her. "Tell me, Erin," he said evenly, "what made you decide to become a doctor?"

She swallowed her last bite before answering. "Oh, I don't know if any one thing triggered my decision. I think it was a lifetime of environmental influences." She looked away. It had been more than mere influences. Parental pressure that last year of high school had been overwhelming.

His brows arched and he nodded a single time. "Then I assume your father must have been a doctor."

"Yes. And my mother." She had been unable to disappoint them, to dash their hopes. And so she hadn't. Now she had to put it back together again, as much for them as for herself.

He hesitated before concluding that short conversation with, "I see." Then he was on his feet clearing the table and pouring two cups of coffee, one of which he placed in front of her with the question, "Would you like anything in your coffee?"

"No," she said with a soft laugh. "After years of nearly living off the stuff I've discovered it's a shame to spoil good coffee with cream and sugar. And if it's not good, cream and sugar won't help it."

He smiled, reseating himself with his own cup of

plain black coffee, his eyes catching hers directly. "What made you discontent?"

Catching her off-guard with that question, she floundered. "Ah—who said I was discontent?" That was one of those questions better answered with a question. She had no desire to delve into her personal history with him.

"Something must have prompted the move from land to sea, your decision to leave your area of specialization, which I imagine you trained many years for."

She shrugged slightly, an almost imperceptible shift of her shoulders. "Oh, I don't know." Her words trailed off as she looked to his large window. "You have a lovely view from here," she said in an attempt to change the sensitive topic of conversation. He was getting to her, the handsome captain. He was too damned perceptive for her own good. But she had no intention of reviewing her past with Kurt Garisen. She was suddenly conscious of the quiet that had fallen between them, and her gaze swung back from the window to him.

He sat staring at her. "You're very beautiful," he finally said, his eyes shining, his expression intent.

She knew it was time to leave. "This has been very nice, Captain. . . ."

"Kurt," he interrupted softly. "Kurt, Erin. And you aren't going anywhere yet." Taking her hand, he leaned forward and looked at her. "This is a marvelous opportunity for us to get to know each other, and I would like to know you." He ran his fingers gently over the back of her hand. "We're going to be shipmates for the next year, and I see no reason for us to remain virtual strangers. Isn't that right?"

She withdrew her hand from his and placed it in her lap, clasping it with the other. She had to firmly remind herself that this was the same man who had treated her so shabbily the day she reported on ship. An elephant had nothing on her when it came to remembering. Still, he was correct in stating that they would indeed be shipmates for the next eleven and a half months, so it would only be smart to make the best of a questionable situation. A distracting quality about Kurt Garisen made her intensely aware of him, aware of him as a man and of herself as a woman. She shook her head. "I must go."

He moved to the edge of his chair, leaned forward, and put his hands on her bare shoulders. He peered at her inquisitively, his face softly shadowed. "I don't think so, not according to Ben Franklin. There are only two musts, and to go isn't one of them."

She smiled faintly, moving backward. The room was suddenly silent.

He smiled and turned his head to one side. Then his hands let go of her shoulders and he stood up. A moment later there was the soft sound of music floating through the air, and on the way back to where she sat he turned down the lighting so that only the outside deck lights glimmered inside.

Erin grew restive, aware of the quickening rhythm of her heart. Rising from the chair, her only thought was to leave. Now.

Slipping from his dinner jacket, he tossed it onto the sofa, saying in jest, "You don't mind if we spare my coat this time, do you?"

Turning to face him, she murmured, "I'm going to do you a favor and spare more than your coat."

"Are you refusing this dance? Are you going to

86

waste this beautiful music?" Even as he spoke he moved toward her, shaking his head.

"Kurt, I need to go." Some instinct alerted her to the fact the time to leave had long passed.

He placed his hands at her waist, and she did not draw back when he brought her into his arms. His embrace was strong and comforting as he began to dance smoothly with her. They had only moved a few steps when his lips brushed her cheek, her temple, and touched her hair. She trembled with a combination of sudden excitement and awareness. "Please, don't do that," she whispered, pulling her face back to look at him. She was upset now—upset by herself, by her own response. It went deeper than she cared to admit.

For a moment they stared at each other silently. Then he stepped forward and placed his mouth gently over her lips. She felt the warmth, the moistness, and immediately tried to disentangle herself from his overpowering arms, his crushing embrace. She was stunned and filled with disquiet.

Well aware of the creeping desire for him, she attempted to push it back. "Kurt, I—" The words died as he reached up to silence her, touching her mouth with his fingertips.

He studied her a moment and slowly shook his head. He moved his mouth over her face, to the hollow of her throat, wrapping her tightly in his arms. He moved his hands over her, to the soft flesh of her shoulders, down to the fullness of her breasts. Then his hands were back at her throat while his mouth covered hers with fragile kisses. Every line of his body pressed against hers, and he was on fire.

Her arms curved around his neck; she buried her

87

fingers into his thick hair. She no longer had any thoughts as they kissed faster and deeper, the tempos of heartbeats increasing until the music faded away completely. The pulse of their hearts became the same—thunderous and rapid.

Under half-closed lids she felt his experienced hands removing her clothes. She felt the slight trembles in his hands. Then he quickly shed his clothes. But she was totally unprepared for the sensation when he drew her close and naked bodies met in a firm embrace. She was a weightless flame and her fingers buried into the hard muscles of his shoulders.

Together they moved to his bedroom and he gently pressed her onto the bed. Leaning forward, he kissed her as her head touched the pillow. Once more she felt the strength of his arms and she returned his fiery kisses without reservation.

Hands, mouths, bodies, touched—exploring, struggling for a greater closeness, and at the same time fighting to control the overpowering emotions. His hands slid from hers to touch her, to delicately brush her flesh until she groaned in pleasure. His mouth moved over her breasts, his tongue bringing a raging passion to life.

She cried aloud, her body arching to meet his, and she gave way to the true delirious joy of merging desires. Their breathing was harsh and piercing as for the first time they shared the beauty and strength of the unimaginable moment. Their arms tightened around each other and they followed the beating of their hearts. Erin had given in to an elemental force of nature, something she had never done before. But she didn't care. At the moment she had no cares.

When they lay in quiet contentment, he wrapped

her tenderly in his arms. "I think I would like it if you dined with me more often."

"I'm sure you would," she said, smiling at him.

He laughed and started to say something more, but just as his lips parted the telephone rang. Grimacing, he released her and reached across and lifted the receiver to hear Rachel Lawrence inform him that a patient suffering chest pains had just signed into the hospital. "Is Dr. Barclay there by chance?" the nurse asked hastily.

Without a word he handed the phone to Erin. A moment later he sat up, naked and wide-eyed, and stared at her in disbelief.

She dressed in a flurry, then looked back over her shoulder and smiled. "Sorry. I'll see you later."

He did not have time to react before she dashed out the door. After she was gone he fell back against the pillow, feeling a huge depression rise up from the bottom of his stomach. He was damned near paralyzed by what had just happened. He couldn't believe it. She had leaped out of his bed as if nothing at all had transpired between them. Never had he known such a moment of terrible frustration. Why did he have the feeling that if the call had come a few minutes earlier while they were making love, her response would have been the same?

Getting out of bed, he slowly dressed, grunting a string of profanities under his breath. "Damn," he uttered, pulling on starched white workpants. He should have known a female surgeon would be about as romantically inclined as a tongue blade. Yanking on his shirt, he had to wonder about his own wisdom in luring her to his bed. It was obvious it hadn't turned out to be his finest hour.

His hand touched one button and halted in a frozen position. She was a doctor. She would have to leave when it was required of her. He couldn't believe this sort of thing would not happen again. He buttoned his shirt, wondering if he really wanted to become involved with her. Deeply involved. Tonight should have taught him something. His body still trembled from her closeness, but where was she? In the damn hospital, he thought angrily, and probably happy to be there.

Slamming out of his stateroom, he could not shake his thoughts of her. He was astonished by her quick reaction to the phone call. It was the first time he had ever made love to a woman who had leaped out of his bed as if it were on fire. Of course, if he happened to be the passenger suffering chest pains, he would be happy to have a physician so adaptable to change in mood. But he wasn't that passenger; he was the man left behind with his blood boiling. It was all very upsetting, very upsetting indeed. He had the feeling that getting to know her would be like chiseling a rock. And once he had chipped away the surface, what would he find? More rock. He'd probably never know her, never understand her. Shaking his head, he set off to find Mark Payton.

"Dinner went smoothly, Kurt," Mark announced confidently, then with a broad smile inquired, "How was your evening?"

Kurt stood with his hands behind his back on the bridge. He pursed his lips with some thought before answering. "Interesting."

"You did have dinner with—er—Dr. Barclay, didn't you?" A tentative smile appeared as he examined the captain's face.

Kurt cleared his throat and after a long moment finally nodded. "Yes, we had dinner."

Mark regarded him inquiringly. "Were you disappointed?"

Kurt glanced at his junior officer and shrugged. "The meal was fine."

Laughing, Mark said, "I wasn't talking about the meal, Kurt."

"I know," Kurt groaned softly. "But let's just get off the subject." He looked out over the water, frowning.

"Whatever you say," Mark said, then suggested with a sly grin, "Say, the buffet is being served. Want to go down and catch some shrimp?"

"Hell, no," Kurt sighed in dismay. "I seem to have lost my appetite."

A while later, after leaving the bridge, Kurt went by the weather room, then proceeded down to the hospital unit. With anxious eyes he pushed open the door and entered the bay area to see Rachel swing a quizzical look at him. "How's the patient?" he asked with a mouth so dry it surprised him he could even speak.

"Fine," Rachel answered factually.

Kurt looked at the empty beds, a question in his eyes. "Where is he?"

"In his room. It wasn't a heart attack or anything serious after all. Just a delayed allergic reaction to some local anesthetic the doctor used to suture his hand earlier."

Kurt's jaw fell and hung limp a long time before he managed to get out, "Are you telling me that Clar-

ence Hudson was the life-threatening emergency?
Clarence Hudson!"

"Right." She smiled. "The man came in here with
a pulse of a hundred and sixty and complaining of
chest pains. I figured the doctor needed to check
him out. She gave him an injection and sent him to
his cabin. She seemed happy that I called her. She
was humming under her breath all the time she was
checking Clarence, and that's a first for her." She
looked down, making notations on the chart she was
carrying. "I would say she didn't seem too annoyed
at being called away from her evening with you."

"I doubt she was all that unconcerned."

"Why, Kurt, I do believe you're upset," Rachel
chided, moving toward him. "What's the matter?"
She swept his cheek with one finger. Their eyes met
in a subtle staredown. "You did use all the right
lines, didn't you? It couldn't be that you're slipping
in your old age? That couldn't be it, could it?"

"That's enough, Rachel." He gazed at her a moment,
then turned and left the room.

Walking to the elevator, his face registered surprise and disappointment. *Humming under her breath*.
It had not bothered her in the least to be pulled from
his bed. He felt reduced to an object.

In the elevator entrance he stood and looked back
at the hospital unit. If she was humming under her
breath tonight, he'd damn sure try to give her something to sing aloud about tomorrow.

Erin felt unnaturally calm. Seated on her bed in
her nightgown, she relived the sensation of melting
into the warmth of his lean muscular body. Falling
back, she stretched out in her bed and smiled. It had

all been part of his great plan—the dinner, the music, the bed. She could still feel the way his hands moved over her, exploring her bare flesh until she welcomed his passionate lovemaking.

She closed her eyes and turned her face into the softness of the pillow. Kurt Garisen had a dangerous charm. She had not expected the night to turn out as it had. He was the masterful lover, full of experience and self-assurance. That thought brought an uneasy feeling to her. She had never aspired to be part of his harem.

Shifting fretfully, she fell into a sleep of near exhaustion.

CHAPTER SIX

Erin was very much astonished when Kurt didn't show his face in the hospital the next morning. She had the impression that once he developed a routine, nothing short of death would alter it. Her mind wandered back over the evening in his cabin. Was this how he treated a woman once lovemaking became a part of the relationship? Like an old shoe? Her mind flickered with a quick spark of anger. She had expected him to come by her office with his cup of coffee and his insignificant small talk just as he did each morning. Was he upset because she had received the call from the hospital?

Feeling a chill, she got up from her chair and stared blankly at the wall. She shook her head. Surely that wasn't it. It couldn't be. He was the ship's captain. He, above all others, knew what duty meant. No, that couldn't be it.

S.L. stuck her head inside the office and looked over to Erin. "I'm going down to the gift shop to replenish my paperback supply. Want me to pick you up anything?"

Erin's fingers slid into the hair at her nape. "Yes,

if you don't mind. I could use a big fat book to get lost in right now—maybe something with spies. Here, let me get you—oh, never mind, I'll just come with you." She glanced at her watch. Eleven o'clock. Obviously, Kurt Garisen was not dropping by this morning. It bothered her tremendously, but not enough to sit and wait for him.

On the way to the gift shop S.L. gave forth a dimpled smile. "Guess whom I had breakfast with this morning?"

"Miss Woodson's aged Romeo?" Erin replied, a teasing sound in her voice. She was not going to dwell on Kurt's strange absence this morning.

"Goodness no. I wouldn't be caught dead with that old octopus," she returned cheerfully, then paused before announcing, "Mark Payton."

"Oh, really," Erin commented. "That's nice. Mark is a terrific young man."

They walked on a few steps before S.L. inquired, "How did you dinner date go?"

"It was fantastic," Erin said woodenly. "We couldn't wait to see each other this morning."

"Then it didn't turn out so hot, huh?"

Erin shook her head, wondering to herself what had really happened. "I wouldn't say hot."

"That's too bad," S.L. sighed forlornly. "I was hoping the two of you would—uh—well, maybe find some common interests." She made a defeated clucking sound.

"We do have a common interest, S.L.," Erin went on jokingly. "He doesn't particularly care for me and I don't particularly care for him, and that's about as common as you can get." She forced herself to be light, but she didn't understand it at all.

"Then you won't be going out with him anymore, is that what you're saying?"

"Well, all I can say is would I be buying a spy novel if I believed my own life held any thrilling moments in the forecast?" She tried to keep the flat resentment from her voice.

"You disappoint me, Dr. Barclay," S.L. groaned.

"In that case, you may call me Erin. I like to be on a first-name basis with people I disappoint." Erin smiled at her. "Don't look so down and out. After all, it's my life."

"I know." S.L. endeavored to make the next point as tactfully as possible. "But you do know that Mark is somewhat fond of you."

Erin's lips twisted knowledgeably. "Is that what's worrying you? Come on, Mark is a very nice young man, very nice and very young. I have no interest in Mark other than being a friend. Okay?"

"It will be when he understands that," S.L. muttered. "But I don't think he does, not yet."

At midafternoon, stretched comfortably on a deck chair, Erin was caught up in the latest escapades of James Bond. She had been reading for an hour or so, completely oblivious to the movements around her, when a hand reached down and lifted the book from her. She looked up into the smiling face of Mark Payton.

"You know, Erin," he joked, "we have never had a cruise with so little illness."

"Word must have gotten out that I was on ship," Erin quipped with a spreading smile.

He knelt beside the chair. "I don't think that's it,"

he said. "If that were the case, I think the hospital would be full, especially with men "

Her eyes widened. Could it be that the junior captain had a better line than the captain himself? At the moment, looking into the desire-filled brown eyes, she concluded it was indeed possible.

"Now that the captain is out of the way," he continued smoothly, "how would you like to join me for dinner and dancing?" His eyes stalked her face.

She straightened. What did he mean *now that the captain is out of the way*? Had Captain "Ahab" Garisen met his Moby Dick? Had one tumble in bed done him in? Suddenly aware that Mark was waiting anxiously for her answer, she smiled bleakly. "I don't think so, Mark. I don't want to risk my reputation by doing in all the captains."

He smiled. "You won't do me in, Erin. I think we could have a wonderful time together. I'm much more resilient than the old guy. Try me, you'll see."

"Not tonight, Mark," she refused as tactfully as possible. "Maybe on a later cruise."

Disappointment plain on his face, he placed the book back into her hands. "All right," he said softly, "I'm not going to pressure you, but I'm not giving up either. At some point you and I will have our evening together."

After he had moved on, Erin sat holding the paperback in her lap. Mark's words, *Now that the captain is out of the way*, kept ringing in her ears. She knew that their evening had not concluded on the most pleasant of notes, but prior to that telephone call she had believed they shared some special moments together. Now she seriously pondered the time shared with him. What had she done to send him off the deep end? Failed to neglect a patient who had possibly suffered a coronary? She stirred and sighed a loud dismay. Damn it, she would just stop thinking about it.

With a deep frown on her face she went back to James Bond. She read only a few pages before it dawned on her that Bond was a despicable womanizer, just like most men. Rising from her chair, she stalked over to the rail and flung him into the ocean, muttering under her breath, "Now, get yourself out of that one, Double-O-Seven."

She went back to the hospital and was greeted by a long-faced S.L., a long-faced Rachel Lawrence, and a pair of sleeping orderlies. Shaking Hal's shoulder, she snapped, "If you're going to sleep, then go to your rooms, both you and Johnny. This is a hospital, not a hotel." She closed herself in her office and stayed there until she was feeling a little calmer, more controlled.

When she went back into the bay she found herself completely alone. She was just about to leave when the door swung open and who walked in but the elusive captain of the *Royal Princess Star*.

He looked at her coolly, hesitating a moment before saying, "I just dropped by to see if everything is smooth."

"As glass," she answered quickly and equally as coolly.

He touched one corner of his eye awkwardly. "Well, in that event, I'll be on my way."

"Captain?" She stopped him with a mockingly sweet voice. "Before you go, let me take this opportunity to thank you for last night. I want to apologize for my untimely departure." She took a step in his direction, her eyes widening. "I didn't get a chance to tell you the food was magnificently prepared and quite delicious, the music divine, and of course, your love-making was nothing short of fabulous. . . ." The amazement on his face stopped her words. She stood looking at him with mock admiration.

He simply stared at her as her gaze moved from his eyes down to his lips, then back to his eyes, which were wide on hers. "Thank you again for a lovely evening," she whispered, touching his lips with one finger.

He continued to stare at her.

She sighed, and with her lips slightly parted, gave him a spontaneous brush across his mouth. Just as she touched him the doors opened and in walked her complete staff. They all stood bunched in the doorway, glaring. Erin flushed and Kurt looked blankly over his shoulder at the newly arrived foursome.

Not to be intimidated, Erin said softly, "The captain had something in his eye." She looked back at him and smiled, saying, "There, I don't think it'll bother you anymore."

"Uh—well," he stammered, and backed up awkwardly. "I'll be on my way." He gave an embarrassed nod at the hospital staff and hurried from the unit.

One by one the unexpected intruders filed past Erin, who stood watching the door close. Rachel was the last, and when she passed Erin she said quietly, leaning toward Erin. "Didn't look like a speck to me, looked more like a mouth."

Erin cut a sharp glance at the nurse but made no reply. Instead, she reached into her pocket for her cigarettes, then went to her office and smoked half a dozen.

That night, by invitation, she dined at the captain's table. Throughout the evening he kept giving her quizzical but intent looks. The entertainment was thoroughly delightful and she tried to ignore his persistent glances by giving the group on stage the best part of her attention. But when he was on the dance floor with other women from the table, she riveted her full attention on him. He was certainly one of the most handsome men she had ever seen, if not the most handsome. His uniform stretched perfectly across his broad shoulders and back, emphasizing his exceptional physique. She watched with great attentiveness the litheness in his movements, the way he smiled into the eyes of whichever woman he held in his arms at the moment.

And while her thoughts swirled with him on the dance floor, his own thoughts rested back at the table with her. He didn't feel at ease thinking about her. She was such a mixture—a surgeon, a woman, independent, desirable. Now that they had shared a night of intimacy, he was more unsettled than ever concerning her.

He was slowly working his way around the table to her, and when her time came he held her firmly in his arms and whispered, a hint of teasing in his tone, "I have another speck in my eye."

She looked at him warmly and smiled. "Doctors aren't always known for their diagnostic ability on a moment's notice."

"Oh," he grinned, "I hadn't noticed. If not instant diagnostic ability, then you do seem to be a woman with a ready solution, an answer for everything."

"Do I really?" She laughed softly.

"Yes." He brought her slightly closer to him. "And I am wondering if you'll have an answer for this."

"For what?" she asked softly.

"I would like you to have a drink with me afterward, in my cabin."

A sudden veil of doubt clouded her eyes and she was reluctant to answer. "A drink?" she murmured with brows raised.

"A drink," he repeated with a single sure nod.

She smiled. "Yes, I think we could manage that."

As the song ended he took her hand and together they walked back to the table.

A few minutes past midnight they were in his cabin once more, sitting on the sofa and sipping drinks he had prepared. Relaxed and talkative, he was discussing the next voyage southward, down to St. Thomas and Bermuda, an eight-day cruise.

When he inquired if she had ever been to those places, she hesitated a moment before admitting, "Yes, I honeymooned there," she said faintly.

Shock filled his face and his head jerked back as if she had slapped him. "You're married?" he asked.

She gave a little shake of her head. "No, but I was."

"To a doctor?" he asked abruptly.

"No, to a professional golfer."

He looked deeply into her eyes, his own blue irises troubled. "I don't suppose that's something you want to talk about?" His wide gaze was full of questions.

"No," she said softly. "It's past, and talking about it won't help."

"Except sometimes," he offered slowly. "Sometimes

it helps." He looked at her thoughtfully. "Is that why you're here?"

That question again. She smiled to herself. He would never be content until she had laid out all her reasons for being on his ship. But she wasn't ready to do that. It was still too painful and they had thus far shared a pleasant evening. Why spoil it? "Tell me," she initiated a conversation completely different from the last one, "what brought you to the sea?"

Relaxing back against the sofa, his teeth grazed his bottom lip a moment before he said, following a deep breath, "It's what I always wanted to do. I suppose it was in my blood. My father was career navy. His ship went down near the close of the war. Until that happened we had lived in Chicago, but following his death my mother bought a home on the coast of Maine. I grew up with the ocean at my door. It seemed a natural path for me to follow."

"And you've been happy?"

"Oh, yes." He nodded. "I regret to say I don't feel I've missed anything life has to offer"—he raised his eyes to hers—"except maybe"—his hands slowly touched her arms and her fingers coiled into her flesh—"this." He paused. "I realized last night I'd missed this."

She felt the intense currents of his body through his fingertips, then the gentle touch of his lips. He was touching her mouth, breathing her breath, melting her lips. Partially opened lips pressed hers and she felt his trembling in her mouth. For a moment she was unable to think, unable to breathe. She desired him. He knew how to strike all her right notes. But it was happening too fast, much too fast.

She was aware that he was about to make love to her again.

He crushed her mouth fiercely and her arms went up around his neck, touching the back of his head, then his shoulders and back to his hair. There came a dim time when everything fell away from her except the scent of him, his mouth consuming hers, his arms pulling her violently close. He kissed her tenderly, then savagely, and there was nothing but his mouth, his warm moist sensual lips creating tiny vibrations inside her. Her breasts swelled inside her dress as if stroked by invisible hands. But second thoughts kept tearing at her, telling her not to let go.

Determined, silent, he forced her lips apart and his tongue squeezed against hers, bringing an overpowering heat inside her mouth, which made her pull away, gasping for air and wildly shaking her head. He grabbed for her, but she was already on her feet, racing to the door. He remained frozen on the sofa while she slammed out.

Biting the back of one hand, she went only a few feet before going limp against the wall, shaking her head. Her cheeks flushed, her heart thumping like a drum, she gasped for breath. She couldn't do it, not again. She couldn't repeat the same mistake with him. She wasn't ready for emotional involvement and she couldn't make love with him again and not be involved.

Hurrying to her cabin, she rushed inside and bolted the door. Falling across the bed, she felt like she might explode from the sudden overpowering frustration. Never in all her life had she ever felt such a sudden surge of desire. One touch and it was there.

Where had it come from? And more important, what would she do with it?

Burying her face in the pillow, she rubbed the top of her head with both hands. Last night should not have happened. But it had, and had even come close to happening a second time tonight. It had to end. She had to end it.

Back in his cabin, still on the sofa, Kurt stared blankly into the empty space before his eyes. What in hell was wrong with her? Last night she had had to leave, but why had she run out tonight? He felt lost. Erin Barclay wasn't the kind of woman a man could touch one time and then forget. She was the kind of woman who made a slave of a man. "I'll never run after you," he muttered.

He leaned his forehead on his thumb and forefinger and rubbed it. With every part of his body begging for her, he had allowed her to run away. He had not gone after her because there was a stronger part of him that didn't want to catch her. That same part of him didn't want to fall in love with her. That would spell disaster in capital letters. If he was smart, he would leave her alone now before a real disorder was created on ship that he couldn't manage and she couldn't treat. He'd been a bachelor too long to risk it all now. Lord, where was his mind racing to?

Slowly he stood up and unbuttoned his jacket. Realizing his heart was still pounding angrily at his ribs, he gave his head a shake, then looked down at his chest and grunted aloud, "Better to pound a little now than break a little later." He wasn't going by that damned hospital another time, not for any reason. And that could be entered in the logbook. If a situation looked like quicksand and felt like quicksand and you found yourself sinking, then you'd better believe it was quicksand. Erin Barclay was quicksand. He knew it for sure now.

After bandaging an ankle sprain the next morning, Erin moped inside the unit for an hour or so, feeling unsure as to whether or not Kurt would drop by, half-hoping he would and half-hoping he wouldn't. Of course, now that it was morning, her actions last night could be explained quite easily. She was protecting herself. She could deal with anything but another heartbreak at this stage of her life.

They were a day and a half from New York and she was looking forward to planting her feet on concrete. As big as the ship was, it seemed terribly small this morning.

Kurt didn't stop by, and she was both relieved and disappointed. She kept busy making plans for when she arrived back in port. She was going to visit some hospitals and gather up material to do research on during the coming months. This voyage had been her shakedown personally and she knew that in the coming months she would have ample time to work on various projects relating to her profession.

She was surprised when Rachel Lawrence swung into the unit with an unexpected announcement. "I have just turned in my resignation, Doctor," she said with more than a measure of hostility.

Erin looked up from where she knelt counting Ace bandages. "You did what?" She tilted her head.

"I have just handed my resignation to Captain Garisen."

Standing up, Erin was unable to mask her surprise. "Are you resigning because of me, Miss Lawrence?"

"Don't flatter yourself, Doctor," Rachel huffed. "I'm bored with this ship, that's all."

"Well, I'm sorry to hear that," Erin said with earnestness. "I had believed we could all work together here. I'm sorry to realize we can't."

"Oh, don't worry about it," Rachel threw out. "I'm sure you'll be sorry about a lot of things before your tenure is up, just as Kurt is already sorry."

Erin felt the color rise in her neck. "What?" She had never been good at early morning riddles and Rachel Lawrence was speaking in riddles.

"You have cost the dear master of this ship a cool one thousand dollars."

Stunned, Erin's features screwed up. "I have done what?" She was getting short on patience. "I don't understand what you're talking about."

Rachel's face jutted forward and she smiled before saying very softly, "I'm sure you don't. I'm sure you don't know about the bet Kurt waged with Nils Malaney."

"Are you planning to tell me about it?" Erin snapped. "If you are, do it, because I'm about to leave."

Rachel's easy smile widened. "It was just a little wager. Kurt bet Malaney a hundred dollars to a thousand that you wouldn't last a complete voyage. And when we dock you'd better believe Nils will be there at the disembarking with his hand extended."

Erin eyed the other woman speculatively. "It sounds a bit trumped up, if you know what I mean, Miss Lawrence."

"You think I'm lying. Well, just parade yourself up

106

to the bridge and ask the man who's got to shell out the thousand. I'm sure he'd be quick to tell you. No one hates to lose a bet worse than Kurt. And just for your information alone, the reason the bet was made in the first place is because you're a woman. Kurt did not think a woman doctor had the stamina needed for this job." Rachel's face became a questioning mask. "Now, do you think I'm lying?"

A long pause. Finally, Erin admitted, "No. If it allows you to leave happy, I don't think you're lying." The acid effect of this revelation was slowly eating through her. It was true. A man she had become intimate with had placed a bet on her as if she were a horse. It was true. Angrily, she appraised the situation as her brown eyes grew deadly dark.

A searing pain ripped through her and she cursed him silently. How could he have done this? What kind of man was he to play such cruel games with another's life? Even realizing the wager had not been against her as a person, to think he thought so little of her professional ability was equally as devastating. Whatever had allowed her to think for even a fraction of a second that Kurt Garisen was different from any other man? They were all alike. Soul brothers in fact.

Without another word to Rachel she went into the lounge and poured herself a cup of coffee, then went into her office and closed the door. Slowly, she moved to her desk and sat down. For about an hour she sat there, fighting back the desire to act on impulse. She had already been too impulsive with the good captain. Now she had been placed in a position where she felt compelled to leave, to quit. She had been a pawn in two men's game—again.

She clutched her head tightly with both hands. Yes, she would leave. Let them place their bets and play their games with the next unsuspecting person to fill this position.

She attempted to crawl from under the blanket of humiliation that covered her. Self-pity was a luxury she could not afford at the moment. She began to think about what she had to do.

Kurt Garisen walked the decks late and alone. The night was black, not a hint of a star or a glimmer of moonlight. His lean face sported a grim expression. For the last twenty-four hours Erin had avoided him as if he carried the plague. He was puzzled and a bit put out with her. There was such a thing as over-reacting, and that was exactly what she was doing.

He slumped against the railing, deep in thought about her drastic change in behavior toward him. That look in her eyes; he couldn't figure it out. In any other eyes her expression would be close to hate. But she couldn't hate him; he'd given her no reason. He had already concluded that they probably should not have any type of long-term affair, but that didn't mean they couldn't say hello or ask a friendly question. She had severed his head even with his shoulders when he'd stopped by earlier to check on a passenger who had developed problems with a bleeding ulcer. Now he was reluctant to go back into the unit when she was there. He had been back a few minutes ago to have S.L. inform him that the bleeding was under control and the man was resting comfortably. When he had casually inquired as to the doctor's whereabouts, even S.L. had leveled perilous eyes at him with the cool explanation, "Doctors must have nourishment, too, Captain."

And he hadn't even made love to S.L. As best he could tell his entire hospital staff was staging some kind of silent mutiny against him, even down to the two orderlies.

He was a bit relieved when Rachel sought him out on deck. "Well, Rachel," he said kindly, "this is your final night aboard the *Royal Princess*. You sure you're making the right decision? You know this is the top ship of the line."

Rachel walked slowly and purposefully over to the railing. Then she stopped and turned to look back at him. "We've had some good times, Kurt."

He nodded. "Yes, we have," he admitted nostalgically. "We've made a lot of good voyages together, had a lot of good times. I'll miss you."

She eyed him gingerly. "We still have tonight. Care for one last fling?"

He looked thoughtfully at her smiling face. "Oh, I suppose we shouldn't push our luck. Let's just leave it where it is."

"You know what I think has happened?" she said, her dark eyes twinkling. "I think you've fallen for that haint of a doctor downstairs."

He smiled. "Whatever she is, Rachel, a haint, she ain't. She's a very lovely woman."

"But not the woman for you," Rachel maintained.

"What makes you so sure?" he countered. It was one thing to tell himself that, but he didn't particularly care for someone else telling him, not even Rachel.

"She's not your type." Rachel smiled knowingly and winked.

He inhaled a slow, deep breath. "You're probably right," he admitted quietly.

Rachel's smile faded. "Does it bother you, Kurt?"

He gazed down into her inquisitive face. "Nah. I just can't understand the change in her. She looks at me as if I'm some low-life criminal." He shrugged, then narrowed his eyes keenly. "You don't know what's wrong with her, do you?"

"Heavens, no," she replied quickly. "I've never understood her."

"It seems S.L. knows, so I thought maybe you did." He shrugged. "Never mind."

She looked uneasy. "Well, listen, Kurt, I've still got packing to do. Take care of yourself."

He half-smiled and nodded. "You too."

His mind drifted for most of the night. And when the *Royal Princess Star* sailed into New York Harbor in the overcast gray of the following day, he was satisfied that he had done nothing to incur the wrath presently being leveled at him by the ship's doctor. In the restaurant at breakfast that morning she had given him a fixed stare, a look that brutally murdered the smile on his lips.

So she looked upset; it wasn't his fault. He hadn't done a damned thing to her, at least nothing she hadn't wanted done. Strange, he had not figured her to be one of those you-ravaged-me-when-I-was-defenseless types. But apparently she was exactly that. And it was for damned sure she'd have a long wait before he "ravaged" her again.

Watching the passengers disembark, he managed a somewhat bleak smile of farewell. He even smiled when he paid Nils the thousand dollars.

Checking into the hotel that night, the smile remained pasted to his lips. Then when he closed the door to his room he walked over to the mirror and looked at his reflection and frowned—a genuine ugly, grotesque twist of the face. Then he groaned and raked his hands through his thick dark hair.

The morning after docking in New York Harbor, Erin made an appointment to see Nils Malaney. She arrived at his office early and was ushered right in by Julia Conrad.

Nils greeted her with a generous smile. "Dr. Barclay, good to see you."

Erin stared at him unsmilingly. "Mr. Malaney, I'm afraid I don't have good news."

Motioning her to be seated, he asked, "What are you talking about, Dr. Barclay?"

"I would like to be relieved from our agreement." She looked him in the eye and added softly, "As soon as possible."

"Why? What's happened?"

Her head high, she replied, "The captain and I simply do not get along and I don't believe our situation will improve in time."

He studied her face. "What you're asking is impossible, Doctor. At least at this time. I have no one to replace you."

"How long will it take to find someone?" she asked.

Nils gave a little shrug. "To be honest, I don't know." He cleared his throat. "Might I inquire into the nature of your problems with the captain. Perhaps it would be easier to resolve those than to find a replacement."

She hesitated, then said, "I'd rather not discuss it."

111

"I see." Again he studied her. "Very well, Doctor, I'll see what I can do. However"—he paused and gave her a vague smile—"I must ask that you abide by our agreement until a replacement is found. The ship cannot leave port without a medical officer aboard. I'm sure you understand our position."

She nodded one time. "Yes, I understand. I will continue with my duties until you find someone." She rose from the chair.

"It could be a few weeks, maybe longer," Nils said factually. "But when we have someone we'll contact you and possibly have you relieved at some port. We'll just have to see."

"Thank you, Mr. Malaney."

He nodded, and when the door closed behind her he reached for the phone.

Nils went to see Kurt at the hotel. Entering the room, he said curtly, "Morning, Captain."

Kurt stepped back and looked at the much shorter man. "What's up, Nils?"

"As if you don't know," he grunted.

"Excuse me," Kurt replied sharply, "but I don't know. You didn't say much on the phone to clue me in."

Nils looked around the room. "Then I'll make it brief." His eyes came back to Kurt. "Your doctor is a little unhappy, and I want you to keep your distance from her."

Kurt glared at him a moment, then said loudly, "You came here to tell me that!"

"That's right. I want you to back off." Nils gestured vaguely. "I know you tried to win your bet, but that's over, and whatever you've been doing, I want it to stop."

"I didn't notice any complaints yesterday when you took the thousand dollars," Kurt argued hotly.

"No thanks to you, I'm sure, Kurt."

"I don't know what she's told you, but I haven't done a damned thing to her!"

Nils's brows shot up. "Whether or not you have, I'm just suggesting that you put a distance between yourself and her."

"No problem there. It's as good as done," Kurt affirmed solemnly.

"Good," Nils said, then started back toward the door. "I'm on my way to lunch, would you care to join me?"

"No, thanks," Kurt answered in a scornful snort.

His reaction to Nils's visit did not properly register until after the director left. This had been the last thing he expected to encounter—ever. A woman who kissed and told. And not just anyone, but the damned director of the line. Well, he would sure as hell put a distance between himself and the good doctor.

CHAPTER SEVEN

Four days later the ship was readied to depart on the southward cruise. Erin reported to the hospital unit along with the three remaining members of her staff. She had been informed that Rachel Lawrence was not being replaced and would not be until the first of the year and the commencing of the round-the-world voyage. Her first encounter with Kurt Garisen was in the corridor, after she had seen her staff. He merely gave her an empty look, then walked on by. His greeting suited her fine.

Unperturbed, she went into her office, where she began to unpack various materials she had gathered while on shore. She intended to make good use of her time on this cruise until her replacement was found.

S.L. stuck her head in the door and smiled broadly. "Have you seen the passengers, Erin?" The grin widened and she winked. "Boy, have we got some winners this trip. Eligible, handsome men by the dozens."

Erin looked momentarily puzzled. "Really?" she asked, looking up from a stack of medical journals she was sorting through. "Just men? No beautiful, available women?"

She laughed. "Yeah, those, too, but the cruise to the islands always brings aboard a new kind of clientele—romance seekers. These are fun cruises, not like the one we just completed to England or the round-the-world trip. As you saw, passengers who take the longer, more expensive trips are usually over-the-hill, retired, you know. But on these shorter cruises they're young and they're fun. Need I say more?"

"Well, what about Mr. Payton? I thought he had a hammerlock on your heart?" Her twinkling brown eyes looked directly into S.L.'s deep blue ones.

S.L. feigned a look of total disgust. "I marked Mark off. I've decided when a man becomes a captain he automatically gets his fool stripes. In his own way Mark's as big a fool as Captain Kurt Garisen. And that's *big*."

"What's the young captain been doing, betting on you?" Erin laughed and joked.

S.L. grimaced. "Nothing quite so dramatic. He's just ignorant, that's all. You know, when we were on shore he called and asked me to go to the theater with him, and like an idiot I went. Some evening it turned out to be. All I heard was Erin this and Erin that. Really, he has it bad. He asked *me* if I thought *he* stood a chance with *you*. That's why he asked me out. It made me sick," S.L. concluded in a pout.

Erin smiled bleakly. "I assume you gave him the appropriate answer."

S.L.'s face became a haughty mask. "Indeed." She smiled shrewdly. "I told him his chance was one in a

115

million. But to take heart, those were better odds than the captain's."

Both women laughed. Then Erin looked at her watch. One hour till sailing. "S.L., would you send Hal or Johnny over to the purser's to see if he has our supplies."

"Sure thing," S.L. agreed, then paused a thoughtful moment. "But I think I'll go. One never knows what poor lost thing one will encounter in the corridors." The door closed and she was gone.

Erin went back to sorting her journals. She had willed herself not to think of anything but the task at hand and was being completely successful until soft taps sounded at her door. "Come in," she called, expecting to get a report on the supplies from S.L. Instead, the door swung open and Kurt walked in. Looking up, her expression became tense and her eyes turned to ice. "Yes, Captain?" she said.

He stood for a moment, peering at her, an unfathomable expression in his eyes. "I suppose the ship's hospital is shipshape," he said coolly.

How clever, she thought, then smiled sweetly and said, "Indeed it is, sir."

An acute silence followed in the next moments. Then he began, "Erin—"

"Unless it pertains to the operation of this facility, whatever you're about to say, Captain, I have no desire to hear."

He looked at her so oddly and for so long she feared for a moment that her blouse must be unbuttoned. Then, without another word, he slammed out. When the hinges stopped rattling she looked down at her hands resting on the journal. They were trembling. Rage, no doubt. Just the sight of him brought the best of her tempestuous nature to the surface.

She sank back in the chair, wondering how she would ever manage until she was officially relieved of her duty on the ship. Kurt made her weak with anger and it didn't take the physician in her to know that that was an unhealthy symptom.

The first night out she sent an excuse that she would be unable to dine with the remainder of the elite staff at the captain's table. That stirred his wrath. He called the unit and when Johnny handed her the phone, he demanded, "Doctor, I assume you have a valid excuse for your refusal to participate in presenting a unified front to the passengers tonight?"

An unified front. He made it sound as if the staff were at war with the passengers. "Well," she began her excuse, "I did grab a bite earlier."

"And if that's your only excuse," he added, "it won't do. I expect you to be at my table in fifteen minutes, along with the ship's engineer, the ship's purser, the ship's captain of the staff—and others. Do you understand me, Ship's Doctor?"

"Yes, I believe you've made yourself clear, Captain." The drop of the phone from his end almost perforated her eardrum.

Quite undisturbed by his tantrum, she walked boldly from the unit to her cabin, where she changed quickly into her white uniform with the three gold stripes and the caduceus on each shoulder. It was the first time she had worn the uniform, since it had to be specially tailored, and the first voyage had been completed before the home office sent it to the port office for her to pick up. All uniforms had a natural defeminizing effect, but this one fit very nicely.

It allowed ample room for her breasts and the tailored skirt followed her natural lines like a snug glove.

With five minutes to spare she left her cabin and walked up the companionway to the main deck and into the formal dining room, where she walked straight to her command-performance table. Much to her chagrin, an empty chair sat at Kurt's left, the seat vacated by Rachel Lawrence. But there was also a place between Mark Payton and Samuel Tondi. It was to that location she directed her steps.

No sooner had she started to seat herself when Kurt said softly, "Up here, Doctor," and nodded to Rachel's old chair with a slight movement of his head.

With a tight expression on her face she moved around the table. As soon as she was seated where he had directed her, he leaned toward her and whispered, "Nice uniform."

Before she could properly ignore him, Mark called out, "Erin, you look like a swan in that white. It's definitely your color. My compliments to your tailor." He shrugged and grinned. "Or seamstress."

She gave a fleeting smile in Mark's direction and immediately begun scanning the room in an attempt to completely isolate her mind from the manly presence she sensed rather than saw just to the right of her.

Champagne was poured and when the captain proposed a toast to a good voyage, she was tempted to empty her glass into his immaculate lap, but instead she raised her glass along with the others, then sipped while her brown eyes busily moved from table to table. She could see what S.L. meant. There were certainly a lot of attractive people in the room.

118

When Kurt took the floor to make his welcome-aboard speech Erin continued to survey the room rather than focus her attention on the captain. And then she saw him. A most handsome man with rich brown hair and large black eyes and a tan that would make any woman envious. He was dazzling. And when he caught her stare they started to do a little eye-to-eye combat across the room.

No sooner had Kurt reseated himself when he realized what was going on between the ship's doctor and the grinning young passenger. His face flushed a deep red as he observed first Erin, then the man. "Doctor," he whispered harshly, "if you're bored at my table, please feel free to find yourself another place to sit."

Erin's eyes glinted mischievously into the fiery blue ones. "Oh, no, Captain, yours is definitely the best table in the house. The view from here is excellent."

With his jaw clenched Kurt leveled a hostile glare at the playful young man across the room and immediately the game ceased as the tanned face took on a sudden look of interest for one of the young women seated at his table.

That same evening, the first night from port, Erin had the first true emergency of her tenure thus far with the *Royal Princess Star*. Two young men had begun a brawl in the disco lounge and before the stewards could break up the fight, one of the men had lifted a champagne bottle and crashed it across the other's skull. Not only had the blow resulted in a concussion, but the lacerations were severe, reaching the skull in several places.

The entire hospital staff was called from their cabins and were up the remainder of the night. Clad in surgical green, Erin worked over the unconscious young man while S.L. remained at his side monitoring vital signs.

Suddenly S.L.'s eyes fluttered up at Erin. "He's in trouble, Dr. Barclay. His pulse is slowing and so are his respirations. Down to fifty-four and ten, and dropping."

"Oh, damn," Erin muttered behind the mask. "Hal, get the captain."

In less than a minute Kurt rushed into the treatment room. "How is he?"

"We've got to have help," Erin stated factually. "He has definitely suffered a concussion. I also fear the formation of a subdural hematoma; the intracranial pressure is building. We've got to get him to a hospital and a neurosurgeon." She cut her eyes anxiously at Kurt. "And as soon as possible, Captain."

The next instant Kurt was gone. Thirty minutes later a helicopter from the Coast Guard lowered onto the upper pool deck, which had been quickly stripped of furnishings and transformed into a landing pad. Two medics with stretchers rushed into the hospital unit and in less than ten minutes the injured young man was en route inland, along with his assailant, who had suffered a fractured mandible and nose.

The hospital staff stood and watched the helicopter lift away. An uncertain frown rested on Erin's face as she followed the aircraft until it disappeared from view. "Why in the world would something like this happen?" She shook her head slowly from side to side, talking as much to herself as to the others who stood around her.

"They get to jiving and to drinking," Johnny said

in a subdued tone. "And some can't handle it. We've treated cuts before, but nothing like this, not since I've been on this ship." He stood, like the others, shaking his head slowly from side to side.

"Do you think he'll live, Doctor?" Hal asked.

"Of course he will," S.L. answered quickly. "A week from now he'll be good as new, except for maybe a little headache and a bald head."

Erin looked at the optimistic nurse. "Did you send the hair I shaved away from the lacerations I sutured?" she asked, her face heavy with concern. It was the first time in her career she had ever shaved a portion of a patient's head. She had watched the neurosurgeons do it when she rotated through neurology and it always gave her a strange sensation, the care that was taken of the hair. She hoped and prayed that the young man who had just left her care would not have use of it, that he would live to grow himself more hair—that he would live.

Suddenly, her eyes flooded and she darted away from the others and hurried back to the elevators. Reentering the hospital unit, she gazed into the treatment room, at the tray of instruments, at the disarray. For the first time it dawned on her that this was the disadvantage of practicing medicine on a ship. To be faced with a condition, a trauma, that required the advanced technology of land-based facilities.

Clutching her head, she tried to remember if she had done all the right things. She proceeded mentally down a checklist. If she had made a mistake, it would be in waiting to call for help. But then, there was no way to know beforehand the extent of the injury.

"Erin," a voice called from behind her.

121

She spun around and stared at Kurt. Quickly, she wiped at her eyes.

"I thought you might want to know the helicopter radioed back to say John Rainey roused up enough to give his name and address.

"Was that his name?"

Kurt looked at her strangely. "Yes. And it looks like he's going to be all right." He shrugged. "Of course, we won't know for sure for several days."

"It was a terrible thing to happen," she said in a near whisper. "A terrible thing."

"It won't happen again," he countered strongly. "Not on my ship, it won't." Suddenly, he offered in flat tones, "You look pretty beat, Doctor. Could I buy you a cup of coffee?"

She didn't have the strength to argue. She didn't have the strength for any kind of comeback at all. Still in her scrubsuit, she followed him up to the radio room, where they sat with the radio officer and drank coffee until the sun came up. After the last report from the Coast Guard, a positive prognosis, she excused herself and went down to her cabin where she bathed, changed into a nightgown, and went to bed. Her last thoughts before drifting off to sleep were that the captain could be a thoughtful man when he put his mind to it.

Even with the deep anger she still felt at him, he was so desirable, but strictly on the physical plane. His arms offered supreme satisfaction. But that wasn't enough. She turned over in bed and sighed. Or was it?

After the unfortunate beginning, the southbound cruise proved to be a delight. In San Juan Erin bought her first memento with the thought that in each port from now until her replacement came aboard, she would buy a little souvenir to remind her of each place she visited.

From San Juan the ship moved on to St. Thomas, the thirty-square-mile island rich in pirate history. She developed closer ties with her staff and while one stayed on ship the other three would tour the famous landmarks. When they reached Bermuda it was her turn to pull duty and she stayed on ship in spite of the arguments presented that the doctor was not expected to stay behind.

She had already noted that Kurt rarely left the ship and was not surprised when she bumped into him on the pool deck where he stood dripping after coming out of the water. He picked up his towel and rubbed his face vigorously before calling to her, "Nothing here interest you?"

Not sure of his meaning, she asked, "What?"

He gave a shake of his wet head toward the island. "Bermuda. Doesn't it interest you?"

"Since we'll be here three nights, there's no rush to see it," she admitted pleasantly.

"I know a pretty good restaurant on shore," he offered, meeting her eyes. "Maybe we could go to dinner tonight."

There was a long silence before she said softly, "I think we have a good arrangement now, Kurt." She smiled. "Why don't we just leave it at that."

He pulled the towel around his neck. "You're the doctor," he said matter-of-factly. With a hint of a shrug he moved away from her.

* * *

That night he sat in his cabin nursing a Scotch on the rocks and watching the lights on land from his window. There was some activity on ship, but not much. Most of the passengers and crew had become landlubbers since docking in Bermuda. He wondered if Erin was on ship or if she had taken off with her hospital groupies.

His face expressionless, he stretched his long legs and sighed aloud. Nils Malaney's command was becoming increasingly difficult. He was keeping his distance to be sure, but not because he wanted to keep it. The first day or so she had been cold and indifferent to him, and it had been easy. Her feelings about him were impossible to decipher. But for him merely looking at her made him aware of the intense sensations that coursed through him.

Leave her alone, he warned himself. But his flesh hungered for her, perhaps because she had been placed off-limits. He didn't know. All he knew was that it was beginning to wear on him now, and he didn't know what to do about it. But he was going to do something. He just didn't know what or when, or even where. But when the time arrived he would know. He finished off the Scotch and went to bed.

The summer passed with several more southern cruises, two more tours to England, and a northern jaunt to Quebec, Nova Scotia, and Bar Harbor, Maine. It was on the northern cruise that he found her shivering on deck one night around midnight. Leaning against the railing, she had pulled a Windbreaker up around her ears and was looking out at the dark water swirling below. "Having trouble sleeping?" he asked, walking up to her, rubbing his arms in response to the brisk sea wind

"No. I just love the wind, and the sea, and the smell of salt," she said pleasantly.

"You're just at the right place to get all that."

"I know." She looked out at the night. "The time is passing so fast. All the staff is talking about the round-the-world cruise, and it's not far off." Nils had still not hired a replacement for her. The last inquiry had been met with "I'm trying, Doctor." But it had been weeks, and she wondered if he was.

"It's a great time to be on a ship," Kurt stated. "It's different."

"How is that, Kurt?"

"Oh, I don't know, a combination of things. Although a lot of people come aboard in the ninety days, it seems that everyone gets to know everyone else. We have additional staff to come aboard. It's a lot more work." He grinned. "For everyone, including the hospital. On these shorter trips you don't get your hypochondriacs and chronic complainers. But wait until we set sail in January. All the land doctors send their crocks to sea."

Erin smiled, pursing her lips thoughtfully. "I don't believe that. I was a land doctor and I never sent a patient to sea." Her smile slowly evaporated. Did a part of her heart still exist back in that clinic in Baton Rouge? Glancing up at the stars, a troubled look settled on her face. Had she been fair to her patients, those people who had come to count on her, to depend on her skills? She had left them. Would she ever go back? Could she ever go back? So many questions, as many as there were stars. And so few answers. And after these months at sea she still didn't have the ones she needed. She looked around at Kurt a bit helplessly, a look of confusion on her face.

"What is it?" he inquired softly, calm unwavering eyes fixed on her face.

She merely looked at him, then after a while shook her head and breathed, "Nothing." Then without knowing how it happened or why it happened, she found herself entwining her fingers with his, hands locking together. "Kurt," she faltered, "I—I don't want—"

He brought her toward him and before she could say more he had wrapped her in his arms to tight and securely, she no longer had the desire to say another word or make another sound. She felt his lips trail across her forehead—those soft warm lips. His arms were powerful, and for several moments he held her locked in his strength.

Then his hand touched the back of her head, his fingers curled into the thick ash-blond hair, then relaxed and caressed up, then down to her neck inside the collar of her jacket. "Erin," he murmured. "Erin."

She jerked away abruptly at the sound of his voice, pushing away from him. He held out one hand to her and she looked at it as though it were a dagger— dangerous and deadly. He took a step toward her. "I want you so much, Erin." There, he had said it without meaning to, without thinking. He wanted her and he didn't care if everyone on deck heard him.

Apparently everyone did, including Mark Payton who walked up and interrupted with, "Captain

126

Garisen, sorry, sir, but there are some problems in the engine room."

Erin looked around at Mark, then past him at several passengers whose curiosity hadn't allowed them to pass the show taking place on deck. Then she stared at Kurt, her eyes wide and no less troubled than before. She felt like a fool, an utter fool. One word and she had melted in his arms.

As she hurried to her cabin she shivered, from the cold she wanted to believe, but she couldn't quite sell herself that piece of goods. Hadn't enough bad things happened to her thus far in her life? Did she really think she could remedy them if she allowed herself to fall for a man such as Kurt Garisen? And that was just about what was happening. She was falling for him and she had to stop it before she made shambles on top of shambles.

During the days that followed she made certain she stayed away from him, or if she was found to be in his company so was someone else.

During a transatlantic crossing in October they hit a nasty storm, the first truly severe weather since that first voyage. The hospital filled to capacity and Erin and Johnny found themselves making cabin calls throughout the night while Hal and S.L. tended those in the unit. For some reason the wild churning of the water assaulting the ship had no effect on Erin this time. It pitched, it rolled, but she kept her balance and so did her stomach. But this time the storm did not last a few hours; it kept the *Royal Princess Star* in a mess for the best part of two days. The bouillon cubes were brought out and the fancy menus delayed. There was little activity on board except by the hospital staff and other ship's personnel.

Late the second afternoon Mark Payton entered the unit and looked around with open disbelief. "Jeez," his voice echoed over to S.L., "this looks like a Red Cross warship. How does the casualty list read thus far, Nurse Brenner?"

Tired and worn, S.L. said smartly, "We've treated only two hundred and four in the last forty-eight hours, Captain Payton. Our congratulations to you and the captain for keeping us on such a smooth course."

"We're only trying to see if everyone's on their toes," he joked, grinning at her weary face. "However, if anyone in here is interested, the sun has just broken through a heavy barricade of clouds and is now shining brightly on this ship." He chuckled. "Clear weather ahead." Suddenly, he stopped and scanned the unit. "Where is Dr. Barclay?"

"Behind you, Mr. Payton," Erin answered, having just entered the unit from a call.

He flipped about, still grinning. "I was just telling your staff—"

"I heard you," she answered calmly. "But neither I nor my staff are inclined to give you or Captain Garisen credit for the sun shining."

He craned his neck toward her. "Well, you aren't blaming us, are you? I mean, after all, we didn't make the storm."

"We have to blame someone," she quipped. Holding a small black bag in her hand, she passed by him, winking at S.L. before entering her office.

"Damn," Mark grunted. "It seems work doesn't agree with any of you." With those words he made a quick turnabout and walked briskly from the unit.

When he made his report to the captain, he tem-

128

pered it some by saying, "I'm glad the storm is over. The hospital staff is really beat."

"That's what they get paid for, and very nicely I might add," Kurt snapped, raking one hand through his hair. "A little work won't hurt them every now and then. A cruise is supposed to be pleasant for the passengers, not necessarily for the crew."

Mark left his company and moved out onto the deck, watching the glow of the sun grow brighter. He expected the clearing of weather to improve dispositions, not to worsen them. He had never seen S.L. in a grouchy mood. Never. What was happening on this ship?

CHAPTER EIGHT

As a surprise Christmas present Erin's mother and father booked passage on the ship for the Christmas–New Year's cruise south. Erin had no idea they were on board until she was seated at the captain's table for the welcome-aboard festivities. She hadn't thought she would still be on the ship at Christmas and it seemed that her agreement would be fulfilled before Nils found her replacement.

Sipping champagne, she watched as Kurt moved from the table to make his usual speech. He had looked awfully smug the entire afternoon, and she had begun to wonder if he had himself something special stowed away in his stateroom. Having now heard the same welcoming more than a dozen times, she did not pay particular attention to his words, nor even to him, incredibly handsome as he was in his deep blue winter uniform. Theirs had become a somewhat relaxed friendship. She had lost most of her anger about the wager. She hadn't forgotten it, but time had lessened the impact and she didn't think about it much anymore. Once again she and the captain had fallen into the routine of talking of passengers or voyages or other things, but rarely did the conversations relate to anything personal.

The line had presented John Rainey with a free cruise and he and his fiancée were on board. He had come by the hospital to personally thank Erin and the staff for what he called "saving his life." Erin had been pleased to see that his hair was once again rich and full, completely covering the scars that would remain with him for the rest of his life.

John was only one of the repeat passengers. Also on board were the strange trio from the first voyage: Miss Woodson, the elderly Romeo, and his wife. There had been a lot of laughter in the hospital unit when Miss Woodson stuck her head inside and waved with a "Hi, y'all."

"Was that who I think it was?" Hal had said when the door closed.

S.L. and Johnny were bent over double and Erin stood gawking in wide-eyed amazement. She had only shaken her head in reply. She had to give it to the old guy. He not only had lots of money, but even more fortitude to travel with wife and mistress at the same time. What made it unique was the wife and the girlfriend always seemed to get sick, but the aged man remained remarkably healthy. Erin told herself that if he should ever require treatment, it would merely be to pull the sheet up over his happy, smiling face.

While Kurt spoke, her eyes wandered out over the crowd in search of familiar faces. She skimmed a table with only a handsome couple, went on to the next table, then suddenly jerked her eyes back to the couple just as Kurt was saying, "And a special welcome to Doctors Michael and Elise Barclay."

The reunion of parents and daughter went on well into the first night at sea. Ecstatic, Erin cried, "Why didn't you tell me! I really should be mad at both of you."

"We weren't sure we were both going to be able to make it, dear," Elise said. "This is our first real vacation in five years." She smiled and widened her eyes. "Regardless of what the brochures say, this is definitely not like being on land. But I suppose it's nice."

"You should have the feel of it by tomorrow or the day after, Mother. Just wait until you stand back on land, that's really a strange feeling."

"I can hardly wait," Elise laughed. "As a matter of fact, I think I'm going to go roll in my bed awhile. You and your father can continue on if you like."

After his wife left, Michael Barclay looked solemnly at his daughter. "Erin, is this what you want?" He stirred a spoon of sugar into his cup of coffee.

Erin squinched her eyes. "For now, Dad."

"But what about later? You've already been away from the operating room for longer than a year. It's not good for a surgeon to be away too long."

"I'm keeping up, Dad. I have all the latest materials. As a matter of fact, I've put together two papers in the past few months and both have been accepted for publication in the *Journal*. I look on this time as kind of a sabbatical."

"Few surgeons take sabbaticals, particularly a sea sabbatical. I want to know if it's something else keeping you here, away from your profession, your duty."

"Dad, you know what a mess my life was in. I was burned out almost to the breakdown stage. I need the time away. Not only for me, but for my patients.

What good is a broken-down surgeon to anyone. The pressures had me, and I was one inch from exploding."

"Have you seen Bill?" he inquired softly.

She gave a single shake of her head. "No, but I do know Bill's a survivor. As long as there's a golf ball and an iron on this earth he'll be all right."

"Then you don't know he's remarried?"

Astonished, she said, "No, I had no idea. Whom did he marry?"

"Apparently a young woman he was giving lessons to at the club. I understand they're expecting their first child sometime in the early summer."

Erin moistened her lips, saying nothing for a long moment. When she finally spoke she whispered, "I hope it's a boy."

Long after her father retired to join her mother, Erin sat out on deck alone, staring up at the beautiful starlit sky. For the first time in months she felt strangely off-balance with the present and again lost in the past. Somewhere in the stars there had to be an answer for her life.

She suddenly remembered her grandfather's warning: Don't reach too high or stretch too far, or you'll miss it.

"I think I've missed it already, Grandpa," she murmured, "and it wasn't because I reached too high or stretched too far, it's just that I've never known what I was reaching for." It was true. How many decisions in her life had been hers alone? Even the fact that she was what she was had not been her decision. It had been a group deciding her future, and she had only been one of the group.

Warm tears sprang to her eyes and blurred the twinkling lights overhead. Dropping her head, she

133

fought the tears and lost the battle. And then she didn't care that she was crying, and she didn't try to stop herself. It had been such a long, long time since she had cried. It had been years. She had hardened herself to the pain of tears; she had hardened herself to the source of tears. Even with her family on board she had never felt so alone and lost. She knew that deep in his heart her father felt she would never return to the operating room, and he was disappointed in her. But she would go back. She had not spent all those years in training to throw it all away. This job at sea was temporary, and before this voyage ended her father would believe it. She was a surgeon. She would always be a surgeon. Someday she would go back, but the thought didn't make her happy. At this moment it seemed nothing could make her happy.

She glanced at her watch. Two o'clock. Drying the last of her tears, she picked up the cup and emptied it.

"Would you like another?" Mark Payton asked from behind her.

"No, thank you, Mark. Another drop of coffee and I'll be more buoyant than this ship. I was just on my way downstairs."

"Could I talk you into sitting with me a minute?" he asked in a near plea. "I have a few things I'd like to speak to you about."

"Of course," she said in a smooth voice. "Sit down."

He seated himself and remained thoughtfully silent for several moments before he said, "Erin, you realize that in a couple of weeks we'll be traveling around the world together." He hesitated and cleared his throat.

134

Of course she realized the long voyage was just ahead. She had a copy of the schedule just like every other staff member.

"Uh—I'm in love with you, Erin. I think I have been since that first day I met you outside the port office. I would like for the coming voyage to be a special time for us." He words trailed off into the night.

His words took her completely by surprise, and just looking at him at this weakened moment in her life brought the tears flooding back. She suddenly burst out crying, jumped up from the table, and ran inside and down the companionway to the hospital deck.

Mark sat at the table in wide-eyed amazement for the longest time before hauling himself up from the chair and going up to the bridge. He didn't expect to find the captain there at this hour, and at seeing Kurt he merely shook his head.

"What's that for?" Kurt inquired matter-of-factly.

"I don't suppose I'm ever going to understand women," Mark muttered.

"Which one's confused you now?" Kurt inquired with a grin.

Inhaling deeply, Mark said, "Erin. I'm never going to understand her."

"Well, welcome to the club," Kurt announced, removing his cap and wiping his brow.

"I had it all figured out, exactly what to say," Mark went on.

"About what?" Kurt prodded, still grinning.

"I want to have a relationship with her, I mean a real relationship. I'm so crazy about her. I can't keep on sailing all over the world with her and acting like she's no one special. She is special. I'm crazy about her."

The grin vanishing, Kurt stood speechless, staring at the younger captain. Finally, he asked in a smooth voice, "And exactly what was her reaction."

Mark sighed. "She jumped up and ran off, crying." His eyes fixed on Kurt's face. "Do you think maybe she misunderstood my intentions?"

"I doubt it," Kurt answered without ever losing the evenness of his tone. "She's a perceptive woman. I'm sure she knew exactly what you had in mind."

Mark looked with honest sincerity at Kurt. "How do you ever know what could be if you never give it a chance?" He inhaled deeply. "She's never going to give me a chance. I know that now."

Kurt paused before saying, "Then it's best you forget about her," he stressed tactfully. "I don't think she knows what she wants."

"That's precisely my point, Kurt. It's almost as if she's afraid of involvement, any involvement."

"Maybe she is," Kurt agreed. "But that's something she'll have to change. No one can do it for her."

Mark shot him a crafty glance. "It seems you've spent a little time thinking about her yourself."

A wry smile appeared on the captain's lips. "A little," he said.

The Christmas Day banquet was held while the ship was docked at Fort-de-France, the main seaport of Martinique in the French West Indies. Erin went ashore with her parents and they were all amazed at the resemblance the city bore to New Orleans, with its iron grillwork.

"It's astounding that we've come all this distance to find ourselves standing in a city that looks remarkably like home," Michael Barclay said.

Elise smiled thoughtfully. "Reminds me of the song, 'I'll Be Home for Christmas.' I suppose wherever we are there's a part of us home at this time of year."

Erin walked silently beside her parents, feeling a bit like a little girl again. That was the problem with being with her parents. Sooner or later it always led to falling back into old patterns of behavior. Their influences on her life had been powerful—and still were.

Over a late breakfast in the city, Michael smiled over to his daughter. "Erin, while we all have our feet on solid land, there's something I want to tell you, something you may want to give a significant amount of thought to in the days ahead when you're God knows where.

"When this position is over I want you to come home and join me in my practice. Benjamin has been talking of retirement now for the last couple of years and Jonathan and I simply won't be able to handle the practice alone." He cleared his throat before he went on. "Your mother and I want to believe that what happened in Baton Rouge was the result of your inability to cope with a dissolving marriage, and had no bearing on your professional skills or career goals. I realize, or rather we realize, that you would not like to return to the association with Raymond Morrow."

"Dad," Erin said emphatically, "if anything, it was my partnership with Raymond that dissolved my

137

marriage, not the other way around. Raymond Morrow is a lazy, arrogant—"

"Erin," he cautioned her, "we're here to enjoy ourselves. I just wanted to throw out my offer for whatever it was worth. And I want you to think about it."

A flicker of Elise's eyes hushed him, and the topic of conversation changed from medicine to the ports yet to be visited.

That evening the dining room was beautiful. The *Royal Princess Star* was a floating Christmas tree. Bright lights were strung on the decks, giving off a colorful glow that reached up and mingled with the moonbeams filtering down. A Christmas buffet, complete with turkey and unending dishes ranging from rack of lamb to Alaskan salmon was set up. Vegetables and casseroles of all kinds and colors were followed by an abundance of desserts, including beautiful arrangements of fresh tropical fruits.

After the meal the guests joined the entertainers for hours of Christmas carols while champagne flowed freely.

A few minutes past midnight Erin, feeling a bit topsy-turvy, excused herself from the large table of festive singing and sought fresh air, leaving her parents behind with the others, which included her staff. Several people, mostly couples, had preceded her to the open deck. She smiled at several, then went to the railing, where she looked down at the silver haze on the water. She inhaled a deep breath and let it go slowly.

A few minutes later Kurt walked up beside her

and asked softly, "The party get to be too much for you?"

Her brown eyes glistening, she straightened and looked at him, a smile on her lips. "Not the party, maybe the champagne. It has a way of sneaking up and hitting me under the chin."

Reaching out, his fingers touched her chin. "I'm sorry to hear that, you have such a lovely chin . . . and face." His fingers brushed across her lips. "And mouth."

She edged back from his touch. "Kurt," she said in a teasing tone, "are you the kind of man who takes advantage of women who have had too much to drink, catching them when they're weak and defenseless?"

He grinned, though his eyes remained pensive on her face. "That's me," he said in a joking whisper. "My motto has always been catch 'em anyway you can, just be sure you catch 'em."

"Why, Captain, I do believe you mean that."

"I do, Dr. Barclay, I surely do. And it's taken me longer to catch you than any woman I've ever gone after." He moved closer to her and looked into her face, his eyes bright with triumph. "But I do have you now, and it'll probably be a long time before I let you go."

"Kurt, it's not funny anymore." Her words were thick.

"I'm not laughing." His hands caught her neck close to her shoulders. He leaned over her face, and with the softness of a rose petal, kissed her mouth. "Merry Christmas," he murmured against her lips. Then he kissed her and the lights all around them became misted jewels in the darkness.

Her head tilted back and her lips parted beneath

139

his, her mouth straining with abandon as she became completely undone in his arms, overwhelmed by the sensation brought by his lips moving over hers, caressing slow in gentle deliberate exploration, bringing a flaring warmth to her body and at the same time a parade of chills reverberating down her spine.

His lips moved over her mouth again and again, expertly slow, exquisitely sensuous. The barred doors deep inside began to swing open as she pressed against the superb body beneath the deep blue fabric of his coat.

He pulled back and spoke very softly. "Erin, come with me to my cabin." It was a request, a plea, a command.

Her mouth opened, but she stood in silence forever, it seemed, before she whispered. "I can't, Kurt. They're waiting for me."

"Then let them wait," he said urgently. "I've been waiting for you longer, Erin, forever." His words were tense, strained. "I need you, and you need me. The more we fight it, the greater the need becomes. Erin, don't walk away from me tonight. Not tonight."

She jerked her chin a little. "You're asking the impossible."

"I'm asking you to love me, and to allow me the freedom to love you. That isn't impossible; it's only a few steps away. Come with me, Erin. Tonight."

Moistening her lips, she gave a tiny shake of her head. She spoke in a whisper. "I don't expect you to understand, but down there in the dining room are two people who are very important to me, two people who already think I have failed my profession. I would hate for them to leave this ship believing I have no moral attributes either. Now I am going

140

back, Kurt, because they are expecting me and I can at least not disappoint them tonight." And with those words she turned and walked away from him.

He stood unmoving, watching her go. "Erin," he reflected bitterly, "you have a thousand phantoms living inside you, but somewhere in all those phantoms is a living, breathing woman, and I'm going to find her."

He yearned for her so strongly he knew it would never go away. Walking along the deck rubbing one temple, it was a strange thought, almost a fearful thought, the thought she had brought a flame to him that might possibly burn for the remainder of his life, or blaze out into eternity. He loved her and there would come the time when the intrusions between them would be gone. He could wait. He could yield to time.

Propping himself against the ship's railing, he sighed along with the cool night wind.

The New Year's Eve party was held at sea forty hours from New York. The renewed passions inside Erin for Kurt Garisen were building in a near violent intensity. She could not look at him without remembering the touch of his lips, the noble lines of his body, the softness of his fingertips. Now she was depending on her parents to keep her out of his arms again. But in forty hours they would be gone, and who would she hide behind then? She had all kinds of arguments with herself. He had awakened passion, so what? That wasn't enough of a reason to get involved with something she might only regret. What would be the harm in an affair with him? It would only be temporary, until she left the ship, if and

141

when Nils ever came through with her replacement. It wasn't as if she planned any type of permanent relationship with him. Why not abandon herself to his expert lovemaking? He had spent a lifetime perfecting his style, she was sure. She was as strongly attracted to him now as she was when they had made love. Why should she not enjoy him as a thousand other women had enjoyed him? The arguments went on silently; the battles inside her mind waged on.

But as fate would have it, when the clock struck midnight on New Year's Eve, it was not Kurt Garisen's arms in which she found herself. She was dancing with Samuel Tondi, the cruise director. She had never given a thought to the thin wiry man until the band began the traditional song and he almost suffocated her with a long searching kiss. What he bestowed upon her was far from the traditional kiss and for a moment she was tempted to slap his face, New Year's or not. But then, everyone was kissing everyone and she forgot his ill-mannered plunge when Mark Payton swung her around in his arms. "At last," he said with a good-natured laugh, then proceeded to kiss her soundly on the mouth for a respectable time before releasing her.

Then he started back in the direction of her mouth and she scooted away quickly into the crowd. Turning around to catch her, Mark stepped directly into the path of S.L., who had just left Hal Haywood's arms. "Hello, Nurse Brenner," he said with his eyes searching over her head.

She popped him severely in the shin with the toe of her shoe. Hopping in place, holding his leg with both hands, he exclaimed loudly, "What did you do that for!"

"I always try to kick a fool on New Year's," she huffed in his face.

He looked at her with disbelief. "And just what have I ever done to you!"

"Nothing!" she blew back haughtily. "And you never will, in case you're wondering!"

"Well, I think you've chipped the bone in my leg!" he yelled out.

"Get out of my way or I'll chip the one in your head, and there's enough stone there to lay all new markers in Arlington Cemetery." Pushing him aside, she, too, disappeared into the crowd.

Mark stood there holding to his leg and shaking his head.

When Erin saw Kurt coming her way she turned abruptly and stood face to face with the aged Mr. Donovan, Miss Woodson's sneaky old man.

His drawn face wrinkled into a radiant smile. "Why, Dr. Barclay," he said trembling, "would you care to dance?"

She didn't take time to answer. She just grabbed him up and headed to the dance floor with him. Kurt Garisen was not going to kiss her in this roomful of people, not if she had to dance the rest of the night with the fox-trotting octogenarian she was holding at the moment.

CHAPTER NINE

January 18 was a bitter cold, overcast day in New York Harbor. For the past two days snow flurries had drifted softly on the huge liner, which was busily being prepared for the ninety-day voyage. Tons of food had been stored, along with every other imagined item that might be called for in the three months at sea.

Erin's dilemma had not been solved. All of Nils's excuses sounded plausible, but she wasn't convinced he wasn't merely dragging his feet until her agreement with the line was up. He had certainly had sufficient time to hire another physician for the ship.

Her complaints to him were met by, "I promise, Dr. Barclay, I'm doing my level best. It just takes time."

"But it's been *months*, and now the world cruise is coming up," Erin answered.

"Tell you what, you continue on with your duties and I'll see that you get replaced at some point during the cruise," Nils promised.

She was beginning to wonder why she'd ever asked to leave the ship. With the enthusiasm for the coming voyage becoming more infectious, she was tempted to withdraw the request. But she didn't.

Through large horn-rimmed glasses she studied the list of drugs just presented to her by Arthur Swinney, the ship's pharmacist. Then she compared Mr. Swinney's list with her own that she had drawn up from the latest *PDR*. To her happy surprise the two lists were almost identical.

One thousand and thirty passengers had been booked for the world cruise and not only did the staff find themselves buried under a hundred pounds of medical records, there were also inoculations and vaccination records for each person on ship. Her own arms were sore from the immunizations required for the Far East portion of the cruise. Up-to-date passports were required for the cruise, though the line had received blanket visas from some of the ports of call, while others had to be obtained by the individuals. Erin had turned over her documents to the dreary-eyed purser, as had the other members of her staff.

For forty-eight hours prior to passenger embarcation the eight-hundred-member crew and staff of the *Royal Princess Star* had been on duty. There were standard orders to follow and each employee followed them. Still, there was the excitement, the enthusiasm, present that Erin had not noticed on previous cruises.

The day before the ship was to leave port Kurt came into the hospital and threw the first real kink into the hospital's smooth operation. "The new nurse has arrived," he announced softly. "It's Rachel Lawrence, Erin."

Slowly, she looked up from her desk, removed the

reading glasses, and said totally emotionlessly. "Are you joking?"

He gave a shake of his head. "No. No joke. Nils told me this morning. Seems the other ships weren't to her liking. She asked to be reassigned and the company considered her record and reassigned her. It's that simple. She is an excellent nurse."

Erin only gazed at him, her eyes worried.

He half-shrugged. "I'm just passing on information."

"Thank you," she said, subdued. In a flash she recalled her last conversation with Rachel Lawrence and shook her head. She would shut her mind to the image of that meeting; nothing would be gained by dwelling on it. She wasn't happy Rachel was returning, but she managed to fake a smile. "I'm sure we'll make it fine."

After he was gone she stayed in her office and returned to her paperwork. She didn't have the heart to tell her three wonderful apples that the rotten one was back.

That night, bundled in warm clothing, she stood on the sundeck and watched the snowfall. Then she went by the snack bar and got a cup of hot chocolate before going to her room. She sat down in the lamp-light and watched as the snow thickened outside her window. She wondered if there was a chance the weather would keep the ship from sailing tomorrow, then shook her head. No way. The entire year's schedule was posted and it didn't allow for snow.

S.L. came by and asked if she wanted to go ashore for a late movie and dinner with her and Hal. Erin made the excuse that she was tired, and after they were gone she sat shaking her head slowly. She wasn't tired. She didn't know what she was, but she was in a strange mood for sure.

Only four months to go before she would be back in the real world if Nils didn't find her replacement before then. That thought made her tired. She considered her father's words to her with an increasing sense of dread. He had gone home to New Orleans after extracting a half-promise from her to join his group of surgeons. She had promised to think over his proposal and he had, of course, accepted that statement as an affirmative.

Her eyes were glued to the window, staring pointedly at her future, but she couldn't make out what she was seeing. She only knew it couldn't all stay bottled up inside her indefinitely. When the tap sounded at her door, she said, "Come in."

The door opened and Kurt, dressed in denims and a wool sweater, walked in. "I was hoping I might catch you. Want to go ashore and have dinner with me?"

Looking at him, the knot of tension inside her grew tighter. "It's too cold," she whispered.

"Nonsense. That's what coats are for." He gave her one of his superior smiles and said, "I'm not taking no for an answer." He looked at the cup in her hand. "What are you drinking there?"

"Hot chocolate."

"Sounds good. Come on, I'll buy you another cup."

Rather than argue, she got up and reached for her coat. He took it from her hand and held it while she slipped inside. When her arms slid through the sleeves he turned her around, lapped it neatly, and brought the belt to the front. She stood gazing at him, wondering if he was going to tie the belt for her. Then

147

his eyes flicked up and he remained unmoving for the longest moment, studying her. Then he stepped back, putting the belt in her hands. "You better do that," he whispered.

On shore he hailed a cab and they went a few blocks to a small Italian restaurant, complete with checkered tablecloths and candlelight. After they were seated by a handsome young man with an accent, she smiled at Kurt, her brown eyes lighting up. "Spaghetti and hot chocolate, a nice combination," she said in jest.

He stared at her for a long moment. "That isn't the only nice combination at this table. Actually," he continued smoothly, "wine is equally as warming as chocolate, and it goes much better with spaghetti." His eyes, so very blue, absorbed her in the wavery candlelight.

"I know what you're doing, Kurt." She regarded him with mock suspicion, a twinkle in her eyes.

"I hope so," he breathed, paused, then added, "I do hope so."

The meal was delicious but filled with a new kind of tension as gazes kept fixing on each other and the silence stretched. He was making love to her in that small restaurant with his eyes, with his expression, with his words, and she was allowing it because it was impossible to stop him.

The dinner was followed by pastry and coffee, and the sensations inside her grew. She loved the way he looked tonight, the casual thick sweater, the faded denims, the way the wind had mussed his dark hair. She liked the width of his shoulders and that small round mole on his cheek. She loved the blueness in his eyes, so very blue, and the tiny crinkles at the corners when he smiled. Desire flashed through her and she could feel the beat of her heart in her throat.

The conversation was a bit erratic and rambly. They weren't really saying anything, just relaxed, insignificant small talk—pleasant and polite. Then when the dessert was gone and they had just the two cups of coffee before them, he sat back in his chair, one arm draped across the back, and again studied her soberly. That mask she usually wore was gone completely tonight. The passionate restlessness in him stirred. For months he had seen her in professional dress. She looked the ship's doctor. In the evenings in the exquisite gowns in the dining room, she looked like an unattainable vision. But tonight in wool slacks and thick tan pullover sweater, she looked vibrantly alive—and irresistible. Tonight she looked touchable again. And he was dying to touch her. He loved what the amber lighting from the candles did to her eyes, flecking the brown with pure gold. She had large pretty brown eyes and the most perfect mouth he had ever kissed. He was remembering those kisses, that first night he touched all of her, and unconsciously his tongue reached out to moisten his lips.

She saw the sudden change on his face and her eyes widened in an unspoken question.

"I—I think we should go," he whispered, his blue eyes fixed on her.

"I suppose so," she agreed with a slight nod, then added, "in view of the busy day ahead."

He felt a small tightening in his throat as he fought back the impulse to say, It isn't the day ahead that holds my interest, it's the night. But he didn't say anything; instead, he signaled for the check.

He hailed a taxi and the two of them slid inside. The snow was peppering down with much more intensity now. Seated dangerously close to him, she laughed, reaching up and brushing the snowflakes from his hair. When she touched him the electricity in her fingers crackled in a near audible sound.

He caught her hand, bringing it down to his mouth. His lips brushed her palm, then her fingers. Instead of pulling back, she pressed closer to him and his arm went around her. Nestling her head on his shoulder, she tried to will her body to stop trembling.

Then abruptly, while putting on his brakes for a light, the driver lost control of the fast traveling car and slid across the pavement, bouncing into the curb. Kurt tensed and straightened immediately. "Hey, watch it, fellow."

"Everything's under control, mister, just hold your horses."

Erin caught Kurt's arm. "It's okay," she breathed low. "No harm done."

Falling back, he gave a shake of his head. "I just want to be sure we get back to the ship okay tonight," he half-moaned under his breath.

"Kurt," she chided, "you're more protective of that ship than an old mother hen."

His lips parted, he stared at her with a look of disbelief. He blinked. Surely, she didn't think it was the ship he was worried about. The ship would be there tomorrow, but he couldn't be sure about the captain.

When the taxi halted at the port Kurt reached across her and flung open the door for her to get out. Then he followed, pulling out his wallet as he moved out the door. Bending slightly inside the car, he paid the driver handsomely, saying, "Don't wrap yourself around any poles tonight, buddy."

The driver grinned. "And a good night to you, too, mister." His eyes widened at last. "Say, do you work on that ship?"

"Occasionally," Kurt murmured as he slammed the door and took off after Erin.

Glancing up, her eyes glittered teasingly at him. "I had no idea you were such a generous man, Captain Garisen."

"There are a lot of things you don't know about me, Dr. Barclay. But we are soon about to remedy that."

"Kurt," she began cautiously.

"Don't Kurt me, Erin," he interrupted before she could continue with her argument. "We are going on that ship, and from there we are going straight to my room. And that's the end of that discussion."

She tensed. "That's the most romantic thing anyone's ever said to me."

They were inside the ship at the elevators when he caught her shoulders, his eyes searching her face, eyeing her with a speculative gleam. The flame inside him burned fiercer than it had ever burned. "I've been lonely without you," he whispered.

"That's a little better." She laughed softly.

He looked at her anxiously. "I'm not trying to be romantic, Erin. What I'm saying happens to be true."

Her eyes widened. "Let's don't rush anything, Kurt."

He took her arm and guided her into the elevator. When the doors opened on his deck he all but dragged her down the corridor. "I'm not rushing into anything," he said in a firm voice. "Not at all."

"Kurt, wait a minute!"

Unlocking his door, he was completely deaf to her. He closed the door and bolted it, then turned to her, his eyes feverish with desire. "Now," he said softly, taking a single step toward her, "state all your objections, because you have my complete attention."

"If you think for one minute—" she began.

He caught her up in his arms and kissed her hungrily. When he released her his blue eyes were shining wickedly.

She swallowed and began again, "If you think—"

His mouth buried her words, but this time the tempo of his mouth changed, smoothingly slow and languishing over her lips.

When he pulled away she murmured, "If—" The final and whispered word flickered like a weak flame, then went out. A warmth invaded beyond the heavy coat, the thick sweater, the wool clothing her legs. His room had become a desert and she was burning, thirsting, and he was the soothing breeze, the cool drink of water. She didn't care about tomorrow. It was only a day, an unmoving dream. She was caught up in the now, the moment.

He stood back, gazing into her eyes. He brushed a hand across her cheek gently while the flames leaped and danced in her eyes. "I do love you, Erin." His words floated softly past her ears. "I do love you." Deep, thickening words. She heard them, and at the same time didn't.

He slipped the coat from her shoulders, then pulled her gently back into his arms. He kissed her face, her forehead, her chin, her neck, her mouth, both stroking and caressing her flesh.

Her head fell back in response to his lips at her

neck and she gasped. Then his lips, soft and moist, covered hers, his tongue reaching into her mouth, touching her teeth, sweeping the lines of her lips, then playing velvet games with her own, luring her close to him, so close she pressed into the hard defined lines of his body in a helpless search for intimacy.

Taking her hand in his, he led her into the bedroom, where he slowly, carefully, undressed her, then himself. The anticipation of touching his body, of experiencing his hands on her flesh again took her breath away. And while they stood he did touch her, so delicately, in slow, simple caresses.

Standing apart from her, his hands swept her shoulders, her arms, her waist, her breasts. "You are beautiful," he murmured in a daze. "You're perfect, and you're beautiful."

Barely perceptive of her own movements, her hands went to his chest and pressed the soft growth of dark hair stretching across his expansive body, then up to his shoulders before trailing down the smooth skin covering his narrow stomach and solid thighs.

Her hands dropped away from him and for a moment they weren't touching at all—just two forms standing silhouetted in the darkness, gazing at each other as if they were seeing for the first time.

Did she move? Or did he? Did he reach for her, or did she merely flow into his arms? She didn't know. She didn't care. All she knew was that his arms were around her, his mouth was against hers, opened wide, tongues searching and finding each other.

His hands, spread wide, traveled along her back, bringing flames and chills, making her burn and quiver at the same time, speaking a language of tenderness to her flesh. Then the tenderness was lost to a large blazing fire, one which suddenly swept past, sending them both out of control.

The passionate kiss grew and exploded into a million little kisses, touching her neck, her body, kissing her until she moaned aloud, until she fell back onto the bed, pulling him with her.

He leaned across her, sweeping her face, her neck, her breasts, with wet, erotic kisses. His tongue stroked her nipples delicately, with loving tenderness, prolonging the sweet pain rising inside them.

She had never known this sensation. Not even when they had made love that first time had she felt this complete loss of time and place, this total absorption by another person, this loss of identity. That she was Erin Barclay became a matter of not the least significance. That she was a woman, touching a man, a woman being touched, was all she was and all she wanted to be. She marveled at his strength, at his control. While every nerve-ending in her body hungered for him, cried out for fulfillment, he would not let go and give in to that release they both sought.

She held his mouth to her breasts, her fingers stretched wide in his rich hair. Then holding on to his hair, she moaned and brought his lips back to hers for a brushing wet kiss, her body arching closer to his. She could feel his hardness branding her abdomen, and the kisses became wild, uncontrollable desire guiding her hands to him. She brushed him, she circled him, her fingers up, then down, until his trembling matched her own.

Then he rose slowly and provocatively, placing a knee on each side of her. He touched her with his fingers, and her lips parted in a moan of pleasure. Then she felt the weight of his body, of his magnificent nakedness spreading along her, and still he lingered.

He lowered his mouth to her mouth, taking her lower lip between his teeth. She took hold of his shoulders and her fingernails clung to the moist texture of his flesh in this moment of the greatest weakness she had ever known. She was weak for him. She was trembling for him. Her own needs were so great, she was being ravaged by them.

She arched sensuously toward him, taking control from him. Slowly, he lowered his body in the fusion that made them one. Simultaneous tremors passed through them as she circled his legs with hers. For a moment they weren't born. They were lifeless and motionless. And then with the breath of passion they were alive and moving through the paradise of flesh. Beyond them there was nothing. Between them was the world, the world of hardness, of softness, of deepness, of delirium. While the wind blew snowflakes at their window, a perfect fire blazed inside.

Gripping his shoulders, she gave herself to the most burning ecstasy she had ever known. He was now the conqueror, moving wildly, eagerly, past all barriers, and she was with him in the mindless quest of bodies for that dimension of explosive desire.

He had felt himself completely overtaken by her, and while he fought to delay the all-consuming moment, he became a slave to her will. He felt the welling up inside him and he became insatiable, taking all, giving all as they soared out beyond the snow clouds, far past the night into that part of the cosmos that existed only for the two of them. They held the torch of passion for only that brief moment, for a flash of time, and then it was gone, sweeping back into the darkness without them.

Then it was so quiet, so still except for the quickening gasps for air. And finally they, too, slowed. They lay together, not moving, not speaking, still enjoying the warmth of the explosive moment just shared.

Her eyes closed, Erin nestled her face against Kurt's damp neck. She didn't want to speak, she didn't want him to speak; she just wanted to lie there close to him and not think or talk. She was content just to be there. Over and over she kept fighting the thought, *I could love you, Kurt. It would be so easy to love you. I could love you so much.*

He was silent—spent and silent. Then he raised her slightly and gave a grunt of a sigh. "Am I awake?" he whispered.

She turned toward his face and smiled. "I don't know, are you?"

"I don't know. A part of me thinks I must be dreaming." Smiling tenderly, he gazed into her face. "You're the doctor, tell me if I'm awake."

She stared at him, a faraway, distant stare. "What day is it?" she asked.

He grinned softly. "I don't know."

"Well, then, what's your name?"

"I don't know that either."

She reached up and stroked his cheek, her fingertips lingering in his hair. "What do you know?"

"I know that I love you."

Once again there was silence.

"You aren't awake," she finally murmured. "You aren't even half-awake."

"You're saying that because I said I love you," he

156

chided her, leaning over and kissing her cheek gently. "Is there something wrong with loving you?"

"Don't make it difficult, Kurt."

He brought his fingers to her mouth, stopping her words. "I don't want it to go on between us as it has in the past, Erin. That's what makes it difficult. To want you, to need you. I don't have that kind of fight left in me. I can't love you tonight and tomorrow pretend you don't exist. You do. You exist in my life, in my heart."

Curling her arms around his neck, she kissed his chin. "What about the animal in you I just heard about. Animals don't complicate things."

Playfully, he rolled over and pulled her on top of him. "This animal has just begun to complicate things. You are about to sail around the world with this animal. What do you think that makes your chances?"

Something flickered in her eyes before her lids closed. She thought of telling him she might not be making the cruise, but decided against it. This was neither the time nor the place to admit her plans.

His gaze rested squarely on her closed lids. For an instant his eyes narrowed and his face grew rigid, then relaxed with a long sigh. "What are you doing, Erin?"

"Thinking," she answered quietly.

"About what?"

Her eyes still closed, she smiled, her tongue toying with her upper lip. "Thinking about a lot of things tonight I failed to notice the last time."

He laughed. "Such as?" he prodded, his eyes twinkling.

"Oh," she laughed playfully, "I don't know, a lot of little things."

His brows rose. "Oh, really, care to elaborate?"

"Only if I must."

"Since you have my curiosity aroused, I'd like to hear."

"Those two little moles on your hips for one thing."

"And"—he drew close to her lips—"what else?"

"That little patch of hair at your bellybutton. It's completely isolated."

"From what?" he asked solemnly, fighting back the grin about to break through.

"From the other hair on your body." She laughed. "It's like a little fuzzy island, all alone."

"Damn, Erin, you're beginning to make me sound like I'm deformed."

Her lips rounded. "Oh, no, you are definitely not that. I would say you are the least deformed man I've ever seen."

He grunted under his breath. "And being what you are, you've seen plenty, huh?"

She smiled. "And being what I am, I am observant. It's my nature."

"Since I find myself in a goldfish bowl, do you approve of me or not?"

She gave a sigh, followed by a moment of mock deliberation. "I don't like to form hasty opinions. Why don't we just go back over the same procedure and I'll let you know in a little while."

"It would be simpler just to call in a second opinion, wouldn't it?" he chided.

"It might be simpler," she agreed with a sinister smile, "but it wouldn't be nearly as much fun." She brought his mouth to hers and kissed him long and slowly. "Now, would it?" she murmured against his lips.

"I've forgotten the statement," he groaned, circling his arms around her in a crushing embrace.

Quickly, the hunger was back. As she was held tightly in his grasp her mouth made an irresistible assault on his lips, his nose, his eyes. Her mouth trailed across his neck and his arms fell slack. The night sparkled in splendor. Taking the initiative, for the first time in her life she made love to a man. His beautiful tapered body was hers to do with as she wanted, and she wanted it all.

Reflections in the dark were of her lips softly plying his flesh, sweeping his chest, pressing firmly at his small flat nipples until they were aroused by the raw sexuality of the moment. She was untamed and free, free to touch, free to explore and his wonderfully muscled body became her playground. He was pliant to her touch and the electricity in her hands emitted powerful currents throughout his body.

Then he was no longer content to remain the experiment. His large hands exploded along her body, her beautiful fine-boned body, long graceful legs, full, aroused breasts, smooth, sculptured hips. Breathing had entered into a state of near frenzy as their bodies strained together, following the sensations that raced toward the inevitable sacrifice of fulfillment. The flame was intense and they both fell away burned, seared, and breathless.

Then he gently rocked her back and forth in his arms and a flow of words echoed against her ears. But her mind was still locked, her senses swimming in the aftermath of desire.

A few minutes passed and he got up and poured them each a glass of wine. Sitting on the side of the bed, he handed her one glass as his eyes moved slowly over her face. "Would you like a cigarette?"

She nodded and smiled.

He removed her pack from her coat pocket, took one out, and put it into her mouth. Then taking her lighter, he lit it.

She took a deep drag and blew the smoke out slowly. "Tastes good," she said, her eyes moving to his lips.

She held the cigarette out to him and he leaned over and took a puff. Blowing it out, he said, "Back to all my old habits."

"Which one did you give up?" She laughed playfully.

"Smoking." He grinned boyishly. "Of Scotch, cigarettes, and women. I decided it was the easiest to give up." His brows rose. "Of course, I had about decided all I had going for me was Scotch."

She poked him in the ribs with her glass. "I believe that, but then I also believe the world is flat."

"I had," he argued with a short laugh, "about given up on ever holding you again, and I suddenly found myself without the desire to hold anyone else."

She raised herself up on one arm and sipped from the glass. "Is that true?" she whispered.

He nodded, a solemn expression covering his face. "Yes, it is true. I love you, Erin. I really love you."

Her eyes moved along his profile, but she didn't say anything more. She sipped the wine and together, in the dark, they smoked the cigarette. When the glasses were empty, he took her in his arms and they stretched out side by side on his bed.

"Where to now?" she asked softly.

"How would you like to go around the world with me?" he whispered into the dampness of her hair.

"I feel as though I just did," she murmured against his cheek. They lay embracing each other for a long time before she got up and dressed and left for her cabin.

She felt miserable for not telling him about the replacement request to leave the ship, but she had been dreadfully aware of the confrontation that would no doubt follow. He would not have understood. Maybe Nils would not find anyone to take her place; then Kurt would never have to know.

CHAPTER TEN

The sailing was scheduled for four thirty. Erin was in the hospital unit with S.L., Hal, and Johnny, the latter three putting away the last-minute supplies which the purser had sent up at seven o'clock. She was also staying busy. She had to stay busy or lose what little mind she had left. The night with Kurt, beautiful as it had been in one way, had been equally devastating in another. She had been unable to sleep, not the first short wink.

Kneeling in front of one of the cabinets with a box of insulin syringes in her hand, she just knelt there frozen, staring blankly at the box. She didn't have the intelligence of a severed grubworm this morning. Outside, the sun was shining brightly, melting the slush on the pavements from last night's snow. She had to force herself into the unit this morning. She wanted to get off the ship and run in a dozen directions.

She had dressed casually this morning in dark blue slacks and white sweater following an hour's soak in her small tub. But it hadn't worked. She couldn't wash him away—not his scent, nor his touch. He was in her blood.

Finally, placing the box on the shelf alongside the other syringes, she told herself that it was only a superficial shipboard romance, with a possible lifetime of ninety days. Actually a hundred and twenty days. If Nils found no one to replace her, she would still have a month with the line after the completion of the long cruise.

The other three members of her staff were chatting happily among themselves, having finished with the last of the supplies and started putting clean, pressed linens on the beds in the bay. When Mark Payton waltzed in, everyone in the unit ignored him, the three bedmakers on purpose, Erin because she didn't realize he was even there. When she slowly rose to her feet from the cabinets and looked around, he was merely standing in place, one side of his mouth twisted out of shape. She smiled and said, "Hello, Mark."

"Hello, Erin," he said, his mouth returning to a normal position. "Is it all going well?"

She nodded.

He glanced over to the busy threesome. "Where's Rachel?"

Erin shrugged. "Sleeping, I imagine. I understand she reported on ship last night, but we've yet to see hide or hair of her."

The entire unit fell deadly silent. S.L. walked from the side of the bed and leveled a hostile glare at Mark. "Did you say Rachel?" she asked threateningly.

Mark nodded. "Actually, I did."

"Rachel, like in Rachel Lawrence?" S.L. persisted, not batting an eye at the lank young officer.

"Actually, I didn't say Lawrence, but yes, if I had mentioned her last name, I would have said Lawrence.

But fear not, save her some work. If she isn't here by now I have a good idea where she is. I'll see if I can round her up for you."

"Well, don't play cowboy for us," S.L. said coolly. "We can wait."

Mark's eyes focused on the pretty, smooth face. "Which side of the bed did you get up on this morning, Nurse Brenner?" Turning, he started out the door. "Why don't you try the other side tomorrow," he called back, swinging out the unit.

S.L. stood leering after him, then went back to the bed, slowly shaking her head. She cut her eyes to Erin. "Rachel is back?" she asked very softly.

Erin merely nodded, then turned and went into her office just as the phone rang. She answered, "Hospital, Dr. Barclay."

"Hello, Dr. Barclay." It was Kurt. A slight pause followed. "Have you had breakfast?"

"Yes, thanks. I picked up a danish and a cup of coffee on my way up from the lobby."

"Have you had dessert?"

She smiled. "I don't usually eat dessert with breakfast."

"Well, I have something special for you here in my room," he said good-naturedly.

"Am I supposed to guess what?" she replied with a suspicious laugh.

"Indeed not. And get your mind above your smooth, hairless bellybutton. I'm talking about a cup of steaming chocolate, with marshmallows." He laughed. "Come on up."

She deliberated only a moment before returning, "Do you have time? I mean, the passengers are

164

already coming on ship by the dozens. Have you been to the purser's lobby?"

Kurt laughed. "I try to stay away from there during embarking. Now, do you want to come up here or shall I bring it down to you?"

She hesitated only a moment, "Be right there," she half-whispered. Dropping the phone, she shook her head fleetingly. Of course it was harmless. For goodness' sake, she scolded herself. *We are taking on passengers by the hundreds today. This afternoon we're sailing.* Certainly the captain of the ship did not have time for hanky-panky, not on this particular morning.

Stepping out of her office, she called over to the others, "I've got a meeting with the captain. Be right back." She wasn't sure, but for some unknown reason it seemed all their eyes followed her out the door.

Going up to his room, she felt alive, so very alive. And if it was wrong, she couldn't help it. Her heart was beating like a schoolgirl's with a first crush. If she had been totally coherent and in her right mind, she would probably have been embarrassed.

Reaching his door, she raised her arm to knock, but the door opened and his hand grabbed her arm, hauling her inside, where he embraced her tightly, the door still half ajar. Then with his foot he closed the door at the same time his mouth lowered to hers. It was suddenly as though she had never left his arms. Then he was kissing her face gently and she felt the trembling in his lips, in his arms.

She drew back dizzily. "This is a lot like the chocolate you bought me last night," she accused him lovingly. "What are you going to do when we sail down to where it's too warm for chocolate?"

He smiled, his light blue eyes casting a hypnotic spell over her. "I am the captain; I will think of something. Believe me, I will think of something. However"—he stepped back—"I did not call you here under false pretenses. Madame, your cup." And he motioned to the table beside his sofa.

Without a word, but wearing the smallest smile, Erin moved over and lowered herself to the cushions and he came and seated himself next to her. They barely talked as they slowly sipped the chocolate, which was no longer steaming.

A part of the melted marshmallow stuck near the corner of her mouth and his face broke into smiles. "Messy, messy," he said, his eyes devouring her lips.

Her brows rose. "Could I have a napkin?"

Placing his cup down, he leaned a bit and caught her face in his hands. "Capt'n Napkin to the rescue." And she burst out laughing when his mouth covered hers. But the laugh quickly vanished as he kissed her senseless.

She wasn't sailing this afternoon, she was sailing now, away in his arms. Her lips parted beneath his and her arms folded around his neck and she clung to him. The feelings were so high between them, her head, her thoughts, were spinning from his closeness.

Together they lowered themselves full-length along the cushions as his lips gently passed over her mouth, her face, her neck. The outside morning light flooded the room brightly through the light drapes, but they were blind to it. His hands slowly slid under her sweater and he carefully unfastened her bra, pushing

166

it away to touch the softness of her breasts, moving his hand over her until the tips were no longer soft and supple, but taut and arching to his fingers.

"Kurt," she murmured, "are we really going to do this here . . . now?" Her words slid past his parted lips and echoed in his mouth.

"Nah, you're safe." He smiled against her lips, whispering back into her own mouth while his hand slowly unzipped her pants. "Most of me is still asleep." And he kissed her again, then again.

She pulled back from his mouth, snorting with laughter. "If any part of you is still asleep, then it's your mind, not the part that needs to be." Her hands went to his waist and she slowly unfastened his trousers, raking her hand slowly over him. "Tell me how safe I am now," she murmured suggestively, her tongue sweeping the lobe of his left ear.

He groaned, kissing her wildly, and when he softened against her mouth, he said breathlessly. "Not very." His hands ran down her body, savoringly slowly, taking her clothing with the movement until they lay only partially naked, the pressure of him burning against her flesh making her gasp and press closer to him.

Then while they kissed and lay clinging to each other the phone on the table rang. For a moment he didn't move and when he finally raised his head, he muttered, "Who would dare call at a time like this?" He frowned and glared hostilely at the telephone, which was in the process of ringing a second time.

"You'd better answer it," she said gloomily, closing her eyes.

"Captain Garisen," he said in a deep voice, then

paused. "Just a moment." He placed the phone to her ear.

Her eyes shot open and she rose up slightly. "Captain Barclay," she said professionally into the receiver. Kurt's eyes widened and his hand went over his mouth.

There was a dead silence in Erin's ear to the phone. After a moment S.L. said in a somewhat strange tone, "Is Captain Barclay also known as Dr. Barclay?" she began reluctantly.

"Wha—" Blushing brightly, Erin realized her error. "Oh, don't pay any attention to me, S.L., I don't know where my mind was. Uh—what is it?"

"A passenger, Mr. Homer Vlasic, is here. He wants to talk with you. He's not feeling well and he wants your opinion about making the cruise. The purser sent him here."

"Vlasic, like the pickle?"

S.L. giggled. "There's no relation except in appearance." Suddenly, she was the all professional again. "Should he wait for you, Doctor?"

"Yes. Have him wait in my office. I'll be there shortly." With a sigh she placed the phone back in Kurt's hand.

Still fighting laughter, he said, "You have a sick pickle, Doctor?" Then he laughed loudly, stopped, and said, "I figured that out all by myself." Again, he burst out laughing.

A tiny smile broke on her lips as she started to get up, pushing him back. "You are really a very clever man. I'm impressed."

Suddenly he was serious. "Where are you going?"

Edging from under him, she began reaching under her sweater to put her bra back in place and fasten

168

it. "That's something else for you to figure out." She gave him a challenging grin.

He argued on as if he hadn't heard her. "But you can't leave me now, Erin, not now. If you do, you'll have two patients on your hands."

"Your illness I can treat later, Captain Garisen, but I can't keep the overwrought Mr. Vlasic waiting." She finished dressing, then leaned over and pecked Kurt on the lips and stood back and looked at him. "If I were you, I would wait a few minutes before I mingled."

He lay back on the sofa and shook his head from side to side as she went out the door.

Walking down to the unit, Erin fluffed her hair out with her hand and swept her face with her fingers, then straightened the bottom of her sweater and hand-pressed the rumples from her slacks. She entered the unit courageously and smiled with amazing earnestness at S.L. and Hal. Then, sighting Rachel, she continued to smile, but the light in her eyes faded. "Rachel," she said with a small nod.

Rachel, immaculately groomed in a sparkling white pants uniform and perfect coiffeur, smiled and at the same time gave a complete once-over to the physician from head to toe. "Hello, Doctor," she said in a purr. Then she turned her gaze to the office door. "Mr. Vlasic is waiting for you."

Erin cocked her head to one side and acknowledged her with a low "Thank you." She moved to the door at the same time Rachel sauntered over toward her causally. Reaching for the closed door, Erin looked quizzically at the nurse, who was now at her elbow.

"You know, Doctor," Rachel said out of earshot of

169

the others. "I have a pair of pants exactly like those and I can't keep my zipper up either."

Erin's eyes dropped to her waist, then lower. Their eyes met as Erin casually reached down and remedied her situation, then with complete smoothness said, "I've been meaning to send this pair to the tailor. Thanks." Then she went on into the office, where she conferred with a nervous little man of seventy who was in better health than she was at the moment.

A little before lunch Hal dropped by the office and leaned in, stating, "I'm going down to the purser's lobby, Doctor, want to come along?"

Erin spun around in her chair, looking quizzical. "Is something going on?"

Hal replied, "Not really. But S.L. and Johnny're already down there. We like to watch the passengers come aboard on this one."

"Where's Rachel?" Erin asked matter-of-factly.

"At lunch. She's dining with the skipper. He called just a few minutes ago."

Try as she did, Erin could not keep her expression from registering the shock she felt, so she quickly turned from Hal's eyes. "I may join you later, Hal, but I want to complete these notations on Mr. Vlasic while they're fresh in my mind."

"Sure thing." And he was gone.

Alone in the unit, Erin actively fought back the sudden frustration that accompanied the news of the luncheon date between Rachel and Kurt. She assured herself that it was nothing, two old friends renewing their friendship. She remarked half-aloud. "I am not playing any jealousy game." And she meant it. She did not have time or a place in her life for the destructive emotion. She was a mature grown woman and Kurt was a mature grown man. Still, she was stunned that he was sharing a meal with the head nurse before they had even set sail.

Seated inside the poolside restaurant opposite Rachel, Kurt stirred sugar into his tea, then took a bite from his hot roast beef sandwich. He chewed slowly, glancing around the crowded room before leveling his gaze on the nurse. He touched the corner of his mouth with a white cloth napkin, then inhaled deeply before saying, "Sure you don't want a sandwich?" He watched calmly as she shook her head.

Straightening her shoulders, she inhaled deeply and asked defensively, "Are you upset with me for asking to be reassigned to this ship?"

His eyes scanned her face. "No, but I do want you to understand the situation is not as it was before."

Her brows rose. "You mean between us?" She gave a start. "I had already figured that out since it's been eight months since I've seen you, or heard from you." Her eyes plied his and she took a deep breath. "I'm not going to cause any problems with *her* if that's what you're worried about."

He concentrated on her face. "I'm in love with her, Rachel, and I want you to be aware of that before we leave port."

"I was aware of that before I resigned, *Captain Garisen. I was probably aware of that before either of you were."

He looked bewildered. "Then why are you back?" he asked with honest curiosity.

Looking across at him with an expression of sadness,

she said, "Because of this ship. I love this ship, Kurt, probably as much as you do. I didn't realize it until I worked on some of the others. You love this ship and I love this ship, but she doesn't. And someday she'll leave to go back to work on land, and we'll still be here. We'll be here because we can't leave it. It's kind of like it's a part of us." Suddenly her eyes met his head-on. "You'll never leave," she said emphatically.

He took another bite of sandwich and the more he chewed the larger the bite became in his mouth. When he finally swallowed, he took a big drink of tea. A heavy cloud had settled over his pale blue eyes. His chiseled jaw then locked, and he stared over his lunch companion. But he said nothing more.

After she had excused herself from the table, he continued to sit there, cursing her words under his breath.

Erin did go down to the lobby and joined the others shortly after Rachel came back into the unit. She sat pensively and watched the passengers come aboard to check in at the desk. There were a number of older retired couples, several smaller groups of elderly women, but, amazingly enough, a large number of middle-aged people and younger. A couple in their mid-twenties caught her eye when they entered the lobby. To be embarking on a world voyage, their expressions were terribly solemn. Something about the pair immediately mystified her and she straightened and watched them wait in line at the desk. The young man was tall and dark, lean, and good-looking. The woman was short and curvaceous with golden-blond hair and large blue eyes. A most handsome couple indeed, and a most unhappy-appearing twosome.

Erin's mind abruptly launched into all kinds of thoughts about them. They were running from something, or maybe from someone. Obviously they were married, as they wore identical wedding bands.

She was still looking intently at them when S.L. came over. "I've seen enough," she declared with a laugh. "Enough to know we're going to be very busy."

Erin laughed. "How can you tell from just watching? I haven't seen anything."

"Just trust me, Doctor. Take my word for it, our unit will not be empty for a single day in the next three months."

Erin's brow rose. "That's what we're here for, to care for the sick." From the corner of her eye she still watched the young couple. The man had leaned over and said something to his wife and Erin could see the young woman fighting her tears. Merely looking at them made her very sad and she couldn't imagine why.

S.L. had started across the lobby alone when Mark Payton reached out and caught her arm. Then with a grin, he said, "Say, aren't you the famous Nurse Brenner, the one known the length and breadth of this ship for her loving bedside manner?"

"That's me," she replied smartly. "Just get yourself admitted to the unit and find out for yourself."

Suddenly he reached up and rubbed his right temple. "Well, you see, I've had this nagging pain in the side of my head for a couple of days now."

"Sorry, we don't give treatment in the lobby." She flipped around and walked off, leaving him standing, rubbing his head. A few steps from him she halted and threw back seductively, "But feel free to come up and see us sometime."

He gave a half-smile, lifting one side of his lips. "Thanks, but I think I'll just suffer."

An hour before the ship left harbor the activities on board were wild. Parties were going on in the lounges, and smaller individual ones in the cabins and staterooms. Erin made her way through a couple of lounges rocking with gala festivities, then following one glass of wine, went down to her room. She had not seen Kurt since their episode this morning, not so much as a glimpse of him. Had her call to the hospital angered him? She stretched out lazily on her bed and wondered.

For a fleeting instant she was back in her marriage with Bill. There had always been interruptions and he had not coped at all. Then she reproached herself for thinking about him and her thoughts skimmed over anxious Mr. Vlasic and the young couple at the desk. Suddenly, she smiled, thinking then of S.L. and Mark Payton. She had been within hearing range of their exchange with each other and she thought their sparring was cute. And she also imagined there was more there than met the eye, even their own eyes. But whatever thought entered her mind, it was soon replaced by Kurt. It was obvious to her that she loved him, but to what extent she had no idea. She would not have made love to a man she didn't love. Or would she? No, she loved him. Of that she was sure, and then she didn't know what she was sure of or what she would do. Thinking about it before they even left port wasn't helping anything, so she tried

174

to put it out of her mind. She would simply love him for as long as she could, and let it go at that.

She took a short nap, then got up, showered, and dressed in her uniform. They had pulled from port while she was sleeping and when she looked out the window there was nothing but water and sky meeting her eyes.

With the sea as smooth as glass she was met with two cases of seasickness before they were an hour from New York Harbor. She understood her patients' desperation and talked with them for a long while after giving them medication for their queasiness.

Following their departure she glanced at the clock and looked over to Johnny. "Are you attending the welcome-aboard party?"

He gave a single shake of his head. "No. I think I'll just stay here. I traded tonight with Hal. Besides, after you've been to a thousand of those things, they can get kind of boring." Suddenly he looked around and his eyes widened. "Not that the captain isn't interesting." He grinned.

She started out the door, then stopped and looked back over her shoulder at him. He had already turned back to his crossword puzzle and was busy penciling in a word. Moving on out into the corridor, she wondered just how much her staff knew. For damned sure it was hard to keep a secret on a ship.

She did not have a single minute alone with Kurt that first night out. Finally, at midnight she gave up, left the party, and headed toward her room. But before she went down she walked out on deck and stood silently in the near freezing temperature, breathing in the fresh air.

Suddenly, the violent tone of voices snapped her

attention to the right of where she stood. The couple she had watched earlier in the purser's lobby were in the midst of an argument. From where she stood she could see the agitation on both their faces in the dim deck lighting. She saw the young man reach to grab the woman, only to see her jerk from his touch and yell out bitterly, "Don't touch me. I told you this wouldn't work. Now you've spent your precious hard-earned bonus, and nothing's changed."

Suddenly he was calm, maybe too calm. "Beth, it's only been a few hours. Let's give it a chance." Suddenly, he must have felt there was nothing more he could say. He strode across the deck blindly, passing Erin and pulling open the door leading back inside the ship.

The woman now had a name. Beth. And she stood there in the cold, the defiant look still hard on her face, her jaw set firm. Then she looked over and saw Erin standing a few feet away, bundled warmly in her heavy winter coat. The two women looked at each other several fleeting moments before Beth flung out across the space separating them, "There's nothing like a romantic cruise to put everything back in its proper place, is there?"

Erin kind of gave a weak half-smile, but said nothing. Then when Beth hurried past her, the younger woman said softly, "Marriage is like a terrible disease. It eats at you until you are nothing."

Erin opened her mouth to say something, she didn't know what, but it was too late anyway, Beth had followed the path of her husband inside the ship.

Minutes later in her room Erin slowly undressed and pulled on her nightgown. For some reason the last remark hung like lead in her mind. She wasn't thinking of her own ill-fated marriage, but rather of her terrible partnership.

She brushed her hair for a few minutes, then dropped the brush and went to bed. Lying there in the dark, she could take Beth's remark and change it to fit her own life. Medicine itself had been the disease in her life. Her profession had eaten at her until she felt she was nothing. She hadn't had time both for Bill and the unending demands of her partnership. So she had pushed her husband aside. But lying calmly several hours out in the Atlantic she wondered if she had ever really loved Bill. She had possessed such perfect ideals of what life could be like—successful in her practice, a warm, loving, understanding man to share her home. But it hadn't been that way. She could admit to her successful practice, but it all stopped there.

Her lips straightened in a smooth, determined line. Suddenly the thing she had fought so hard to attain was her enemy. It was strangling her. She had pulled away merely to survive the discord that had become her life. But she couldn't run forever. Her mind was going back and forth, from past to present.

Flipping over to her stomach, she buried her face in her pillow and tried to sleep. The past was just a memory of chains. Chains now broken. She was free and she was happy. But for how long? Undoubtedly the day of decision was approaching with a swiftness she did not care to think about.

She had dozed into a kind of twilight existence when the knock came at her door. Glassy-eyed, she raised her head from the pillow and heard Kurt call her name out. "Erin?"

Quickly she flung back the covers, got up from the

bed, and opened the door for him. He stepped in and smiled at her. "Were you asleep?"

"Kind of," she replied, stifling a yawn behind the back of her hand.

"I was wondering what happened to you. You just disappeared. I looked up and you were gone. Did you mean to leave without telling me good night?" he asked in a half-whisper.

"You were busy," she explained. "I told Mark to tell you."

Kurt smiled. "He did, but somehow it wasn't the same." He drew her into his arms and snuggled her close. "I could hardly stay there knowing you were gone. I love you, Erin," he said, burying his lips in her hair. Then he drew back, tilted her chin, and found her lips in a soft, searing kiss that woke her to her toes.

She drew back, her face glowing. Then, placing her arms around his neck, she pressed into his embrace and trailed her mouth across his. They kissed wildly for a moment, then he fell back away from her. "I—I still have several matters I must attend to," he explained breathlessly. "Can I come back later?"

She grinned teasingly. "It's now or never. In my business there are no rainchecks."

Reaching for the door, he gave her a lopsided smile. "I'll be back," he said softly.

When he returned an hour later he found her in the hospital treating a rotund little woman with a chronic gallbladder condition, acutely aggravated by overindulging at the midnight buffet. He looked over to Erin with huge disappointment on his face.

She smiled helplessly back at him.

178

CHAPTER ELEVEN

It was a baffling time for Kurt Garisen. It was five days into the voyage when the ship made its first port call at Cartagena, Colombia, and to his disbelief he and Erin had spent very little time together since leaving New York Harbor. Anytime he had a free moment, she didn't, and when she was free of patients, which had been rare, he was tied up with some operation of the ship. Even the nights weren't theirs to share. Erin was always exhausted or being called in the middle of the night, so they had agreed to sleep in their separate quarters. His spirits delved to a new low for him. He was beginning to think the night in New York hadn't actually happened. Outwardly he was the confident, knowledgeable captain of the vessel, radiating the security that was so important to passengers and crew alike. Inwardly his nature was undergoing a radical change, a change he did not readily understand. His quiet sense of contentment, his inner tranquility, had run amok. They had already wasted so much time. Eight months. And now that they had really discovered each other, time was wasting them. In a sense he supposed this was some kind of poetic justice being leveled on him, when he thought of all the casual loves that had drifted through his life. But Erin wasn't a casual love, and she wasn't drifting. She had given him the most steadfast emotion he had ever known and it was creating a new kind of tension within him.

The weather had changed from the intolerable cold to the bearable cool. Soon they would sail into a warmer climate, taking the all-warm-weather route with the exception of the time they would spend in China. Without any clear route to his thoughts, however, he pulled up a chair in the control room and sat down, gazing out at the sunlight.

Suddenly, he felt tired. At forty-three it was not a feeling he had often or could deal with effectively. Always a man of enormous energy, he could not imagine what was draining him, unless it was his emotional upheaval concerning Erin. He knew she was a doctor. He had known that from the beginning. But why did that trouble him so now? Why did he wish she weren't, that she was anything other than what she was?

He sat very still, looking out the sweep of windows, and was still sitting there when Mark Payton entered and said, "Kurt, all those going ashore have disembarked."

Kurt nodded and said, "Good. Any problems?" He looked up and caught Mark's eye.

"No, everyone seemed happy to be touching land for a while."

There was a brief silence. "Anything else?" Kurt asked.

Without invitation Mark straddled a chair and leaned

180

forward, arms folded across the back. "Could I ask you kind of a personal question, Kurt?"

"You can ask." His words trailed off, but not his meaning.

Mark ducked his head. "I've had a nagging headache for several days. Aspirin don't help anymore. And I wondered if you have ever had that kind of headache."

Kurt's eyes fell full on Mark's face and for a moment he said nothing. Then he gave a slow shake of his head. "I've never been bothered by headaches, Mark, nothing other than the kind that accompanies a hangover. Have you been drinking a lot?"

"No. No more than usual, and that's not much. I don't know what it is; it's just in one side of my head. It never completely goes away."

"Maybe something's wrong with your eyes. I understand that eyestrain can cause headaches. Why don't you have Erin check you?"

Mark gave an abstract shake of his head. "Oh, it'll go away I'm sure." He flushed and started up from the chair. "I'll just buy a larger bottle of aspirin."

After he had gone, Kurt looked out the windows again. For the last day or so Mark hadn't looked one hundred percent healthy. The young officer had deep circles under his eyes and an expression of discomfort on his face most of the time. When Kurt saw Erin he would mention it to her. Maybe Mark needed to be checked just to be on the safe side.

His eyes narrowed as he wondered why Mark was so hesitant to make use of the hospital facility. It wasn't, of course, a hard question to answer. Some men were modest about women physicians checking them, and he supposed Mark Payton was one of those men. But that within itself was a bit strange. Of all men, he would have thought his younger captain of the staff would have jumped at the opportunity to avail himself of Erin's services. After all, he had been head over heels in love with her.

He felt a sudden awkwardness thinking about Mark and Erin. Then his thoughts switched to Erin and himself. He would never propose marriage to her, simply because she would never accept his proposal. She loved him less than she loved medicine, and that was what was getting to him at this particular time in his life. In reality he was playing second fiddle to her profession. But then, on the other hand, could he truthfully admit that he loved her better than his own life's work? Did he love her better than the sea, the ship, his position? Raking a hand through his hair, he stopped the questions entirely. The answers would come soon enough.

Lifting the phone in the control room, he dialed the hospital. To his surprise, Erin answered. He smiled. "Do you have an empty bed with a curtain around it?"

She laughed. "Better than that, I have all empty beds. I have just this minute discharged Mrs. Holt. Are you feeling poorly, sir?"

"I was, but after hearing your unit is empty, I am suddenly in amazingly good health. How would you like to accompany me ashore and I'll show you where the pirates once stalked the Spanish Main?"

"Sounds like something I've always wanted to see." She laughed happily. "Let me change and I'll meet you in fifteen minutes."

Replacing the receiver, he moistened his dry lips and inhaled a deep breath. He was tempted to race down to her room, but instead he went to his own stateroom and changed into civilian clothes—khaki pants and a lightweight pullover sweater—and met her in the lobby.

Arm in arm, they left the ship and walked along the cobblestone streets that wound around markets and plazas over four hundred years old. He had not truly seen the real beauty of the magnificently preserved Spanish colonial architecture before this moment. But holding her hand, it was truly beautiful. Maybe it was because the woman at his side made everything seem more beautiful. She was beautiful and she made the world seen ever more so. She looked like a dream in the casual cotton skirt and tailored blouse with blossoming sleeves. Her thick ash-blond hair was parted at the side and fell softly past her shoulders in long loose fluffs. From the corners of his eyes he looked at her perfect features; her nose, her matchless lips, the large velvet golden-brown eyes with thick black lashes. Then he had the incredible thought. *How could anyone let her go?* How had he, her husband, let her go? Then without thinking, he asked, "What happened to him, Erin?"

Not understanding his question, she looked up at him. "Who, Kurt?"

Aware that she was unable to read his mind, he gave a quick shake of his head, then said after floundering a moment, "Oh—Mr. Vlasic. I haven't seen him around the past few days."

Erin laughed softly. "Oh, he's fine. He spends most of his time in the library reading about medical disorders. He came in this morning utterly convinced he was getting scurvy. He'd read where it was a common disorder of sailors. Of course, he didn't take into consideration that it occurred a hundred years ago, but rather than argue with him I just prescribed a lime a day for the remainder of the voyage."

"And that made him happy?" Kurt laughed, revealing perfect white teeth.

She nodded and sighed. "Yes. He's not hard to treat. He's just persistent."

Kurt leaned into her. "That's not a bad trait. I'm not doing so well myself."

Looking up at him, her smile dazzled in the sunlight. "I suppose not. Do you need a lime a day?"

Clasping her hand tighter in his, he whispered, "Give him the limes, I'll just take the doctor. I need her every day." Leaning closer, he kissed the side of her neck, brushing past her hair.

Chill bumps leaped to her arms. "Kurt," she whispered, "we are in public." She gestured to the castle of San Felipe. "And we'd better not go in there. I'm sure a castle has too many dark corners. I would hate to get deported from our first port of call." She laughed teasingly.

Catching her wrists, he pulled her close to his face. "Then the tour is over, my darling," he murmured and brushed her lips. "Because the tourist is driving the guide crazy. And unless the thought of making love on a cobblestone street appeals to you, I would suggest we return to the ship post haste."

Her lips curved slightly with amusement. "Kurt, anyone listening to you would think you've been locked away for the last twenty years." She surveyed his face slowly and her smile changed and she moistened her own suddenly dry lips. "But now that you mention it, the ship does sound inviting."

Fifteen minutes later he was back in his cabin

alone. Clutching the sides of his head, he sat tense and silent. They had no sooner come back on board when the steward looked up from the lobby desk and said, "Dr. Barclay, they've been paging you to the hospital for the past fifteen minutes or so."

Kurt's eyes wide with disbelief, he had gone with her to the unit and then left her there, along with Rachel and Johnny and a young woman who had just recently sprained her ankle up on the sports deck playing tennis.

He finally got up and fixed himself a light drink and turned on the music piped throughout the ship. The fact that the latest rendition of "Happy Days Are Here Again" was playing sloftly above his head didn't help his feelings in the least.

Erin read the x rays of Beth Randle placed on the reading panel by Johnny Manning. Satisfied that no fracture existed, she went back into the treatment room and removed the ice pack from the swollen, discolored ankle. "We'll put a support around this for you, Mrs. Randle, and it won't hurt to keep ice applied for the next few hours. However, you will have a few days of discomfort, so my advice is to lie around and keep your weight off it. I'll also write you two prescriptions, one for pain and one for the swelling."

Beth Randle sat motionless on the edge of the examining table, her eyes fixed on Erin's in some kind of silent mental search. Then after Erin handed her the prescriptions, she asked softly, "Doctor," she hesitated, "were you by chance out on deck that first night we left New York?" Her brow furrowed as she watched Erin's face.

185

Erin smiled blankly. "That's been so long ago, I can't remember." She smiled easily. "But probably. I frequently go out on deck at night."

"It was you," Beth stated.

Erin nodded. She looked back at Beth Randle's expression, unable to decipher whether the injured woman had wanted a denial or an admission.

But before any other words were spoken, the door opened and a troubled young man peered inside. "Beth, are you all right?"

Beth turned her head and gave a melancholy gaze. "Yes, just a sprain."

"She'll need to stay off it for the next day or so," Erin threw in, turning to the good-looking face peering in the doorway.

After the woman had hobbled over to her husband, she handed him the two prescriptions. "Perry, would you go to the pharmacy and get these filled?"

His arm slid around her waist for support. "Sure thing."

After they had gone, Erin looked over to Johnny, who was placing the x ray in a folder. "Whom was she playing tennis with, Johnny? Do you know?"

Johnny twisted his mouth. "Yeah. Samuel Tondi brought her into the unit."

Erin merely shook her head.

"That's what I thought," Johnny agreed. "He's on the make. I've seen them together several times." He blew out a long breath. "Boy, her husband is sure stupid."

After washing her hands, Erin left for Kurt's stateroom. The last thing in the world a troubled marriage needed was Samuel Tondi's wiry influence. He was a detestable man, lurking and slinking all over the ship. She could imagine he played a good game of tennis. She could imagine he played a good game, period.

She entered Kurt's room without knocking and he looked up to her from the sofa, his face somewhat gaunt. "Emergency over?" he inquired, rubbing two fingers across his forehead.

Standing just inside, Erin gazed at him. "Yes," she said following a prolonged silence as her eyes narrowed at him in concern. Whatever had led her to believe that he was the considerate, understanding man? He was sitting on his sofa pouting at her, and she was in no mood for it. Without another word she spun around and reached for the door.

"Where are you going?" he called out, rising swiftly to his feet.

"Back to the unit . . . out . . . anywhere." She opened the door.

He was immediately behind her, reaching past her and closing the door again. "There was something I failed to mention to you earlier," he said, his tone strained. "If you have a minute."

Her back to him, she replied quietly, "What is it?"

He gave an abbreviated report on Mark's complaint of headaches, concluding with, "What do you think?"

"I can't be sure, the symptoms are too vague. I wouldn't venture a guess until I speak to Mark. I need to check him." Suddenly, she turned and looked eye to eye with Kurt. "And while we're discussing your officers, is there anything you can do about Mr. Tondi?"

His eyes widened. "I don't think I know what you mean. What do you want me to do?"

She proceeded with the story. "There is a young couple on this ship, and apparently their marriage is in trouble. Why, or for what reason, I don't know, but I do know that Mr. Tondi's interest in the wife will not help their situation in any way."

Now his eyes narrowed, then widened. "Oh, what do you suggest I do?"

"I don't know, but you're the captain and I would think you could do something," she stated blandly. "Or perhaps," she went on after a short pause, "I'm overestimating your control over your staff."

His look of despair deepened. "It is one thing to cast a value judgment on a situation, Erin, and quite another to alter it. I would imagine that since you have just come up from treating Mrs. Randle that you are speaking of the Randles. I have seen the two of them together. I have no control over their marriage, or of Mr. Tondi's action in the matter. They are all grown, consenting adults. I can't reprimand them and send them to their cabins." He gazed at her suspiciously. "Nor can you."

She sighed, reached up, and caught the bridge of her nose, then dropped her hands lightly. "I suppose you're right," she muttered, "but it's a shame."

"Why should it matter to you, Erin? It's not your concern, nor mine. I would think by now you've become accustomed to fair-weather romances on ship. It's all part of the cruise. Think back, how many couples have you seen connect during these voyages?" He nodded and answered his own question. "Plenty. I can tell you, plenty."

"But this is—" she began, and stopped. She had

started to say *different*, but maybe it wasn't. She didn't know the Randles. But now she was no longer thinking of the couple. Rather, she was thinking of his words. Fair-weather romances. That was what they had. How could she have thought it anything different?

In the silence that followed, they merely looked at each other. After a long while he swallowed and said, "Erin, let's don't have this tension between us. Our time is too precious."

"Kurt," she sighed her reply, "a certain amount of tension seems to be a hazard of my trade." Her large brown eyes dwelled on his face. "I thought you would understand, but you don't. In reality, you don't."

He took a deep breath. "Yes, I do. Maybe it doesn't appear that I do, but I do. It isn't easy to love you, Erin, the way I love you, and know that I'm not first. It isn't easy to know that my place is behind the fractures and the sprains and the indigestion. In time I'll deal effectively with it, I'm sure, but now it's hard." He looked at her thoughtfully. "Can't you understand what it's like for me? Each time I want to hold you in my arms something, or should I say someone, comes between us. And if you can understand this, it isn't you I'm impatient with, but rather myself for my impatience. When I want to hold you, I want to hold you, and I'm selfish. I don't want Mr. Vlasic's psychosomatic scurvy or Mrs. Randle's sprained ankle or Mrs. Elliott's gallbladder condition coming between us." He reached out and caught her gently at the shoulders. "I love you and I want to be first with you. And if that's wrong, I'm sorry."

She put her fingers on his lips and stood looking at him a long time before saying, "Shhh," stopping his words and her heartache. His sincerity, his passion, blazed on his face as he looked at her.

Her hand dropped from his mouth and her lips parted slightly. When he reached for her she eased quietly against him and raised her mouth to his. He kissed her and she kissed him back hungrily. And then the hot thrill was there, racing through them, bringing the closeness that had almost escaped.

Bodies writhed, pressing together, sparked by the single kiss that had not yet ended. Mouths and breaths and tongues, bringing pain and pleasure; the pain of need, the pleasure, deep and sweeping in its desperation.

Kurt smoothed his palm across her shoulder, then caressed the flesh of her neck with his fingertips. Cradling her in his arms, he drew back and looked at her and what he saw was the most romantic, beautiful woman he could have ever dreamed of holding in his arms. Eyes closed, she was poised weightlessly in his embrace, her expression so extraordinarily calm and peaceful, as though she lingered somewhere beyond his touch, between the heavens and earth. He smiled.

Her eyes fluttered open. "What are you doing?" she breathed questioningly.

Without a word he grasped her hands and led her into his bedroom, where they reclined on the thick pillows and sea blue bedspread. They lay embracing a long time, not talking, not moving. Erin turned her face to him and eyed him with uncertainty, the look of wonderment unveiled in the flickering brown eyes.

His eyes were directly on her face, a hint of a

smile on his lips. Finally, he breathed, "You are the loveliest, most exciting woman I've ever known."

She felt the color rise to her cheeks and she returned in soft jest, "I can tell. That's why we're just lying here."

He smiled slyly, his blue eyes growing feverish. His tongue moistened his lips slowly. "Time seems too short at best." Leaning forward, he kissed her, knowing that the touch would devour their time. And he was right. Her taste, fresh as raindrops, came into his mouth, dissolving the last of his resolutions, dooming his intentions. The pangs of hunger for her were greater than his self-control. Senses of touch and feeling became overpowering. The barrier of clothes fell away, removed by hands free and weightless, until they lay naked together.

Then the kisses were longer, harder, and filled with urgency, and the real world dropped away behind a transparent haze while they rose together toward the clouds. His lips, his mouth at her neck, at her breasts, made her giddy, unaware of her movements, of her moans, of her cries. When she murmured, "Kurt," only a moment passed before she felt his lower body yielding into hers and she clasped him there and held him, reveling in the heat of him, the glow of him inside her body, reaching deeper than flesh.

There came the illusion of ascending skyward, of being suspended, unsupported, unencumbered by any emotion other than that of desire alone. Enraptured, they moved upward to the heights, held aloft in each other's arms until the true dimension of ecstasy caught them in one overpowering quake that sent them both back to earth slowly and lightly as summer rain, rinsing them, enriching the warmth they shared with a plummet of chills along their beings.

Erin lay back breathlessly, softly raking her teeth across her bottom lip while his head lay at her neck, his hair a tumbled mass. "You know," he half-groaned between his teeth, "I feel as if I have just won the Olympics, as if I have achieved some victory." The very tips of his fingers played at her hair.

She gave him a tender smile and rumpled his hair even more. "Anything worth having is worth waiting for," she quoted philosophically, smiling.

He raised his head and looked into her face. "And was it worth the wait, fair lady?" he asked her. His blue irises were still firelit and his face was damp with perspiration.

"Worth the wait and more. Though I'd rather we don't hold off for quite so long next time."

He moved beside her and they lay sated and relaxed, going on for some time with nimble little quips at each other. Then Kurt rose on one elbow and looked solemnly at Erin a long moment before saying, "I would like to ask you something, Erin."

Studying his expression, she replied in an unsteady voice, "All right."

"Do you love me?"

She turned her gaze slightly, avoiding looking at him. "Yes," she finally whispered, "I love you."

"And how much do you love me?"

Slowly her tongue moistened her lips. "I don't know," she finally answered.

He remained unmoving, quietly looking at her. "Do you think of it as a weakness?"

Her eyes widened and she looked back at him.

"That's a strange question. I'm not sure I know how to answer it," she said sadly.

"I'd like you to try."

She stared at him thoughtfully. "Why?" she asked softly. Outside, the daylight was waning and she knew in a short while it would be dark and they would both be back at their posts of duty. Why was he wasting their precious time with unanswerable questions?

"Because, Erin, I think that somewhere in your thoughts you associate love with weakness, that you are supposed to be superhuman, and superhuman beings don't allow love the rightful place in their lives."

Her chin rose slightly. "I don't think you're being fair, Kurt. I have never considered myself to be superhuman, but rather at times the opposite. A failure." Slowly, deliberately, she went on. "Have you considered that I am a surgeon, but I'm not operating. I'm the medical officer on this ship. I am running, Kurt, and I have been for longer than a year now. And I *want* to live the life of the skilled surgeon I am."

"Do you?" he asked worriedly. "Is that really what you want?"

"Yes," she answered assuredly. Suddenly, her gaze drifted past him, faraway. "It's very difficult to talk about and I have never talked about it with anyone, but my marriage failed because my husband couldn't accept the demands of my career, and my partnership failed because I couldn't accept the demands of my partner. And suddenly I was surrounded by failure. And I didn't expect it." Her eyes misted. "A superhuman person would have coped, but I'm not that person, Kurt. I didn't cope, I ran."

His arm went around her and he nestled her head against his naked shoulder. With one finger he lifted her chin and kissed her mouth. "I'm glad," he whispered. "I'm glad you ran. Listen, my darling, I love you and I'll always love you. And someday when you're back in that operating room you will have the security of knowing that somewhere out on one of the oceans there is a man who loves you more than anything else in this world."

Her eyes crinkled as she smiled sadly at him and a single tear escaped from one corner. She understood something he didn't. Yes, he loved her. She believed with all her heart that he did love her, but not enough to give up his oceans for her, nor would she ask him to make that sacrifice.

Easing her lips slowly against his cheek, her body inched closer to his, for that feel, that touch that would erase the conversation that just passed between them. The only time in her life she had become obsessed with the thought of being superhuman came with the brief moments she shared with him. The intimacy of their bodies made her superhuman. Her desire for him was incredibly overpowering, reaching a point of near agony.

Her long hair swirled backward as she lifted her mouth to his and he leaned down to meet her lips. They pressed together again, clinging to each other, and simultaneous moans escaped them. They made love again, but this time with a bittersweet passion that had not been present before. More tender than ever before, more explosive than ever before because the words of tomorrow had been spoken and they were not there together. Tomorrow would come and they would not share it. And that knowledge made the moments they shared now sweeter and dearer.

After she had gone, he lay there in a distant silence. He could see himself as a boy on the rocky coast of Maine looking out at the sea. The hours he had walked and looked out at that water and dreamed of conquering it! And hadn't he done it? Wasn't he now in port and tomorrow wouldn't he be en route again around the world? His dreams had been realized with each night under the star-laden sky with nothing but water around him for a thousand miles.

But now something was tearing at that dream, and he fought to keep it from becoming nothing but a thought of nothingness. His love for her was clouding his mind and blowing at him like an angry sea wind. He could close his eyes and see nothing but that beautiful face, and it tortured his mind. Was it so terrible to give up a dream? Was it? Was he already, with his thoughts, in the process of letting it go?

Escaping from his thoughts, he went to the radio room. He was just coming through the door when the cable from Malaney to Erin came through. It said simply:

Doctor, am still unsuccessful in securing you a replacement. With your agreement now so near to the date of termination, am wondering if you would consider completion of the current cruise an inconvenience? Please reply. Nils Malaney.

Kurt was puzzled. "What is this?" he asked the communications officer.

"Another of Malaney's delay tactics," came the laughing reply. He extended the paper to Kurt. "Want to deliver this one?"

Kurt straightened his shoulders. "How long has this been going on?"

The officer raised one brow. "Months." Again the laugh. "The doctor doesn't know, but Malaney never had any intention of replacing her. These radio games are just his way to placate her and make her think he's trying. You know how he is about anybody trying to get out of a contract. It just never happens."

Kurt stood reading over the message just received. "Why haven't you told me?" he grunted.

"Hell, Captain, I thought you knew." He shook his head feebly. "I've received each one; I have the reports."

Suddenly, he was too angry to speak, his mind still not quite taking it all in. He knew there had been messages relayed to Erin from the director's office, but he had assumed those dealt with hospital directions, or payroll deductions, or some senseless crap Malaney was always relaying to various members of the staff. But not this! Anger washed over him. She had requested to leave his ship! He couldn't believe it.

He exited the room, and in the corridor, crinkled the paper into a tight ball. She had betrayed him. Used him. And all the while had not even hinted that she had asked to be replaced. His first impulse was to cram the wad of paper down her throat. But that would be too simple, too easy.

Kurt's anger had changed into brooding when he knocked heavily on her door. Several moments passed before it opened. "Kurt," she said quietly, her face,

196

her eyes, revealing the fact he had awakened her from a sound sleep. She paused, then asked, "What is it?"

"May I come in?"

"Certainly." She yawned and stepped back, then closed the door after he was inside. "Is something wrong?" she asked in a quiet tone.

He fought to keep the annoyance out of his voice when he replied, "Should there be?" He met her eyes then for the first time since entering the room. "Just consider me the ship's messenger," he went on with a halfhearted smile. "I'm here to tell you that Nils has been unsuccessful in finding a replacement for you." He inhaled deeply. "And furthermore, he would like you to complete the term of your contract, since it'll be up soon anyway." He fell silent.

"Oh," she said, startled.

His eyes flashed. "What is 'oh?' " His eyebrows rose. "Is that, 'Oh, Nils can't replace me,' or is that, 'Oh, Kurt's discovered the devious little game I've been playing with him'?"

Determined not to argue with him, she said softly, "I haven't been playing any games with you, Kurt."

"Like hell you haven't!" he exclaimed sharply, then was suddenly calm again. "Why did you ask to leave?"

"I asked a long time ago."

He stood rooted close to her. "Why didn't you talk it over with me? Why did you go over my head?"

"It seemed the thing to do at the time."

"You're being evasive, Erin. Why can't you come out in plain talk and tell me your reasons?"

She tossed her head in defiance, and when she spoke her words were firm and positive. "Let's face it, Kurt, you're not going to give up the sea for me, and I'm not going to give up medicine for you."

"And that's why you asked to leave?" His brows knitted close.

"I love you, Kurt," she said factually. "And it's a miserable kind of love. A love which began on that first voyage. I was merely trying to save myself another heartbreak. I wasn't interested in sacrificing my emotions to a relationship which was, and is, quite hopeless." She gestured helplessly toward him. The reason she had given was far more truthful than admitting she knew about his wager with Nils. That bet had ceased to be important a long time ago. That wager had merely made her face the pointlessness of continuing a relationship with him.

"Then why have you changed your mind?"

"I don't know," she said with a weak smile.

He smiled and touched her hair, pushing it back from her face. "Don't give up on our love so easily, Erin. It may prove stronger than you think."

She caught his shoulders with both hands, stepped forward, and kissed him tenderly on the mouth. Then brushing his lips, she whispered, "I'll notify Nils tomorrow that I'll complete my agreement with the line."

He took her hand and she felt the tenderness pass between them. He grinned and said quietly, "Let's not wait until tomorrow, let's do it now."

"But, darling, it's very late in New York."

His smile widened. "I know."

198

CHAPTER TWELVE

The next morning the *Royal Princess Star* entered the Panama Canal and was raised to a height of eighty-five feet above sea level through various locks, and then was lowered back to sea level on the Pacific side of the Canal. It was fascinating to a sleepy Erin, who watched at stages and listened to Samuel Tondi's commentary on the ship's public address system when she was in the hospital unit. Some of the more adventurous passengers had gone ashore for the overland tour along the canal and would come back on ship at Balboa.

Erin looked from the deck at the engineering marvel, then glanced around. The first person she saw was Beth Randle, alone on a deck chair with her arm resting across her eyes and her leg propped on a pillow. Erin made her way to the chairs and sat down. "How are you, Mrs. Randle?"

Beth's arm dropped away and she looked over and smiled. "Fine, Doctor. It's really not too bad today." Her large blue eyes widened. "But last night was bad."

Erin looked around. "Are you alone?" It was not

her nature to pry, but she had been going against her nature a lot here lately.

Beth gave a little shrug. "Perry's on shore. He wanted to traipse through the jungle."

Erin shifted uncomfortably in the chair and cleared her throat, but she didn't say anything.

"It's all right," Beth said indifferently. "I'm used to him not ever being around." Suddenly switching topics, she went on cheerily, "You know, you don't look like a doctor. That's why I was so surprised to see you in the clinic yesterday."

Erin smiled and said rather lamely, "Oh."

Beth laughed and said, "I don't mean any disrespect. I think it's great. Really. Once in my life I used to dream of being a doctor or lawyer." The mirth disappeared from her eyes, left her expression. "But I fell in love. I was a sophomore in college. . . ." Her words drifted away.

Erin's mind began racing. Beth was opening up and she wanted to keep the conversation going. "So," she said with interest, "you got married and dropped out of college?"

Beth twisted her lips and nodded. "How right you are." She glanced nervously at Erin. "And now here I am, twenty-six years old and I'm nobody—nothing but Perry's wife."

Erin inhaled deeply. "Is that bad?" she inquired lightly.

Beth groaned. "It wasn't, but Perry is a damned workaholic. It isn't enough for him to make a living, he has to be best, always. He's a sales representative for a national office supply corporation and he has to be the top man every quarter. Each time he opens his mouth it's to say he's got this copier sold or this word processor, or some bank is switching to his computers." Her tone became impatient. "You can't imagine what it's like to live with a man who each time he opens his mouth you get this feeling of getting a computer printout." She raised her upper body and leaned on the armrest in Erin's direction. "We're on this cruise because I asked him for a divorce at Christmas." Her eyes rolled with dismay and she shook her head. "If you can believe this, at the dinner table at my parents' he talked my dad into buying an electronic typewriter. While the rest of the family was gathered under the tree opening presents, Perry and Dad were down at his office picking up the typewriter."

Erin smiled helplessly.

Beth went on. "So when we got home I told him I wanted a divorce. And you know what he did? He went right to the phone and called the district manager of the company and asked for a leave of absence. He took his bonus checks for the past year, money he had intended to invest in his own office supply outlet, and booked us on this cruise." She shook her head. "I don't know what to think of him."

Erin peered at her curiously. "You're here. I would think by that you're both trying to salvage your marriage. Aren't you?"

Beth sighed. "I don't know if we can." She took a deep breath. "I just don't know."

Erin was still sitting there talking with Beth when she glimpsed Samuel Tondi come out on deck. His eyes were immediately drawn to the two women, but seeing Erin he snatched his glance away and went back inside.

Erin sat there a good while longer before she got

up and returned to the hospital. She had for some unknown reason taken an interest in the Randles the moment she first placed her eyes on them in the ship's lobby. Why, she didn't know. Nor did she know how she was going to keep Samuel Tondi from increasing their problems. But she did know that somehow she was. Demons danced in her dark eyes.

That evening, wearing a soft lavender silk dress with a darker shade jacket, Erin was walking femininity as she entered the formal dining room. She smiled at Kurt, who was busily entertaining at his table and then she was escorted to the table she had arranged for earlier in the evening. She had decided the best way to get a wolf's attention was to provide him new bait. Herself.

Five minutes later, dressed in a splendid evening jacket, in walked the man of her thoughts, complete with sexy heavy-lidded eyes which widened only a bit at seeing her. "Erin," he said smoothly. "I'm happy to be dining with you at last."

Neither saw Kurt's head turn sharply and his lips part in surprise.

"I know," Erin answered softly. "It's been much too long." When he was seated and grinning over to her she said, "I took the liberty of ordering you a glass of wine." Again she smiled.

"Fine." He grinned. "I'm sure anything you selected will be outstanding."

Across the room, Kurt gave his head a little shake, fighting back the despair he felt as he looked at her. She had never looked so beautiful. Despite his efforts to remain attentive to the conversation taking place around him, he could not keep his eyes from their table. What was she doing with Tondi? He gave his head another little shake, trying to clear his senses, fighting back the natural instinct of jealousy.

And then when the Randles came into the dining room, he saw the sweet smile she gave them, and at that precise moment she reached across and clutched Tondi's bony fingers. Then he knew what she was doing and he wanted to choke her, along with the cruise director.

Following the late dinner, in the glow of soft light and to the mellow music of the combo, he sat and watched Tondi take her in his arms and dance with her. And as they danced, a smirk appeared on Kurt's face as he watched her fight against the closeness Tondi was trying to impose on her. His eyes then went to the Randles' table and remained there long enough to see them leaning close to each other in the candleglow, holding hands and smiling lovingly.

Then his eyes went back to the floor just in time to see the lithe man bury his lips at the side of her neck. Up he came from the chair and excused himself from the table. He walked onto the dance floor and interrupted the ship's newest twosome mid-dance with a tap on Tondi's shoulder. "Do you mind?" he asked in a harsh whisper.

Tondi stepped back and relented without a word in return. Clasping her tight, Kurt spoke between his teeth. "What in the hell do you think you're doing?"

She gave him a beautiful smile. "I was dancing with Mr. Tondi."

"It looked more like an orgy to me," he replied in a hot whisper. "He was all over you."

"That's what I was trying to tell you, darling," she said softly, but with a smile. "The man is like glue."

"Well, he had better find him someone else to stick to because he definitely isn't sticking to you," he asserted, still in a whisper. "And it should make you happy to know that the Randles were seemingly enjoying their evening together, so much so they left a few minutes ago, just the two of them."

Her brows rose. "So, you're watching them too." She laughed in soft accusation.

He pulled her closer to him, his lips brushing against her hair. "Don't do this again."

She drew back and looked directly at him. "Is that an order?"

He inhaled and grimaced. "Don't do it again, please."

"I won't. It wasn't that much fun, even though it was for a good cause."

When the dance ended he went back to his table and she returned to her own, finding that her date had left her. She listened to the music a while longer and cast loving glances at the ship's captain. Then, sitting there alone, looking at him, she had the most unlikely thought she could have ever imagined having. Her mind said to her, *I wouldn't mind if he asked me to marry him. I wouldn't mind becoming his wife, bearing his children.*

Her hand spread at the base of her throat and she fought back the wild impulsive play on her mind. It was an absurd thought—impossible. It was frightening. Suddenly, she leaped up from the table, turned abruptly to the doorway of the domed room, and hurried out. Her love for him was getting out of hand; and it was only at this moment she realized it.

Twisting her hands nervously, she went by the hospital before heading for her room. She didn't want to be alone with her thoughts. She found S.L. sitting comfortably in the bay area reading a novel.

Looking up, S.L. smiled. "My, you look pretty."

"Do you have coffee made, S.L.?"

"No, but I'll make some. Won't take but a minute. Johnny finally cleaned the coffeemaker." She placed her novel on a shelf and rose from the chair. "We always wait until it gets so clogged it takes two hours to drip through, then we play the waiting game to see whose nerves it gets to first. Johnny lost this time." She laughed cheerfully.

Erin followed her into the lounge. "I'm surprised we've gone twenty-four hours without anyone checking in," she said, still uncomfortable with herself.

"I think it was the canal." S.L. glanced back over her shoulder. "Anytime we're somewhere interesting it takes a real emergency to bring them in here."

As she spoke the door to the unit opened and Mark Payton, dressed in dinner clothes, entered, holding tightly to the right side of his head. "Anyone here?" he called out.

Erin stuck her head out of the lounge door. "Yes, back here." She smiled, then the smile faded and her eyes grew wide. "What is it, Mark?"

"I don't know," he groaned. "But if I didn't know better, I would say I was having a stroke." He fell back against the wall. "I've never had such a pain. And it won't go away."

Erin rushed out, S.L. on her heels. Quickly, they helped him into the treatment room, one on each side of him. Looking at the wild helplessness in his eyes, the heavy perspiration on his brows, Erin said to S.L., "Check his vital signs first." Hurriedly, they began to undress him.

"Can't you call one of the men in for this?" he muttered, looking at S.L., then up at Erin.

S.L. gave a little push at his bare shoulder. "For goodness' sake, Mark Payton, we're professional women, we aren't going to look at anything you've got." She smiled wickedly at him. "Except with a professional eye. Now, lean back here and let me take your blood pressure." She guided him back on the table with her hands.

With another moan of pain he allowed himself to lie back as she placed the blood pressure cuff around his upper arm. Her eyes darted away from the reading and she said low to Erin, "One eighty over eighty."

"Mark, explain your pain to me," Erin said quickly.

He pointed to his eye, then along the side of his head. "It's a pain. It's been kind of a throb, but now it's like a knife, sharp."

"You've had it for several days, haven't you?"

He nodded stoically. "But not like this."

Peering into one eye, then the other, with the ophthalmoscope, she asked, "Have you had any blurring of vision, dizziness?"

"No, not really. But I've been nauseated."

"Vomiting?"

"Yes. All day, to be exact."

Erin looked at S.L. "You need to call Hal in for the bloodwork, and we'll need Johnny to do skull x rays." She hesitated, then inquired softly. "Who does the EEG?"

"Johnny," S.L. replied, taking the electronic thermometer from under Mark's tongue and looking at the readout. His temperature was almost one hundred and two, and Erin read the alarm in S.L.'s eyes, along with the monitor.

The night passed slowly and all of the hospital staff was in the unit with the exception of Rachel Lawrence, who was off-duty. Kurt came in a little after midnight and positioned himself in an armchair in Erin's office.

From the x-ray table, Mark, now heavily sedated, had been moved to a bed in the bay and S.L. bathed his feverish brow with a cool cloth. Erin studied the x rays on the lighted panel. Johnny, standing beside her, said, "It's negative, Doctor. Nothing abnormal."

"Okay, Johnny, thanks." Erin said, eyeing the film. Shaking her head and sliding her hands into the lab coat pockets she had put on over her evening wear, she walked into her office.

Kurt's chin rested on his chest, and he looked up in tiredness at her. "Well?" he asked, his brow knitting at her expression.

She reported factually. "As best I can tell, Mark is suffering a migraine headache. He has some transient neurological findings, but I don't believe they're of an organic nature. Right now I'm worried about his temperature, which no doubt is due to dehydration. I've started him on IV fluids and vasoconstrictors."

"A headache?" Kurt straightened in his chair.

She nodded and smiled bleakly. "Yes, but a very severe one."

He folded his arms across his chest. "He'll be all right, won't he?"

She sighed. "Yes, I think so. Of course, he's allowed himself to become quite ill. This has been going on for some time."

"Damned fool," Kurt grunted impatiently. "He's let himself go until he gets in this kind of shape, and do you know why!"

Erin's eyes widened and she gave a brief shake. "Why?" she whispered, barely audible.

"Because he didn't want to come in here—" His words stopped abruptly.

Suddenly, his meaning became clear to her clouded mind and she paled. "Because of me," she uttered in total disbelief.

Realizing what he had done, Kurt leaped to his feet. "No," he said, reaching out and clasping her shoulders.

"Yes." She wrenched free and stepped back. "Because I'm a woman, that's what you're saying, Kurt. That he went days in agony rather than allow me to treat him."

"Now, Erin, that isn't it," he tried to explain. "Let me finish."

"Don't try to placate me, Kurt," she said bitterly. "His condition speaks for itself."

"Erin," he grabbed her harshly, "you *will* listen to me. What kept him out of here had nothing to do with your skills, but rather that you were the woman he fancied himself to be in love with. Months ago he was very serious about you."

She gave a shake of her head. "I didn't know."

Kurt nodded again. "Since that time he's realized our situation. But, hell, I have no idea whether or not he's still nursing his fantasies about you. He didn't want you to see him sick. I do know that."

"This is unbelievable." She sighed, on the verge of tears.

The tension between them began to dissipate and he caught her up in his arms, hugging her close.

Long after he was gone she sat in her office, pondering the impossible. She was relieved when S.L. stuck her head in and said with a smile, "His temp is normal, Erin, and he's rousing up from the narcotic. And brother, is he a grouch."

Erin smiled wearily. "Well, I think if he's improved to that extent I'll take myself to my cabin. You can call if you need me."

S.L. nodded. "He'll be all Rachel's in about an hour. They should make a lovely combination. She has absolutely no patience with whiners. And I can tell from the onset, he's going to be a gold-medal one. That's the way it is with all these macho types."

"Well, tell Rachel to make sure he stays in bed. The moment he feels relief he will probably try to return to duty."

After Erin had gone S.L. sauntered back out to the bay and sat down beside the bed, lifting her novel from the shelf, where she had placed it hours ago.

Mark turned his head to her and batted his lids heavily. "What are you doing?" he grunted.

"Reading," S.L. returned smartly. "I always do that when there's nothing interesting in the unit."

"Sara Lynn," he said weakly, "have you ever considered for one brief moment that I am your superior? I am in charge of the staff on this ship, and you are a member of my staff."

Her eyes flickered over the top of the pages. "Why didn't you say 'for one brief shining moment,' Captain Payton, and then I would have thought you were Camelot?"

"Oh, hell," he moaned, and flipped over to his side.

"Don't pull out those IV's," she said threateningly. "I have too much fun starting them over."

"Don't worry," he grunted into his pillow. "You won't be touching me any more than is necessary. I once owned a yellow dog that wasn't as mean as you."

The next afternoon, when S.L. returned to the unit, Rachel tossed her head and declared dramatically. "He's all yours, and I do mean literally. Another five minutes with him and I'll have a migraine myself!"

"I can imagine," S.L. laughed cheerfully, then suddenly became serious. "Has Erin seen him today?"

Rachel nodded. "Indeed. Everyone on ship has seen him. He's beginning to develop a celebrity complex. It's been a crazy bunch coming in and out of here all day. Even to Kurt. He came in and sat with Mark as if your Mr. Payton were number one on the critical list. Can you believe that! The captain of the ship, no less!" She shook her head. "I think I'm going to get falling-down drunk tonight."

S.L.'s eyes scanned the unit. "Who's in the other bed?" she asked, seeing the pulled curtain.

Rachel sighed. "Mr. Pickle, who else."

"For goodness' sake, what's wrong with him?" S.L. inquired, then added, "Now."

Rachel huffed. "That old man has been eating so manly lemons and limes in the past few hours he's lost the inside of his mouth to the acid. We're preparing him mouth rinse three times a day. Lord"—she rolled her eyes heavenward—"this is the real ship of

210

fools." With those words she flounced out of the unit.

Smiling broadly, S.L. went to check her two patients. Pulling the curtain back at Mark's bedside, she said teasingly, "Rumor has it that your pain is subsiding, that you are able to party at bedside. Any truth to it?"

Mark glared hostilely. "I am not going to tolerate any insubordination from you, Nurse Brenner, not today. If you so much as look at me sideways, I'll put you on report."

"Oh, I wouldn't dream of being insubordinate to such a sweetie." Smiling at him, she crossed her eyes, almost losing them completely behind her nose.

"That did it! You're going on report!"

"That wasn't sideways," she argued teasingly. "That was cross-eyed, and you didn't say I couldn't look at you cross-eyed."

"No, you didn't," came a weak voice from the adjoining bed. "I heard what you said and you said sideways."

Hearing that, Mark pulled the sheet up over his head and groaned aloud.

He was still lying like that when Erin came into the unit after a midafternoon snack. She stood eyeing her patients in momentary silence, the tension from last night completely gone from her features.

Sensing her presence, Mark jerked the sheet from his head and called out to her, "When can I get out of here?"

She pursed her lips thoughtfully. "Oh, I would say three or four days. You're still running a slight temperature."

"But I'm feeling fine," he argued. "I don't see any

211

reason to stay here. My headache's gone, at least the one I came in here with. I'm fine, really."

"You're not fine, not yet," she said matter-of-factly. "In a few days." She raised her brows, adding, "Maybe."

"A few more days in here and you can roll me down to cold storage." He grunted and turned to his side, then raised his head and looked back over to her. "I don't want to miss Acapulco. It's one of my favorite spots."

"That's three days away," Erin replied factually. "You won't miss it if you behave yourself and do as you're told. You came in here very ill, Mark, and you aren't well yet."

S.L. walked between the two beds and asked, "Would you gentlemen like me to turn on some music?"

"No," Mark breathed in disgust.

At the same time Mr. Vlasic said, "Yes, that would be nice. I think some music would lead to a more peaceful environment."

S.L. grinned mischievously at the younger man. "Would you mind putting your fingers in your ears," she said with silent laughter in her voice, then walked over and turned on the piped-in music.

Several minutes later she entered Erin's office and said, "Do you know what I think?"

Erin's brows shot up in anticipation.

S.L. nodded emphatically. "I think Mr. Vlasic is lonely. He needs someone to occupy his time, a companion of sorts. At present we're all he's got."

"S.L.," Erin said dubiously, "let's don't add match-making to our other duties."

The nurse's mouth curved. "I think it would be

nice. And since the ratio of women to men is about two to one, I don't think it would be difficult." Her neck craned forward a tiny bit. "I was thinking of Mrs. Elliott in particular, if you know what I mean. Or Mrs. Holt. They both have chronic gallbladders and with his list of ailments there would never be a lapse in conversation."

Erin inhaled deeply. "But if you're going to do this, and I can tell that you are, then why not introduce him to someone healthy."

S.L.'s eyes brightened. "That is a good idea." She stood thoughtfully a moment, then snapped her fingers. "Miss Decker. She's perfect."

Erin's eyes narrowed in a quick mental search, then suddenly widened. "Oh, no, her health is too good. She jogs and works out daily in the fitness room. The other day I saw her press a hundred-pound weight. I don't think he's up to her. Really."

"Okay." S.L. turned around, then glanced back. "But I'll find someone."

Turning back to her work, Erin didn't doubt it.

The next day, when S.L. came on duty, she found Mark up walking around the unit. Once again he was alone. Rachel had helped in the search for Miss Right for Mr. Vlasic, and he was on deck sunning his mouth with a retired librarian from Independence, Missouri. Thanks to Rachel. She had known immediately the person for the chronically ailing man.

In exceptionally good spirits, S.L. smiled at Mark. "Practicing for Acapulco?" she threw out lightly.

He half-grinned. "Could be. The nightlife there is something else." Suddenly, their eyes fixed on each

213

other and each stood motionless for a moment. "Maybe you'd like to come ashore with me."

She gave a swift toss of her head. "I don't think so."

"Why not?" he asked, genuinely surprised.

She was somewhat hesitant before saying diplomatically, "Because I'm not your first choice, and I refuse to play second fiddle to you, or to any man. If I can't be first, then I won't be at all."

"But I haven't asked anyone else," he argued back, taking a step toward her.

"And that's because you knew she would not accept. I know whom you want to ask; you're not fooling me or anyone else on this ship."

There came a moment of silence. "All right, I'll admit I once had a crush on Erin. Does that make you feel better? I'll admit it."

"A crush! You were a falling down blubbering fool! I was embarrassed for you."

"It wasn't that bad," he interrupted hotly. "And besides, she never had a second glance for anyone from the moment she boarded this ship except Kurt Garisen. They are deeply in love, in case your eagle eye hasn't noticed."

"My eagle eye noticed a long time before your blind eye did. Think back to just a few weeks ago to New Year's Eve. You were about to chase after her and make a complete fool of yourself if I hadn't stopped you." Her eyes grew large. "And that was only a few weeks ago. So there! Don't feed me that I'm-over-Erin bit, because I don't believe you! You and Samuel Tondi are just alike. You go ape over any woman with two legs and a half-curve."

His face flushed fiery red. "Don't you compare me

214

to Samuel Tondi. Don't you ever compare me to him!" he yelled out angrily.

"You'd better watch your blood pressure," she said calmly.

"And you'd better watch your mouth!"

"Or what!" She didn't bat an eye.

He stood glaring at her in total frustration. They were standing like that when Erin came in, looked over, and said smilingly, "What's going on?"

"We were just talking about the fun we're going to have in Acapulco," S.L. answered readily.

Mark looked stunned, then he blinked his eyes, gave a quick jerk sideways, walked over to his bed, and fell onto it in a heap.

That night Erin and Kurt bypassed the formal dining room for a film showing in the ship's theater. When the feature ended they went up on deck for a leisurely stroll beneath a beautiful starlit night. The night was warm with only the hint of a breeze sweeping the crowded area.

"Why don't we go up to my deck?" Kurt suggested, and several minutes later they were standing at the wing of the bridge staring up at the night sky.

"I wonder if it's still snowing in New York," Erin said, feeling the soothing breeze in her hair.

He nodded. "Probably," he answered, his eyes resting approvingly on her.

She looked up at the sky. "All the stars are out tonight."

He smiled. "Just for you."

Her fingers played at the railing. "It's exhilarating, isn't it?" She glanced up at him. "Being here," she added softly.

215

He reached over and placed his hand over hers. "With you, it is." Then he turned his head slightly and looked deeply into her eyes. "I don't know how I'll go on without you," he said as softly as the wind in her hair.

"Kurt," she began, her voice tight with a strange sadness, "don't."

"I'm going to tell you how I feel, Erin. I love you." His voice vibrated with feeling. "And I can't imagine ever saying good-bye to you. I don't know why we should allow our love to be compromised by our careers, our happiness jeopardized. When you think about it, it doesn't make sense."

She didn't want to agree with him. She couldn't allow herself to do so. Her eyes were wide and searching. "Kurt, we have such a long way to go, let's don't put barriers in our path so early. Let's just enjoy the night, and the stars, and each other. Can't we?" she whispered almost pleadingly, her tone one of disquiet.

He inhaled deeply. "All right, Erin, but I'm going to say this, then I'll hush." Holding her hand in his, he gazed steadily out over the water. "I used to believe I knew my purpose in life, to sail all over the world. And I loved it. I loved the feeling of being at sea, but in these past months I've come to realize I love you more and I think perhaps that's my real purpose. I have never been happier than now, with you. It's as if suddenly my life has new direction and purpose, and I'm richer for it. I feel if we let each other go, we'll have shortchanged our reason for being at all. I know we can't see beyond tomorrow, we can't look over the horizon, we don't know what awaits our future, but we have today and we are at this moment standing on our horizon." His words died away and he hovered close to her face. "I love you, and somehow I think that is most important of all." He bent and kissed her tenderly.

An immediate warmth surged through her and her mouth quivered beneath his. This longing, this terrible longing, was all for him. She closed her dark eyes and went with the moment, swaying in his arms. Someday she would be able to sort out all her feelings, and with some clarity say, This is most important in my life. Someday, but not tonight. Tonight she didn't want to play with her thoughts. She just wanted him. His lips, his kiss, his touch, his body.

Her long, tapered fingers enclosed the back of his head, slipping into the thick dark hair, and she pressed closer to him.

His fingers tightened at her back as his lips grazed her hair and buried against her ear. Fully aroused to her closeness, he murmured, "You certainly know how to shut me up." And then his mouth was on hers, crushing hers fiercely with a near violent intensity.

Moments later in her cabin they surrendered completely to undisguised passion, naked and raw and flaring with sensuality. But even as she found herself swept away on a sea of whirling desires, she could not keep his words from tearing at her mind. Was he most important in her life? Was he more important than her professional obligation?

The torturing of her mind put new incentive in her lovemaking, until she finally freed herself of any thoughts, fighting them away, and she was totally absorbed by the delight of his body.

They made love several times throughout the night, the last when the sky in the east lightened and drove away the stars. When she awoke it was midday and he was gone. But his words remained to haunt her.

CHAPTER THIRTEEN

The *Royal Princess Star* had been at sea almost a full month. Behind lay Acapulco and Hawaii as the ship plowed into the beautiful aqua oceans surrounding the South Pacific islands. Erin's first thought was that paradise had to be here, and after touring the first port of call at Pago Pago, she thought, it still is.

Kurt had been tied up on ship's business and she and Hal and Rachel and Johnny had rented a car for an island excursion through forests filled with flowering trees and a variety of wildflowers. They had picnicked beside a cascading waterfall, then had spent the afternoon visiting a Samoan village where Rachel and Erin had bought a carload of souvenirs that made the purser shake his head when they came through the ship's lobby. He called out to them. "We still have two months to go, girls, and there's just so much room on ship."

They both bestowed him a look of mocking contempt and continued up to the hospital deck. "I wonder just how old we'll have to be before he calls us women?" Rachel muttered, glancing at Erin.

219

"We'll probably never be that old," Erin replied back.

In the elevator they encountered Arthur Swinney, the ship's pharmacist, who shook his head slowly at Erin and volunteered, "I think we've got a baby growing on this ship."

Erin tilted her head and said, "What?"

He sighed. "The Randles. They've bought about all my pregnancy test kits I had stocked. I've got only two left. Each day one or the other comes in and buys one."

"Well, I wouldn't worry about it," Rachel interjected, "she's about the only one on ship young enough to get pregnant."

Arthur Swinney ignored her, saying to Erin, "I figure they must not be following directions. There's two tests in each kit, so I know they've done at least twelve tests. I suggested to Perry Randle this morning that they come to see you."

Erin smiled bleakly, but made no reply. Pregnancy was another condition somewhat out of her range of expertise.

She was relieved when the day passed and the ship set sail for Suva, Fiji, without the Randles following Arthur Swinney's advice. That night in Kurt's arms she mentioned the Randles, telling him what the pharmacist had said on the elevator.

He chuckled. "That's great." His blue eyes danced at her. "A ship's baby—that's a position we rarely fill."

"I don't know," she said solemnly. "If there are no problems, but . . ." Suddenly her voice failed and she lapsed into silence.

He looked at her questioningly. "What is it, Erin?"

She lay in silence several moments before answering truthfully. "I don't know, but for some reason I don't feel good about it, and I didn't from the moment Arthur mentioned it."

His face broke into a wide, knowing smile. "And if you're worried about the father, don't be. If she's pregnant, then it's her husband's and not Samuel Tondi's."

Distress registered on her face. "I hadn't given that a thought, Kurt." She sighed. "As I said, I don't know what it is."

He stroked her hand gently with his fingertips. "Physician's intuition." Suddenly he bent and kissed her. "Come on, Erin, women get pregnant every second of every day. If she's pregnant, she'll be fine, and if she's not, then you will have worried needlessly. You're not a mama hen and the Randles are not your babies. If they need you, you'll be the first to know."

"I suppose you're right," she murmured. Still, she couldn't shake the uneasy feeling. But in the next uneventful days that followed, she did. Slowly, she put it in a far corner of her mind and forgot about it.

At Suva she and Kurt went ashore together and spent an entire afternoon sunning and swimming. It was beautiful and relaxing. The water was blue and the sand sparkled with sunlight. A fragrance of honeysuckle filled the air around them. Allowing the sand to drift through her fingers, she said with a faraway glaze over her eyes. "My grandfather had a farm outside of Atlanta and the honeysuckle grew wild all around. In the summer it smelled so wonderfully fresh and clean."

With his eyes closed he said, "I thought New Orleans was your home."

She smiled. "It was. But my mother was born near Atlanta. My grandfather remained there until he died. I would spend a part of every summer with him." Rolling over onto her stomach, she rose up on her elbows and looked at Kurt's squinting face. "He didn't want me to become a surgeon."

Kurt's eyes opened and fastened on her face. "Did he give a reason?"

"Hmmm." She stared thoughtfully. "He didn't come right out and say it, but I could tell why by his reaction."

He raised himself up on one elbow. "Why did you?" he asked point-blank.

"Because I thought it was what I wanted to do." Her face was serious. "For a while I was happy. I didn't even mind my residency, and it was awful. Sometimes I went two full days without a wink of sleep. But I had this feeling of doing something so worthwhile, it made my own personal sacrifices seem insignificant."

"What happened? When did it change for you?" he prodded, eyeing her solemnly.

"In private practice it all changes."

"How is that?"

She pursed her lips a long moment, then said, "With my partner, everything was monetary. A cholecystectomy was worth so much, a gastrectomy so much, and on and on. He saw the part and not the person. I had not been raised to that kind of thinking. My father never referred to a person by their diseased or injured part. My partner never referred to the person. And then I found myself thinking, Today I have a thyroidectomy, a gastrectomy, a common

222

duct. I had started doing it. I fell into his routine and I began to become disillusioned with myself."

"Isn't that normal for a surgeon, Erin? I would think your father was the exception and not the rule." His brows rose hopefully. "Isn't it possible that you chose the wrong field of medicine? You are not at all my image of a surgeon."

She cut a quizzical glare at him. "And what is your image?"

He smiled. "I don't know exactly. But I do know you're not it."

She looked at him oddly. "If I am not your image of a surgeon, Kurt, what am I your image of?" She smiled teasingly. "Or dare you say?"

Smiling calmly, he shifted on the sand. "To me you are the perfect example of a woman in search of herself." He gave her a long serious look. "And that's good. You've taken time out for yourself, to find out who you are and what you want out of life. And you gave up quite a lot to do it. You think of it as not coping, Erin, or running. But I see it, I see you as someone dropping everything and saying, Wait a minute, world."

Her eyes remained steady on him. "I think you are being overly kind in your assessment of me and my situation," she said after a while with only a faint hint of a smile.

"And perhaps you're being overly hard on yourself," he said to her without hesitation. "You think of yourself as a failure, and I don't think you are. You spent all those years preparing yourself for your career, busy years, and probably during all that time you didn't allow yourself the one most important question, Is this what I want? And then you had it, with all the trimmings. And it wasn't what you wanted. That's obvious, even to me. I admire what you've done, Erin." He smiled, then his face sobered. "I admire you. And I love you," he concluded in a whisper.

His eyes immobilized her and suddenly the fragrant atmosphere was filled with a tantalizing new warmth. He leaned forward, pressing his mouth to hers and her breasts rose visibly with the deep gasp of air. She felt his soft lips on her forehead, on her cheeks, on her eyelids. Rising to his knees, he held her face between his hands and kissed her softly before falling back into the sand and glaring up at the crystal-blue sky.

Her eyes opened and focused on his face. "What are you doing, Kurt?" she murmured.

He merely shook his head, and after a long while said, "As many times as I have been around this world, it's as if I'm seeing it for the first time."

"Now, Kurt," she said with a challenging smile, "don't tell me I have improved your vision." Stretching out beside him, her face lingered close to his. "You have seen all this before many times."

"But not like this." He sighed. "Never like this."

Two weeks passed and so did New Guinea and the Philippines, and the *Royal Princess Star* was on a course to Hong Kong. Time was fast slipping away and leaving its mark on Erin. Instead of dispelling the doubts that tore at her relentlessly, a small sense of panic began to take seed deep inside her. Her sense of obligation to her profession was as strong as ever, but not strong enough to promote a feeling of well-being, of knowing for sure which course her life

224

was on. She sensed she was on a collision course with herself.

The weather had turned cooler again and as she walked along the deck as she always did at night, she pulled her collar up around her neck. It was late and she felt the slight roll of the ship beneath her feet, hearing the water fall away far below, and from the ship she heard the late sounds of music, laughter, and cheerful conversation.

Chilled, she smelled the salt in the air and her expression became even more disturbed. She looked out on the night with an empty, desolate look, a sense of melancholy filling her. The cruise was half-over; her tenure with the line was drawing to a close. Two and a half months remained. She was looking forward to her bleak future when the pager at her side beeped, then the radio officer said. "Dr. Barclay, please report to the hospital."

Almost grateful for the interruption, she hurried back inside and down to the unit. The first person she saw as she walked inside was Perry Randle. who looked around at her, bewildered. "I—I'm glad you're here," he said.

"What is it?" Erin asked, approaching him.

He moistened his lips nervously. "It's Beth. She's in there." He nodded toward the treatment room.

Erin could see his struggle to remain calm as he went on, yet the panic was clear on his young face. "I—I think she's losing the baby. Something's happened."

Hurrying past him, Erin opened the door to the treatment room and at seeing both S.L. and Rachel inside, said calmly, "S.L., would you go out and see to Mr. Randle. Perhaps take him into my office."

S.L. nodded and left immediately. Erin looked to Beth Randle, who lay coiled on the table, biting the back of her hand, tears of quiet hysteria flowing down her cheeks. Rachel's eyes sought out the doctor's and she gave a quick shake of her head. "I've called Hal to do a type and crossmatch. There's a significant blood loss."

Approaching the treatment table, Erin lifted Beth's cold hand and at the same time acknowledged Rachel's statement with a nod. "Beth," she said calmly, "tell me what happened."

"I'm losing the baby," Beth choked out, wept violently a moment, then swallowed and continued amidst sobs. "It was something like the cramps, so I went to lie down. And when I did I had this terrible cramp catch me, and then I could feel the blood. . . ."

Just then Hal rushed in and took her hand from Erin's, placing a tourniquet around her arm. A second later he had drawn two vials of blood and was hurrying out.

Rachel, on the other side of the table, was monitoring Beth's blood pressure and when Erin looked up, mouthed, "Eighty over forty."

Erin's eyes traveled over Beth's face and for a moment she mentally assessed the situation. Then looking up to Rachel, she said, "Start a drip."

Rachel nodded and turned to the cabinet, where she removed a bag of solution. At seeing the dark stain on the examining table widen rapidly Erin gasped to herself and felt the sudden lurch of her heart. What she had on her hands was not only the loss of a baby, but a life-threatening situation. Beth Randle was hemorrhaging, and severely. Rushing to the door, she called out, "Hal, do you have me a blood count?"

"Just getting it," he called back. "Hemoglobin, seven grams; hematocrit, twenty."

"Seventy over thirty," Rachel called from behind her.

"S.L.," Erin called out as calmly as possible, "could I see you a minute."

S.L. rushed from the office and Erin said half under her breath, "Set up the OR. We're going to have to do a D and C, and now!"

S.L. nodded and hurried into the area not used by the hospital staff since Erin had come on ship. Turning back inside the room, Erin saw that Rachel had placed Beth in shock position on the table.

Hal rushed in. "She's a B negative. We don't have anything that'll match."

Erin spun about. "Call the captain. There's got to be someone on this ship with B type blood. And hurry, Hal." Now she had only one thought—to save Beth Randle's life. The baby was gone. But she couldn't think about that now.

Only a second passed before she heard Kurt's voice on the ship's public address system. "May I have all attention, please. Attention, please. Anyone with type B blood please report to the hospital at once. I repeat, anyone on ship with type B blood please report to the hospital unit."

Johnny rushed into the treatment room, "What's going on!" Then seeing Beth Randle, asked, "What do you want me to do?"

Erin answered calmly, "Help S.L. in the OR, and fast. We're bringing her in shortly."

Johnny left the room promptly and disappeared down the hall.

Turning around, Erin saw Beth's eyes flutter, then

close and remain closed. "Unlock the wheels," Erin snapped. "We've got to go with her."

A second later they were rolling down the corridor to the operating room. Once inside, Erin said to Rachel, "Get a signed permit for the D and C, also blood transfusions." Turning to the others, she said, "Let's get her on the table and up in the stirrups."

Twenty minutes later the procedure was done. Rising from the stool, Erin inhaled deeply and straightened her shoulders. The bleeding had almost stopped completely. She looked up to S.L., who said, "She's stable at eighty over forty." Slowly removing the mask from her face, Erin stared vacant-eyed, then shook her head.

Rachel stuck her head inside the door. "There's no one on this ship with blood compatible with hers," she said, alarmed.

"It's all right," Erin muttered. "I think now that the bleeding has stopped she'll be okay without it."

"Want to move her?" S.L. asked from the head of the table.

Erin gave a little shake of her head. "Not just yet. Let's watch her awhile." She clasped her hands together to stop the trembling, slowly pulled the stool around beside the table, and lowered herself back onto it. She looked up to check the second intravenous bag and saw it was flowing well. She watched S.L. pump up the blood pressure cuff and let the air out slowly.

"It's coming up." She smiled behind the mask. "Ninety over sixty." Reaching up, she removed her mask.

An hour later Beth Randle was sleeping soundly in

the ward with Rachel at her side monitoring vital signs at frequent intervals.

Erin entered her office and found Perry Randle sitting, clutching his head. There was horror in his eyes when he looked at her. He sat mute, staring up at her. The tension eased only slightly when Erin half-smiled. "Beth will be fine."

"What happened?" Perry asked. "Why did it happen?"

"I am sorry, Perry, but I don't know why."

"You don't know!" he demanded. "Why don't you know, you're the doctor!"

"Perry," she stated matter-of-factly, "when something of this nature happens it's usually because something has gone wrong with the development of the embryo. And I would guess that's what happened here. We don't know why something goes wrong, we only know this is the result when it does."

"Beth almost died," he groaned. "I could tell by everything going on out there, all the activity, and then the call for blood. I was afraid to move, afraid if I did she would die." Suddenly tears blinded him and he bowed his head. "It's all my fault. She didn't want to get pregnant, not yet. But I wanted her to because I was afraid she was going to leave me. And when she missed her period she was happy." He lapsed into a choked silence.

Erin walked over, pulled out her chair at her desk, and sat down. For a long while she refrained from speaking, staring directly at the top of his head. "Perry," she said softly, "not a one of us can second-guess nature. Why Beth miscarried is something we'll never know for sure. But I do know that she's young and she's strong."

"She'll never be pregnant again!" he cried out, shaking his head violently. "She'll never be pregnant again!" he repeated and leaped to his feet. "I *know* she almost died!" He glared straight into Erin's eyes. "Tell me she didn't."

Erin said patiently, "Your wife hemorrhaged, and that is not uncommon. It will take her a few days to regain her strength, but she will regain it. If she was happy about the pregnancy, then she will no doubt be depressed over what has happened. I only hope that you will be a help and a support to her when she awakes. If you go out and tell her that she will never be pregnant again, I don't think it will help her at all."

Erin was alone in her office when Kurt came by late at night to bring her a cup of steaming coffee. Placing it on her desk, he closed the door and sat down. "Rough night?"

She nodded numbly. The trauma of the night had indeed settled around her like a heavy black cloud. Taking a sip of coffee, she shuddered a bit.

Kurt slowly drank from his cup, eyeing her across the top of it. "Sometimes, Erin, not often, but sometimes, we have passengers die on ship. In the past few years we've had two heart attack victims and a—a—an—when the big vessel explodes."

"An aneurysm," she answered in a whisper.

Kurt nodded. "Yes. That happened to a man a couple of years ago."

"Kurt," she asked solemnly, "is this your pep talk?"

"No. But it is the truth. Things happen to people on ship just like they would if they were on land."

"But on ship the treatment is somewhat more

230

limited." She sighed, shaking her head. "Tonight, for instance, what if we had been unable to do without blood? She would have died. As it was, we controlled the bleeding, but what if we hadn't? Where would Beth Randle be now?"

He quietly sat looking at her. He drank his coffee without saying anything else concerning the practice of medicine on ship. But when he rose he looked over to her. "It's been a long night, think I'll go up." He hesitated, then asked, "Care to join me?"

Without looking at him, she merely shook her head. When she heard the door close, she glanced up, and seeing he was gone, every fear she had repressed while he was there came back to the surface. She glanced anxiously around the office, feeling frightened with her thoughts. Beth Randle had frightened her. Now she questioned her skills, not as a surgeon, but as a doctor. It seemed her ability had been stretched to the limit since taking this position.

She was still sitting there unmoving when S.L. tapped on the door. "Beth Randle is awake," she whispered. "She wants to talk with you."

Erin inhaled deeply. "Is her husband with her?"

"He just left."

"I think she probably needs to rest, S.L. Tell her I'll speak with her tomorrow."

S.L. looked puzzled, then nodded, and pulled the door closed again.

Lowering her head on the desk, Erin rested her face on her arms. She didn't understand all the strange twists life takes. Of all the people coming on board the ship, she had been most interested in the young couple with sad faces. And now after coming in contact with them she was sadder than they had ever

231

been. That couple had forced her to take a long, objective look at her ability to manage a ship's hospital and she found herself lacking. Slowly her eyes closed and she fell into an uncomfortable restless sleep.

But the next morning, after going to her cabin and taking a bath, she felt better about the night just past. She had tiptoed past Beth Randle's bed and had felt a slight turn of her lips at seeing a hint of color return to the pale cheeks. Beth had been in a sound sleep and she didn't disturb her.

She was in her robe when the loud knock came on the door. She answered it and Kurt entered, bodily lifting her aside. "I didn't sleep well last night," he said in a near grunt as he slammed the door. Turning back to her, he continued. "There are some things that need to be said, and I am going to say them. First, the last medical officer on this ship was an alcoholic. Did you know that?" He paused, waiting for his words to sink in. "Anyone in your unit can tell you what a hell of a time we had with him. Anytime we really needed him, he was drunk. And before him we had a playboy, a man who made Samuel Tondi look like a monk. He left the line when he married one of the rich widows. He was a fair doctor, but medicine was hardly his main interest. I could go on and on, Erin, but what I came to tell you is that you are the best damned doctor the *Royal Princess Star* has ever sailed with. And I'm saying that not only for your benefit, but for the staff in your unit and on behalf of all the passengers. So when you're sitting around feeling inept, you might want to consider this. I would think you've had enough of indecision in your life. You are the best thing to ever happen to this ship and certainly the best thing to ever happen to me." Suddenly his voice dropped to a whisper. "Erin, this life you chose put you in the position of continually weighing life and death, pain and happiness, and that's unique to medicine." He smiled forlornly, lifting his brows. "The rest of us just weigh those when it applies to us. Like now, I'm weighing my life and my happiness. Don't leave this ship, Erin. We all need you."

"Kurt," she began in a low, strangled voice, "please don't. Don't do this.

Taking a deep breath, he repeated, "We all need you."

She opened her mouth to speak, then didn't. What could she say? That she didn't love him? She did. That she could stay? She couldn't.

His intense blue eyes did not waver as he stood there observing her quietly. Then slowly a look of perplexity filled those same blue eyes and his dark brows knitted close together in a frown. He cleared his throat. "Aren't you going to talk with me at all?" he finally inquired.

Very deliberately she moistened her lips. She did not feel clear, she could not see clearly, but she did know that he was asking her to give up her career, to stop being a surgeon, and a part of her resented it. She had not come on this ship to give up anything, but rather to sort through everything, and now he was clouding all the issues and making it impossible for her. "Kurt," she said very softly, "I'm tired. I've been without sleep a very long time, and I would like to sleep now."

With a slight nod of his head he went over to the

door and let himself out without looking back, without saying another word to her.

Distractedly, she walked to her bed and lay down. Following a long intake of breath she closed her eyes. But she did not sleep. She was much too preoccupied with her thoughts. It had been a mistake to love Kurt. Such a mistake. Now she was filled with a restlessness that equaled the one she had left behind in Louisiana. If she had not fallen in love with him, it would have been easier. If she had not fallen in love with him, it would not have been at all.

Suddenly, her thought switched and she remembered the Randle baby, that little embryo lost forever, washed away by its mother's blood. Wearily she counted back over the days, wondering if there was something she should have done. She had known about the tests from the pharmacy, but she had not sought Beth out. It had been easier to ignore her condition and now she felt a guilt for having done so. But she had been right in one respect—she could not interfere with nature. With a sigh of resignation she turned over, and after the longest time, she slept.

She did not go back into the unit until dusk. Rachel was alone in the bay area with Beth. At seeing Erin, she smiled and said, "Mrs. Randle was just asking about you, Dr. Barclay. I was just telling her you must have jumped overboard."

Erin smiled bleakly, thinking, *That's something I haven't given proper thought to*, but said, "How are you feeling, Beth?"

Beth smiled. "Not too great, but not as bad as I thought."

"Oh." Erin's hopes leaped skyward.

Rachel walked from beside the bed. "If you don't mind, I think I'll go into the lounge for a cup of coffee."

Erin nodded. After the nurse left she pulled up a chair and sat down beside the bed, touching her brow thoughtfully before saying, "You're looking much better than the last time I saw you."

Beth sighed aloud. "I want you to tell me what happened, and why?"

Erin gestured helplessly. "I don't know. No one will ever know I'm sure."

Before she could continue, Beth interrupted, "Please don't say it was just one of those things. That's all I've heard. It sounds like a line from that song, and it wasn't. It was my baby's life." Suddenly, her large blue eyes filled and she gnawed at her lower lip. "Perry told me what you told him and I suppose it makes sense. Something was wrong in the development or I wouldn't have lost . . ." She stopped speaking and swallowed. "You know I hate to say 'it' like it was a thing, and yet I can't say him or her."

"No," Erin agreed readily. "The stage of development was not such we could discern the sex."

"Well"—Beth wiped at her eyes with the sheet—"I'm going to think that whatever happened and why was for the best. Even if I don't think that now, I will in the days to come." Her voice quavered and she sniffed. "When we found out that we were going to have a baby we both tried to act happy, but we weren't. Not really, not deep inside. We were still trying to sort out our feelings. Perry told me today that he wanted to get me pregnant because then we would have a moral obligation to each other and to our child. But he wasn't really happy about what he had done, or how he had done it."

"Beth." This time Erin shifted and said, "You don't have to tell me."

"But I need to. I need to tell someone uninvolved. We'd had too much to drink and we were being silly, and I think our baby wanted parents more sure. This was its retribution against us for using it as a means to hold us together. And as you said, there is no way anyone will ever know why. But deep inside I know, and so does Perry, that you can't make a life to save a life, or two lives. You can't use life that way. It won't allow you to."

"I see," Erin breathed, staring at Beth as if in a trance, although she wasn't sure she did understand.

"But—but we have learned one thing from all this. We do love each other, and having been through this together, we'll be stronger now." Again her voice shook. "We had a long talk today and we understand each other better. We have a lot of mending to do. In fact, we've got to start all over. I've got to put some meaning into my life before I can be a good mother, and Perry understands this at last."

Erin tilted her head. "So the two of you aren't giving up." She smiled a sincere warm smile.

"Oh, no," Beth said, smiling radiantly. "We may kill each other in the months to come, but we won't give up because we've found out that our love is real, and lasting. It's just too bad it took a tragedy to teach us this." She paused a long moment before saying timidly, "I don't think Perry did, but I want to thank you for saving my life. I thought for a moment I might die, but I remember thinking as I was passing out, *She won't let me die*. And you didn't. Thank you."

Rising from the chair, Erin smiled. "It was never quite that serious," she lied.

Beth laughed softly. "You're telling that to someone who saw an angel hovering at the end of that bed, standing right behind you?"

Erin looked quizzically at her recovering patient. Then, pursing her lips thoughtfully, she went into the lounge and had a cup of coffee with Rachel.

Late that night Rachel found Kurt alone on the bridge and called out, "Can we talk, Kurt?"

His hands were behind his back as he turned to the nurse. "Sure." He smiled bleakly. "What is it?"

"Kurt," she began hesitantly, "I don't know how to say this, but it's over between the two of you, isn't it?"

He stopped dead still. "I don't know what you're talking about." He voiced his objection strongly, eyeing Rachel with sudden irritation.

"I'm not here to say I told you so, Kurt, believe me. It's just that I sense the change in her, and I see it on your face."

"Rachel, I still don't know what you're talking about," he implored. "And I'm not in the mood for riddles," he said harshly.

"I've gotten to know her pretty well these weeks at sea," Rachel began softly, "and I no longer dislike her. As a matter of fact, for a woman doctor, she is okay. But today we were in the lounge together and she said something that made me think she was talking about the two of you, even though at the time we were speaking of the Randles."

237

He stared at her, a wondering expression on his face. "What did she say?" he snapped.

Rachel hesitated, then said very softly, "She said, 'Dreams perish, it's a fact of life.' And she wasn't talking about Beth and Perry Randle. I know she wasn't. I could tell by her expression that she wasn't. Then she started talking about going into practice with her father, and Kurt, she has never mentioned any plans before—never, not to any one of us."

"Rachel, you're reading a meaning into her words, a meaning of your own choosing," he argued, fighting back a growing frustration with the entire conversation. "Now, I really am busy, so if that's all you came to say."

"All right, Kurt," she said in an assertive voice. "I won't say more, but I know what I heard, and I saw the way she looked, and I know she's leaving. But that's all I will say about it."

After Rachel left Kurt remained on deck pacing. Yes, she was planning to leave, he knew it, too, but he couldn't bring himself to admit it, not to Rachel, not to anyone. Dreams perish, yes, they do. Indeed, they do.

Suddenly, he was so damned confused he couldn't manage a single clear thought. All he could think about were the long, empty nights ahead of him when she was gone.

CHAPTER FOURTEEN

Erin told herself that she must start the severing process and she knew that she was not wrong. She could not continue to immerse herself in him mentally and physically until the day she left the ship. If she did, she would never leave the ship.

The weather had turned biting cold in port at Hong Kong. She stayed with the ship while all of her staff, with the exception of Johnny, went with the tour to the People's Republic of China. Most of the passengers disembarked, only a handful remaining behind for various reasons, health not being the least.

"You didn't want to go with the others, Johnny?" she inquired, looking up from a chart.

"Man, no," he answered with a short laugh. "I saw all of this part of the world I ever wanted to see when I was eighteen."

"Oh." Her brows rose questioningly.

"Vietnam," he said.

"Oh," she repeated as she lowered her brows. Her brown eyes flickered toward him, but she said nothing more. Of all her staff Johnny was the one she knew the least about. And looking at him she wished she knew that little about Kurt. But she didn't. She knew him so very well. He had brought the greatest emotional upheaval to her life yet. And now she wondered if she would ever be content. She had lowered all her barriers to him and now she was having one hell of a time erecting them again.

She did not go up to his stateroom anymore, nor did he come down to hers. Still, she could not glimpse him without the feeling of desire and passion stirring within her. And that look of bewilderment in his eyes kept her wide awake at night and restless throughout the day.

The first night in port, with the moonlight streaming in her window, she lay there thinking about him. She wished she had met him when she was eighteen and loved him as much then as she did now. At that time her path had not been so rigidly set and she could have sailed off into the sunset with him and lived happily ever after. Wild thoughts, she knew, but somehow consoling ones. Her love for him would pass in time, she told herself. All things passed in time. Their love would be no different from a million other loves. *But it is different,* another part of her countered. *It will never pass.* She sighed deeply and looked to her window.

The next morning she ran into him in the dining room at breakfast. He gave her a forced, unnatural smile and asked, "How are things in your unit?"

Her smile was equally as strained. "Going well," she replied.

He hesitated, then said, "Would you sit with me, Erin?"

She, too, hesitated, and against her better judgment answered, "Certainly."

240

He waved the steward away and guided her to a table, his fingers squeezing her arm a little. Once they were seated opposite each other, conversation completely died for a while. They were as awkward and ill at ease as strangers would have been. After the longest time he said, "It's too bad you couldn't have gone into China with the others. There is so much to see." He looked at her tenderly. "Did you know the Great Wall is the only manmade object that can be seen from outer space?" Then he smiled sadly. "But then, that wall is not much greater than the one you've put around yourself these past weeks."

There was silence again. After a while she said, "And from here on to Thailand."

He nodded, his eyes roving over her.

She lowered her eyes to the table and said, "Let's enjoy breakfast, Kurt." She was fighting the overwhelming desire to get up and run from him, and maybe even a stronger desire to run to him. The anxiety of the moment was terrible.

Then to her surprise he gave her one of his old smiles, his eyes reflective as he studied her lovely face. "I know your mind is made up, Erin. I know you'll be leaving, and I know you're angry with me for asking you to stay."

"I'm not angry, really," she quickly replied. The current was there, springing back and forth across the table between them.

"Then you think I was unfair."

"Well," she said softly, "maybe a little. I didn't ask you to give up your ship because I understand you can't. It would be the same as asking you to give up your life, and I don't want that. And I want you to understand that what you ask of me is equally

241

impossible." She pressed a finger to her lips and said around it, "Let's don't continue with this drift of talk; we both know it leads nowhere."

He managed a weak smile. "Perhaps I've been tactless and thoughtless, but we do have some weeks left together. Let's don't spend them apart. Then when you go we will have at least had all the time that we could have had. Share these last weeks with me, Erin. Please." His eyes pleaded with her. "It won't be more difficult in the end, and maybe it will even help." His eyes were clinging to hers now, and she heard the sincerity in his voice. "I know you don't want to torture me because I know you love me, but, darling, you are torturing me." His brows lifted slightly. "You don't mean to, do you?"

The pounding in her chest almost drowned her words. "No, Kurt, I don't mean to." Her eyes burned into his. "I love you," she breathed in a whisper, looking closely at his pale blue eyes, the strong neck, the high cheekbones, his full, sensual mouth. At that moment she realized how thoughtless, how cruel she was being to both of them. Wasn't some time better than none? And avoiding him was tearing her apart, and him. With her eyes she told him that the separation was ended.

That afternoon they went sightseeing in a rickshaw and that evening had dinner aboard a floating restaurant. He laughed. "I don't know why we would think this is unusual, all our meals are in a floating restaurant."

Midway through the meal Erin's pager sounded with the message that she was needed in the hospital. She grinned. "Why, this is exactly like dining on the *Royal Princess Star*."

Fifteen minutes later they were back on ship and on the way up on the elevator. He gave her a rakish grin. "I think I'm learning to put my feelings on reset. I'll go up and make us a drink." When the door opened across from the unit, he said, "You will be on up, won't you?"

Glancing around at him, she murmured, "Yes, but hold up on putting ice in the glasses, I hate a watery drink." She gave him a vague smile and disappeared through the doors.

When she arrived inside she found Johnny in the treatment room busily applying a boot cast to the leg of the torch singer from the piano lounge. When Erin looked over he explained, "She fell off the piano. The x rays are on the panel. A little hairline fracture at the distal end of the tibia."

"I did not *fall* off the piano," Ritzie Duprey huffed. "When I stepped down the heel on my shoe broke and I fell."

Johnny glanced up at the curvaceous black woman and slapped another roll of plaster on the cast and began smoothing it with his hands. "If God had meant for lovely women to sit on pianos, he would have made the bench on them and not under them, right, Dr. Barclay?"

Grinning, Erin looked around. "For goodness' sake, leave me out of this." Her eyes went back to the x-ray panel.

"This fool says this is a walking cast," Ritzie complained loudly. "But it's going to weigh four hundred pounds. I don't know how I'm supposed to walk on it. I won't even be able to drag it."

"Well, for sure," Johnny grinned, "you won't be sitting on the piano with it. If you do, you and the piano will be flat on the floor." Clapping his hands together, he rose to his feet and turned to Erin with a look of pride on his face. "It's all done, Doctor, but you'd better give her instructions, then I'll help her to her cabin."

"That's what you think!" Ritzie mumbled contentiously. "The stewards will help me to my room, if there are enough left on ship to do it!"

Johnny stepped back, glaring at the newest patient with wide-eyed innocence. "Just trying to be of help," he said quickly.

Erin stepped forward and gave Ritzie instructions and a prescription for pain medication with the advice, "When you're taking these tablets, don't drink any alcohol."

Ritzie nodded and took the prescription from Erin's hand. With glacial eyes she then looked over to Johnny. "Since I have to stop by the pharmacy, I suppose you will need to help me to my room."

Erin watched Johnny roll the singer out of the unit in a wheelchair, hearing him ask, "Can I sign your cast? I mean, after all, I was the one who sculpted it, and it is a work of art."

The door closed as Ritzie mumbled up at him, "There's enough plaster on my leg for everyone in Hong Kong to sign."

When they were gone Erin cleaned up the remaining mess of plaster and water, then washed her hands before switching off the light in the treatment room. Walking into the ward, she hesitated in the middle of the floor and looked around. *If God had meant* . . . How strange that a young man like Johnny could make her remember her wonderful grandfather.

She locked the unit and when the elevator door

closed behind her she went up to Kurt's deck. Slowly, the door slid open and she stepped out, a dazed expression on her face.

When she knocked at his door, he answered and to her surprise said, "I'll add the ice, then why don't we go out on deck and find a table." He hesitated, then said, "Unless you think it's too cool."

Smiling, she pulled at the sleeve of her cozy thick wool sweater. "I think this will keep me warm."

He grinned and said quickly, "If it doesn't, we'll find something that will."

A few minutes later, seating themselves outside at a table, she looked over to him, amazed that he appeared so very untroubled. She gave him a report on the injury.

He nodded. "I had already been told. At least it didn't damage her voice. She's really a talented woman."

Erin laughed. "The cast doesn't reach quite to her throat."

Looking at her, he smiled. Her laugh was like a deep breath of fresh air. It seemed like forever since he had heard her laugh, and he sat there quietly smiling at her.

They enjoyed the drinks in the cool night with little conversation flowing between them. And when he saw her shiver, he said, "Ready to go in?"

She nodded, and they rose, leaving the glasses on the table. As they entered the corridor he took her hand in his and she stared down at his fingers entwined with hers. When she brought her eyes to his, he said, "Your hand is cold."

She acknowledged with a soft, "Yes."

When he gently ushered her into his stateroom

she felt a nervousness she had not felt in a long time. Once inside the suite, he went into the bedroom and came back out holding a small box in his hand. He handed it to her. "I have this for you," he explained, then went on. "It's not exactly the one I would have liked to give you, but. . . ." His words trailed off, and then he said, "Open it."

She knew from the size it was a ring and her hands trembled as she opened it. Her eyes widened and her mouth parted with the words, "Oh, Kurt." Her fingers shook as she lifted it from the slot of velvet and held it out, admiring the emerald and diamonds held by gold. Slowly, she slid it onto her finger, then held her hand out and whispered, "It's beautiful."

He took her hand and pressed her fingers to his mouth. "I was afraid you wouldn't accept it."

She gazed at the ring near his lips now. "It's incredibly beautiful," she whispered.

"It has an inscription." He sighed and moistened his lips.

Removing her hand from his she slid the ring from her finger and held it up to the light, then touching her top lip with the tip of her tongue she said shyly, "I should have brought my reading glasses." She looked at him guiltily and gave an awkward twist of her lips.

He smiled and caught her face in both hands. "It SAYS, FIRST YOU ARE A WOMAN. KURT."

She lowered her eyes from his and swallowed. "I see, it's a message."

He forced her eyes to meet his. "Not a sermon, just a message, Erin. First I am a man, and then I am a captain, and all other things that I am. But first I am a man. And you are first a woman, then you are a physician, and all the other things that you are. But first we're together, man and woman, or if you prefer, woman and man. I don't care about the order, I just care about what we are."

She was momentarily lost in his eyes, melted by his gaze.

He took the ring and slowly placed it back on her finger. Then he stepped so close to her, their legs brushed together. Then came the gentle touch of his lips tingling her mouth, then touching her forehead. She clasped his neck with her hands and murmured, "Kurt, I love you so."

Instinctively, the muscles of his body tightened and he pressed her to him with a harsh embrace. Then his dark head drew back and he looked at her, his eyes bright and flashing with desire. "I may lose you, Erin, but I will never do it gracefully."

With her arms entwining his neck, they moved into the bedroom, and moments later lay naked on the bed, blinded by passion and clinging to each other. Kissing her wildly, he felt an enormous confusion. He might sail forever on this ship, but he would drown without her. His mind then gave way to the sensuous scent of her perfume and the taste of her soft, full lips. Thoughts drifted away as he covered her body with his own.

Her mouth rained sweet kisses on his face, his neck, his shoulders, while he held her arms stretched up over the pillow. His mouth trailed from her neck to her breasts, tasting her fresh-smelling skin, caressing her nipples with his tongue, his lips, tempting them to hardness. His hands moved from her wrists and strayed over her skin, lovingly, softly, caressing every part of her.

Her long, tapered fingers stroked his hair, his neck, along his chest, and then they were consuming each other with their hands until their bodies had grown rigid and the warmth had turned to a fiery and inevitable tide approaching in a blissful slowness. She was penned by his weight and she held on to his back, her hands moving restlessly along his flesh.

Her eyes were closed and breathing had become laborious and short by the acceleration of heartbeats. When her flesh yielded to his, the only words in her brain were *Love me . . . love me . . . love me*. The night burned with the heat of their bodies. She felt her heart racing, felt the dryness of her mouth as together they moved toward the rose glow sweeping in on them.

And then it came crashing down, burning them, raining on them, an enchantment beyond time until they collapsed in each other's arms and lay gasping, feeling it all ebb away. He had made love to her with his eyes open. He had watched her face, listened to her moans of pleasure, and watching her, he thought the beating of his heart would surely burst it. And then seeing her quiet and still with her eyes closed, he finally closed his own, feeling exalted and satisfied.

When time passed and he did not say anything, she turned her head and looked at him. "Did I put you to sleep?" she chided him.

His eyes opened in narrow slits and surveyed her face, giving her a tranquil smile. "Not exactly." The thudding of his heart had finally slowed. "You're a strange kind of magic," he whispered, moistening his lips with his tongue. "Or perhaps I should say, a perfect kind of magic."

248

"How is that?" she murmured, snuggling closer to him.

"Oh," he began slowly, "I don't know if I can explain it. It's something I feel each time I touch you. It's as if my hands tell me, my lips tell me, my body tells me—she is life, she is ecstasy, she is the perfect half of me that has always been missing, leaving me imperfect and searching. With you, Erin, I feel complete, all together."

"And that makes me magic," she whispered with a tiny smile.

"That makes you the woman I love." He leaned over and kissed her, then cuddled her in his arms. And that was how they slept.

She awoke before he did and found herself still loosely embraced in his arms. The paneled wall of his bedroom was catching the morning sun sliding in his window. She yawned drowsily and gazed at him. Then, raising her hand, she looked at her ring, the diamonds catching the sunlight and gleaming bright.

Slowly, she closed her fingers into a fist, then relaxed them. Still looking at the ring, she felt a fear deep inside her that he was a part of her that she would never be free of, not for as long as she would live. He had loved her as no other man had loved her; he had possessed her as no other man. That was the moral demand of nature—once a love was perfect it could never be forgotten. She knew now that she would never forget him. Her love for him would be as lasting as the oceans he loved.

She looked past his sleeping face to the sunlit window and sighed forlornly. There had to be rules, otherwise each life would be filled with indecision and confusion. She had chosen a career, but she hadn't stayed with it. She had broken the first rule. She had ended the commitment to her husband of two years, thus breaking another rule. She had sought success and sacrificed happiness, and in doing so had learned that success and happiness are not one world, but two. And no one person could live in two worlds. She had a place if she could find it. Somewhere she belonged, somewhere she could stay. At this bright moment she was the only place she wanted to be—in Kurt Garisen's arms. But his arms could not embrace the operating room and she could not convince herself that the operating room was not her rightful place.

She lay there staring out the window until the wind blew gray clouds across the sun. It seemed a fitting gesture for the wind. Pondering her thoughts, she glanced down to see Kurt staring up at her open mouth. "What are you doing?" he whispered, his dark hair tousled, his blue eyes sharp.

"Watching the sun hide behind a cloud." She smiled down at him.

He reached up with the fingers of his right hand and rubbed one eye. "How long have you been awake?"

Resting her head on her hand, she answered softly, "Not long."

Leaning his head against hers, he asked, "What are your immediate plans?"

She sighed thoughtfully. "Oh, a bath, then breakfast, a stop by the pharmacy, and then on to the unit."

He pressed forward a tiny bit and kissed the hair near her ear. "But what are your *immediate* plans?"

There was no answer for a moment, then she laughed softly and said, "Probably the same as yours."

When the remainder of her staff returned to the ship they were full of stories concerning the tour. "They allowed Rachel and me to visit a hospital and observe an operation using acupuncture. It was fascinating," S.L. called out from across the bay, straightening a shelf. "Anything interesting happen while we were gone?"

"Not much," Erin replied.

"Unless," Johnny interjected, "you happen to put a cast on Ritzie Duprey's leg. That was pretty interesting." He grinned.

Hal looked impressed. "You mean that singer from the lounge?" He turned his gaze to Johnny.

Johnny rolled his eyes and nodded with exaggerated movement. "That's the one." He glanced at his watch. "As a matter of fact, I'm on my way to her cabin. I have to check her toes daily to make sure the cast isn't too tight. Want to come along?"

"Sure," Hal said quickly and fell in behind Johnny, both men wearing big smiles.

After they left, arms draped over each other's shoulders, Rachel looked at Erin with open disgust. "Since when do we make cabin calls to check toes?"

Erin sighed and shook her head. "Since Ritzie suffered a fracture."

After lunch, when Erin was sitting alone in her office she heard the door open. She slid her chair back and peered out to see Mark Payton.

"Hi," he called over. "You alone?"

"Yes, come on in." She rolled back to her desk and watched him walk inside, smiling.

"It's been a few days since I saw you, so I thought I'd just drop by."

"Enjoy China?" she asked, smiling at him.

His head tilted to one side and he gave a lopsided grin. "As much as you can enjoy anything with Sara Lynn. She's not the most congenial female I've ever met."

Erin laughed. "Is she still giving you a hard time?"

He gave a start. "She thinks she is, so I just let her think it." His brows raised. "Where is she anyway?"

"She and Rachel went to lunch just a few minutes ago."

Mark sat in silence a moment, then asked, "Has she told you anything?"

Erin's brows raised. "Like what?"

"Uh, like we might get married when we get back to New York."

Erin could not hide her shock. "Married?"

He nodded slowly. "Well, it's not definite, but I think we probably will."

Erin's shoulders slumped a bit. "Will you keep on working for the line?"

Drawing his lips together, Mark shook his head slowly. "No. We'll probably settle somewhere along the East Coast. You know, start out with a firm foundation under our feet." He cleared his throat. "I like the sea, but I'm not an old sea dog like Kurt. I don't know that he would survive on land. But I think I could be just as happy to look out and see the ocean as to be sailing on it. And Sara Lynn's qualified to work in any hospital."

Erin swallowed and said, "Have you told Kurt? I'm sure he will miss you terribly,"

Mark gave a little shake of his head. "No. And I wouldn't be mad if you told him. I'm not chicken; it'll just be hard to tell him."

Erin shook her head. "I don't think I'll tell him. I know how fond he is of you, but I think he'll understand. Maybe you could just go through channels and submit your resignation."

He stared at her and asked point-blank, "Is that how you're going to do it, Erin?"

She paled. "He already knows about me, Mark."

"Then you really are going to leave after this year?"

She merely stared at him in answer.

That night Kurt was quiet and pensive and she knew Mark had told him. Still, she waited for him to say something. Strangely, he didn't. He didn't mention it at all.

She saw him only a few minutes at dinner, then he left for the bridge. The ship was traveling through a heavy fog and rough waters. A day passed before she saw him again and he seemed to be himself, smiling and happy. All but his eyes; his beautiful blue eyes weren't smiling.

On March 29 the *Royal Princess Star* sailed into port at Cape Town, South Africa, and a week away they would be in Rio de Janeiro, and then begin the northward trek back to New York Harbor, which was now three weeks away.

Once secure in port Kurt sought Erin out. In the unit was one patient, Miss Emma Tiddle, recovering from a severe case of Mr. Vlasic's influence.

"This didn't turn out as I expected," S.L. had

sighed six days ago. "I thought she would make him well; I never thought about him making her sick."

"That old man could make a health poster sick," Rachel threw in, then grinned. "However, they are cute, the way they hold hands and smile at each other. And he's so considerate. After convincing her that she's near death, he brings her flowers every day."

Erin spent a lot of time telling the elderly woman she could find nothing wrong with her and was midway through the last pep session when Kurt strolled into the unit and found her at Miss Tiddle's bedside. He grinned at Erin, then looked with exaggerated astonishment at the white-haired patient, saying, "My, Miss Tiddle, you're looking extremely fit today."

Emma Tiddle smiled shyly up at him. "Do you think so, Captain Garisen?"

He nodded and smiled broadly. "I certainly do, and I'm surprised to find you still here."

She inhaled deeply and slowly. "I don't know that my strength is sufficient for me to leave yet."

He shrugged. "I merely thought you would be going ashore with Homer. He tells me he's planning to visit the vineyards and winery."

Emma straightened. "When?"

"This afternoon, I believe he said. You know the world's largest winery is right here."

Thirty minutes later the unit was empty and Erin and Kurt were alone in her office. "You should have been a doctor," she laughed cheerily.

Catching her in his arms, he brushed her lips, drew back, and said, "I just didn't want her to miss anything. Which is why I'm here." He hesitated. "How would you like to climb a mountain with me?"

254

"That is something I haven't done in a long time," she replied in a whisper. "I think I would like it."

At dusk they ascended famed Table Mountain and looked down on a magnificent view of the ocean at twilight and the city of Cape Town. They were both dressed casually in slacks and lightweight sweaters. Kurt stood behind Erin, his arms firmly around her waist. "This is really beautiful," she sighed, leaning her head back against him. "I'm glad we came."

She was overwhelmed by the exquisite beauty beyond the mountain and the perfect contentment to be in his arms, leaning her head on the side of his face, feeling his expansive chest warm her back.

They stood there for the longest time, not moving, their eyes sweeping the panorama below, and then she felt his eyes turn heavenward and he whispered, "There it is."

She, too, looked upward to the sky, seeing the sudden twinkling of a lone star. She glanced around at him dizzily and saw his clear blue eyes resting solemnly on the single star.

Catching her look, he smiled easily and squeezed her arms. Against her head, he murmured, "Did you ever wish on stars when you were a little girl?"

She nodded her head slowly, her hair rubbing his cheek. "Of course I did. I used to wish for all kinds of things—a bicycle, a pony, and an A in science." She laughed softly. "I got the bicycle, I didn't get the pony, and in fifth grade science I got a B. So much for star-wishing. Did you?" Her head turned so that she could clearly glimpse his profile. "I often wondered if boys did silly things like wish on stars."

He chuckled. "We still do. When I was a little boy I used to sit out on the rocks near the water's edge and wish that somehow my dad would come back. I used to dream that he had made it to an island and was waiting there for someone to find him. Then when I grew older I used to wish that I would be that someone, that I would sail my own ship and search all the islands until I found him." He kissed her cheek tenderly. "And then when I was about fourteen I wished that Martha Watts would let me . . ." He paused. "You know . . ." He grinned sheepishly.

Erin drew back and said with wide-eyed astonishment, "You wished for *that* on a star! Now I know why there are so many stars in the heavens—for nasty-minded boys to sit out somewhere in the dark and make their wishes." She paused and peered inquisitively at him. "Did she?" she asked in a whisper.

Kurt laughed. "I was never one to kiss and tell."

She made a mock grimace at him. "That means she didn't," she said confidently. "Good for her. Fourteen was much too young for you to get your feet wet." Suddenly, she laughed and looked back up to the darkening sky. "If those little stars could talk, what do you suppose they would say? Why, it boggles the imagination to think of all the wishes that have traveled upward." She nestled back against him. "And how many are still up there resting among all those stars."

"I know of only one for sure." Kurt pressed his lips to her temple. "And it'll be there for as long as I live. Somewhere in the stars it'll always be there." He turned her slowly in his arms until they faced each other. "Just as you'll always be in my heart."

She touched his face tenderly. "And you'll always be in mine, Kurt." The lump in her throat was so large, she could hardly swallow past it. Her eyes misted.

Unlocking his arms from around her, he took her hand and after several minutes of standing there in silence they went back and rejoined their guide.

That night in her room their desire was uncontrollable. They were approaching the final days of their time together and the frustration, the sadness, was in their eyes and in the pounding of their hearts. But passion soared untouched, taking complete hold of the two of them.

He lay on his back and watched her take off her clothes in slow sensuousness until she was bare and provocative steps brought her to the bed, where she lowered herself to his firm body at the same time she trailed her mouth across his lips. His dark, brooding eyes caught fire as he felt her breasts pressing against him. Then they were kissing, engulfed by desire, obsessed by the sensations bursting inside.

Eagerly they kissed, their mouths parting and tongues stroking against each other with increasing urgency. Her hands caught the sides of his face and they kissed over and over, until Kurt pressed back in the pillow gasping with thickened breath while the palms of his hands moved up and down along her back, her ribs, the soft flesh of her hips.

Then suddenly he was pushing her away to a distance where he could look into her eyes, and when he did, he whispered hoarsely, "Did you never have the desire to be a mother, Erin?"

The question struck her mute, and she gazed, bewildered, at him. His tantalizing breath was on her face and before she could respond in any way he continued on in the same hoarse voice. "Have you

257

never wanted a child, a baby, a little boy or a little girl, a living symbol of love and life, your love, your life?"

She drew back and cried out, "Kurt, you're not being fair."

"I want to know," he said bluntly, inhaling deeply. "Have you ever had those feelings, or is it just me?"

Now resisting his embrace, she freed herself from him and sat up on the side of the bed, huddling in her own arms and shivering. Then in a strange mournful tone, she whispered, "Yes. I have had the desire to be a mother. . . ." And her words faded away.

He rose up behind her and rested his chin on her shoulders. "To be the mother of my child, have you ever wanted that, Erin?"

Fighting back the hot tears stinging her lids, she nodded and said tearfully, "Yes."

His hands went to her shoulders and he said, "Look at me, Erin."

Slowly, she turned and stared at him past the veil of tears.

He kissed one lid and then the other. "And that, my darling, tells us the depth of this love we feel, and that's what makes it different from any I have known. I have never looked at a woman before and imagined how she would look if she were nine months pregnant with our child. But I have with you. At nights on the bridge of this ship I have seen you carrying our child. And I want it to be."

"Kurt," she cried out, "don't you know how you're hurting me. Please . . . please, don't say anything more."

And then the tears were there in his eyes, too, and he brought her back into his arms, cradling her head against his neck, his hands spread wide in her hair. "I'm sorry," he whispered shakily. "I—I never meant to hurt you. I only wanted to tell you how deeply I do love you. More than anything in this world, Erin." Bringing her head back slightly, he bent and kissed both wet cheeks. And when he covered her mouth she tasted the salt on his lips.

Slowly, she closed her eyes as the tender kiss was succeeded by a firmer one, and then another, bringing the yearning back with an even greater intensity. And all the while they made love she felt the tears slipping from beneath her lids, running from the corners through her hair and when they writhed together in ecstasy, the pillow beneath her head was circled with tears.

CHAPTER FIFTEEN

The disembarking in New York Harbor was a time of mixed feelings, a time of thank-yous and farewells. Erin went to the lobby along with most of the ship's officers to say a final good-bye to the passengers. Sometimes it was a cheery handshake and a well-wish, other times an embrace from those persons she had grown closest to—the Randles, Mr. Vlasic and Miss Tiddle, and others she had treated on more than one occasion throughout the months at sea.

She kept her brave smile and bright eyes when most of the passengers had left the ship, until she saw S.L. and Mark come into the lobby, both dressed in street clothes. Then the smile began to waver and the light in her eyes faded. Moistening her lips, she swallowed at seeing Mark walk up and hug Kurt in a manly gesture, then he stepped back and they shook hands and whatever Kurt said to him made Mark smile.

S.L. approached Erin hesitantly. "Well, Dr. Barclay," she began unevenly, "this past time with you as our chief has been the best time I've known, and that's the best way to end."

Erin replied softly, "I wish you and Mark the best, S.L., you know that."

S.L. nodded and swallowed, and then they hugged, letting go of each other when Mark walked up.

"Erin," he smiled, "you were the best friend I ever had." He hesitated, then added devilishly, "From the neck up." He reached for her hand and she clutched it. "I know you have the Caribbean cruise and the transatlantic to Southampton, and I hope it all goes well for you after that."

She nodded, unable to reply.

Then quite unexpectedly he bent forward and brushed her lips lightly. "Good-bye, Ship's Doctor," he whispered.

Long after Mark and S.L. had vanished from sight, she finally managed, "Good-bye, Mr. Payton." Her hand went to her mouth and she merely stood there.

When she looked around for Kurt he was gone. Then, feeling a loneliness she could hardly tolerate, she rushed up to her cabin, fell across the bed, and cried until her phone rang. Then she sat up, wiped her nose and eyes, and inhaled a deep breath before lifting the receiver.

"Erin," Kurt said softly, "I'm going ashore for a meeting with Malaney. Where can I meet you later?"

"I'll be here," she breathed softly, paused, then added, "Or in the unit. We're taking inventory."

"Good. I'll see you later."

After hanging up the phone she rose from the bed, washed her face, and went to the unit, thinking. *A busy mind, that's what I need.*

Kurt showered quickly and changed into dress pants and an open-necked white shirt. In the taxi he

261

mentally rehearsed what he intended to say to Nils Malaney. His lips were drawn in a tight line.

Entering the executive director's suite, he went to Julia Conrad's desk, leaned over, and gave her a quick peck on the cheek.

She flushed and said, "He's expecting you, Captain Garisen. Please go in."

When he opened the door to Malaney's office, he was greeted by a warm smile. "Great cruise I hear," Nils said exuberantly, motioning Kurt to a chair.

"Smooth as glass," Kurt answered, seating himself. "A few thunderstorms and a twenty-four-hour fog—couldn't have asked for more clement conditions."

"Your supplies for the Caribbean are on their way to the dock now," Nils said in a businesslike tone.

Kurt nodded and pursed his lips thoughtfully, then he leaned back in the chair and said, "I want to talk to you about the ship's doctor."

Nils's head tilted with the quick comeback, "Is there a problem? You didn't mention one at any time we spoke throughout the voyage."

Kurt shook his head. "No, there's no problem. But I'd like to ask you to hold up on finding her a replacement at the end of her contract."

Nils appeared genuinely surprised. "Are you telling me she's staying"—his brows rose—"on your ship?"

Kurt inhaled. "She's an excellent physician. I would like to keep her."

Nils rubbed the top of his head and his brows knitted close together. "Are you Captain Garisen, the same captain who paid me a thousand dollars just about a year ago?" He grinned.

Kurt felt his face redden. "Nils, I'm not here to

listen to a lot of crap from you. I just want to know if you will delay replacing her."

Eyeing him carefully, Nils said, "I could do that, but her contract with the line expires in another month. What if she should leave anyway? Are you prepared to sail without a medical officer on ship?"

After a slight pause, Kurt asked, "Have you found her replacement?"

Nils folded his hands together and rocked in his chair. "Not exactly. What we were thinking of doing was bring the doctor from the *Little Princess* since those cruises are short. A nurse could most likely manage that facility and a number of the smaller ships just rely on nurses."

Kurt sighed. "Then there's no problem." He suddenly smiled. "If she stays then you can keep the doctor right where he is on the smaller vessel and the *Royal Princess Star* will continue with Erin—uh—Dr. Barclay."

Suddenly Nils leaned forward on his desk. "And if she doesn't, Captain Garisen, will the *Royal Princess Star* be in need of a new captain?"

Kurt sat very still, then slowly brought his head down. "It's possible that she will," he said. "Possible indeed." Slowly he got up from the chair and gave Nils an acknowledging nod of his head, then he turned and left the office.

He was halfway across the reception area when Julia Conrad called out to him, "Captain, how's the doctor working out?"

Kurt stopped and gave Julia a reflective smile. "She's some sawbones." He winked. "For a woman, that is."

Julia ran him out with a wave of her hand.

It was late afternoon when he returned to ship and found everything quiet as death. He went up to the bridge and paced, looking out at the city's lights just beginning to flicker on. Holding some reservations about what he had done, he stood there listening to the calm on the ship.

He laced his hands behind him and walked back and forth, searching his mind, staring at the ship and the city and the darkening harbor water. So many years had passed and he never dreamed that he would be facing the monumental decision he now faced. One month remained, one short month. He had spent most of his life doing what he loved and now all those years were passing in review. He had not truly imagined living in a house with a wife and a family, especially a wife who would leave him at all hours of the day and night for an operating room. That would require an adjustment he wasn't sure he could make, and yet he could not ask her to give up that part of her life she deemed so important. She was a surgeon, he could accept that. There would be times she would leave him, he could accept that. The difficult acceptance came with the thought of having the ground under his feet, of walking out the door and stepping on soil and grass and concrete.

Suddenly, he gave himself a twisted smile and looked down, thinking, *The deck isn't making my feet happy, not without her*. If their love required he give up the sea, he would give it up. And with that thought he felt the birth of new hope inside him. There was no reason to lose her, and no reason to ask her to make the sacrifice. If a sacrifice had to be made, he would make it. And coming to that conclusion, his fingers unlaced and slid into his back pockets.

*   *   *

In a private port office, Erin placed her call to New Orleans and waited patiently for her father's voice.

"Erin," he said following the wait. "When did you get back?"

"Today," she answered quietly. "How's Mother?"

"She's fine. She's at a staff meeting at the hospital. How are you?"

"Great," she said. There was a pause.

"Your postcards were beautiful, particularly that one from Seychelles. You know neither Elise nor I knew that such a place existed."

Erin laughed softly. "It's called the Garden of Eden, and when you see it you know why." Switching the conversation, she said, "You're working late, aren't you?"

"Yes, but I just saw the last patient of the day." He hesitated, then said, "Erin, we had to go on and take in another partner, but I don't want you to think that there isn't still room for you. The work load was just too much. Now, I don't want you to be upset."

She smiled, leaning her head over on one hand. "I'm not upset, Dad, really. As a matter of fact, that's why I'm calling. I'm not sure I'm coming back."

"Erin," he finally said, his voice relaying shock, "do you have a better offer?"

She inhaled deeply. "There are several alternatives I'm considering."

He came back with, "Just as long as you come back to your chosen field," he urged. "I don't want you to give up what you worked so hard to achieve. That would be a waste and a shame. Your mother and I are in complete agreement there."

After she concluded the conversation she sat alone in the office for a long time, blinking her eyes rapidly, looking around in dismay.

The three days in port were strange ones. Kurt could not read the look on her face. When he suggested they go ashore for a couple of days, she merely replied, "I'd rather stay on ship."

He nodded, but he didn't understand. Twice her temper flared over nothing. She was a walking time bomb and it didn't take much to set her off.

The last day in port was a beautiful spring day with a clear blue sky. When Kurt arrived in the hospital unit he found Erin busily putting away supplies. "You have a staff to do that," he called over cheerfully.

She raised her eyes, suddenly hot and blazing. "You don't see anyone here, do you? If the staff were here, I'm sure they would be helping me," she replied coolly.

"Erin," he said, flustered, "what is wrong with you?"

"Just quit picking on me, Kurt!" she cried, rising swiftly to her feet.

"I'm not picking on you," he argued, losing some of his control. "I made a comment, that's all. You won't go ashore, you aren't happy here. I want to know what's wrong with you. The only time you've been halfway decent to me since we docked is when we've been in bed."

"I suppose," she said back hotly, "you're moping around thinking I'm using you as a sex object. Is that what you're thinking?"

His sharp blue eyes focused on her face. "Lady, you said it, not me!" he exclaimed, banging out of the unit.

He went up to his room, fixed himself a drink, and sprawled out on the sofa, looking out the window at the sun on the water. It didn't make sense to him. The time they should be closest she was pulling away from him again. Well into the dark he sat staring out the window.

When nine o'clock passed and she did not hear from him, she undressed and sank down in a tubful of soft fragrant bubbles. She knew she was wrong to lash out at him the way she had been doing since the conversation with her father, but each time he spoke to her it seemed to be a reflex action. She felt oppressed and heavy and she was using Kurt as the scapegoat. She knew it wasn't fair, and she didn't enjoy being unfair.

When he knocked on the door she ended her bath, coming up out of the water for a quick rinse. Stepping out, she wrapped a bath towel around her and crossed the room. "Kurt?"

"Yes." His tone was flat.

She opened the door and let him in. He was holding a Scotch on the rocks. Seeing her wrapped in the towel, he merely raised his brows and half-shrugged, sauntering on over to her small sofa, where he seated himself and stared up at her. He came directly to the point. "I want to know your plans, Erin."

Standing several feet from him, she touched her lips with her tongue. "You've known my plans all along, Kurt."

"Nothing's changed?"

She hesitated, then replied, "Nothing's changed."

He was up on his feet. "That's all I wanted to

know," and he started back toward the door, taking a sip of the drink as he walked.

Looking at him, she was puzzled. "You came here to ask that!"

He shot her a quick glance. "Do you know a better question?"

"And you're just going to walk out. You're leaving!" She shook her head.

"I have my answer." He reached for the door.

Her eyes grew dark. "Then go . . . leave!"

Without another word to her he did just that. He walked out, still sipping his drink.

She was wide awake all night. She missed him in her bed. She missed the warmth of his body, the way they slept close to each other.

When morning came she was exhausted and her anger at him grew. The next afternoon she did not go to the lobby to watch the passengers embark. Rachel and the two men were back readying the unit. Outside, the sky was filled with black clouds, a mountain of clouds. The ship left port in the middle of a downpour, but several miles out the weather cleared to a hazy overcast. One lone case of severe seasickness prevented her from attending the welcome-aboard festivities, but she didn't mind, she was far from a partying mood.

When Hal helped the young woman back to her cabin, Erin left for her own personal harbor. Her room. She stretched out on her bed, listening to the sounds that had become so familiar to her, and her thoughts went back to the first voyage and her pounding heart grew calm. She lay thinking how the sea could slip into the bloodstream.

Kurt walked stiffly on the bridge deck. Well past midnight the music and laughter below drifted up to his ears. A cool salt wind blew against his face and he looked out at the hazy dark water. He thought back to his first cruise as ship's captain and the weight of the responsibility he had felt. He had been a young man and *The Poseidon Adventure* incident hadn't helped anything. When he had found out that movie was scheduled to be shown in the ship's theater, he had taken the film and thrown it overboard. He remembered paying for it out of his first check as captain. He had wanted good cruises for his passengers, a time free and uncomplicated for them, a time when they were unchained and free to go and do as they wished.

He half-moaned thinking of the miles he had sailed since then. Bracing himself on the rail with his arms spread out, he felt good about the job he had done since assuming command. He had done his best. He had taken thousands of people beyond the horizon, to new parts of the world. Thinking about it made him smile a little. He would miss it. Some decisions were hell to make, and yet thinking ahead, he felt he had made the right one.

He straightened and began to walk back inside. Moments later, three decks down, he knocked on Erin's door, and when she opened it he could tell he had awakened her.

"Don't you ever sleep?" she asked curtly, rubbing one eye.

He gave her a speculative glare but remained silent for a moment. Then he said, "I would like to talk with you, that is if you don't mind missing a tad of your beauty rest."

269

She turned away from the door, allowing him to enter, eyeing him solemnly.

When he closed the door he turned back to her, saying, "I'm going to bypass the preliminaries and get right to the point. Will you marry me?"

She gave him a disbelieving glare. "Wha—what are you doing?"

He smiled indulgently. "I am making a proposal of marriage."

One hand propped unconsciously on her hip and she stared at him with darkened brown eyes, watching his face intently. Her first impulse was to smell his breath, but she refrained from moving at all. She merely stood there glaring at him.

"Now," he said after taking a deep breath of air. "I wouldn't want you tripping over your words to say yes," he explained patiently, "but there is more to it, if you would care to hear."

When she did not voice an objection, he went on. "I have decided that our place is together, wherever that might be." He gestured slightly with both hands. "Apparently it will not be at sea, so I have decided to resign as captain of this ship so that we might have that life together."

Her lips parted with disbelief at his words.

And still he went on. "I have been wrong in wanting you to give up your career as a surgeon because obviously it is the one thing in life you want to hold more important than all other things." His eyes suddenly narrowed at her. "I don't know that you do, but I believe with all my heart that you want to." He shifted and concluded. "And I don't want us to live the remainder of our lives apart."

She suddenly realized he was very close to her.

She didn't know when he had moved. He reached down for her hands. "I want you to rid yourself of this anger toward me. I don't deserve it, unless loving you is a basis for anger. And I don't think it is." Bringing one hand up, he kissed the back, peering up at her. "And I do love you."

And then he truly was puzzled. Her expression was one he had never seen before and her face had turned chalk-white, as if she might get sick. That was one reaction he had not considered from her and he stood stunned.

Suddenly, she wrenched her hands from his in a violent jerk and cried out, "No! I won't let you do that! You know I would never ask you to give up your ship for me."

She was very close to tears when he seized her shoulders roughly. "You didn't ask me, Erin, you didn't have to ask me. It's something I choose to do." Suddenly, he was calm again. "I want to do it because I love you." His hands slid from her shoulders down to her waist and then he wrapped her in his arms. "Ours could be an impossible love if we allowed it to be, but I won't allow it, and I don't want you to give up anything for me."

Bringing her closer in his arms, she leaned into his warm chest. And then his mouth bit into hers in a kiss of near violence while one hand stroked her neck under her soft hair. Her fragrance mingled with the air he breathed and in that moment he realized he wanted her as he had not ever wanted her, with a desire so strong it was difficult for him to be tender.

He drew back and found himself staring into her bewildered eyes and then he let her go completely. A question remained in her eyes as he slowly backed from her, his own gaze roaming her lovely face. "Kurt," she said softly, "I'm not going to marry you."

He didn't believe her.

A sudden moan escaped from her mouth. "Oh, Kurt, hold me."

Immediately, he was back and she was in his arms. He kissed her tenderly on the forehead, saying, "You will marry me, Erin. You will marry me because you can't live your life without me any more than I can live mine without you." He put his hands on her long silky hair, smoothing it back with his fingers. Physical contact with her burned away unspoken words and in the ashes of those words was born a passion like none other.

There was no protest when he turned off the light and darkened the room, nor when he moved her to the bed and brought her down beside him in the darkness of the night and under the pale shower of faint moonlight. They sank slowly onto the bed and he felt her body relax. He moved his fingers softly along the soft gown, up and down her body, outlining her breasts, the smoothness of her flat stomach, the firmness of her legs and hips.

Bending forward, he kissed her breasts lightly through the lace, soft sweeping kisses, back and forth across the silky material, touching her nipples tenderly, enticingly. Her palms were on his head, her fingers lightly plying through his hair. He removed the gown easily and all the while he undressed himself he stared at her beautiful body with all its curves and angles, and at the same time she dreamily watched his face.

Lowering himself beside her, he reached and touched her face and their gazes locked. "Our lives are most important, Erin," he whispered hoarsely. "Of all things our lives are most important—and our happiness. Without you beside me this ship would be just another lonely boat and I would never be happy here again."

Her voice was silken and soft. "But I don't want you to give up your ship, Kurt."

He smiled tenderly. "Then don't think of it as me giving up my ship, think of it as me gaining a wife, the woman I love. I'm not giving up anything, Erin, I'm gaining."

His lips touched hers and suddenly their tongues were locked in a passionate battle as their mouths assaulted each other, bringing the ache of anticipation into the dark night. And then his mouth moved from hers, devouring her neck and shoulders, sweeping her ear with his tongue, moistening her flesh anxiously as his made a wet path to her full breasts.

Her fingers wandered over his lean back, squeezed his shoulders, wove in and out of his hair. She moaned at the touch of his lips and mouth on her stomach, feeling his breath warming her skin, bringing to them both a growing excitement. And then their mouths were back together in a long, exploring kiss. Her hands swept the muscles of his arms, rubbing into his flesh harshly. Then her mouth moved to his neck, his chest, his stomach, and she felt him shudder from the tingle of her lips. Their desire was mutual and overwhelming. She wanted him as much as he wanted her as he eased his body slowly on top of hers.

He pressed his mouth to hers and they moved together when their tongues entwined. With excruciating slowness their bodies became one, controlled by the incredible force of desire. Everything beyond them faded slowly and the air surrounding them became a furnace. The sounds were still around them, but they didn't hear them.

The ship continued its course through the open sea, but they didn't know it was moving. Passengers were still milling on deck, feeling the wind and staring out at the water, but they weren't aware. They were lost in each other.

Kurt awoke when the night was still dark and lay very still, suddenly wide awake. It was quiet now. The ship slept on a smooth sea. With Erin's head resting on his arm he gazed down at her in wonderment, a feeling of peace within him. With his free arm he reached out and fumbled on her bedside table for her cigarette pack, and finding it, maneuvered one free, and when it rolled onto the floor he shook loose another one. Placing it in his mouth, he groped for the lighter. After lighting it, he inhaled deeply and stretched his legs. He felt strong and alive—and vital.

Looking at the soft, restful expression on her face, he smiled to himself, thinking back to the night he had told her, Don't become my albatross. And she hadn't. She had become his world. And maybe he had known the first moment he looked at that defiant face of hers that this was how it would end with her curled in his arms. All in all, it wasn't a bad ending.

He smoked in the dark, thinking ahead to the things he might find to do on land. There would be no reason for her to go into practice with her father now. She would have him beside her. If they settled in a port town, he would have no difficulty finding a position with some aspect of the shipping industry. He didn't have any illusions about what life would be with her. He had already had a taste of that on ship, but he could deal with it. Their children, if they were so blessed, would probably grow up without seeing much of their mother. He knew Erin would adore their children, but he had no illusions; clearly he could see it would be him and some poor house-keeper making the meals and changing the diapers and doing the washing. He had no illusions as to the demands of her career, or any concerning her first priorities. It would be frustrating and trying, but they would make it.

He inhaled a deep puff and let it go slowly, then looked down at her through the smoke. The odds were definitely in their favor because they had love going for them. And he would always love her. And he supposed he understood her as much as any man could understand a woman.

Grinding out the cigarette, he caught her hand lightly in his and lifted it up, gazing at the sparkling ring he had put on her finger in Hong Kong. He pursed his lips thoughtfully, thinking about the in-scription written in tiny letters. He inhaled deeply. She never understood what he was saying to her, and it was doubtful she ever would.

Edging back down in the bed, he placed his free arm over her and hugged her to him. That was all right too. He knew she loved him, and as long as she loved him, he could handle anything else she threw at him.

CHAPTER SIXTEEN

Instead of being less frustrated, she was more. She had never imagined that a marriage proposal would bring such confusion and guilt. He was giving up his ship and as much as she wanted him, she didn't want that from him.

She missed having S.L. to talk with, and Mark. And then she found herself talking with the one person she least imagined herself ever discussing Kurt with. Rachel.

She had just poured herself a cup of coffee when Rachel entered and asked, "Any left?"

Erin gave a half-hearted smile and nodded to the pot. "Enough for another cup."

Rachel's eyes flashed at her, but instead of saying anything she went over calmly and poured her cup, then slowly turned around. "I have just heard the rumor that following the transatlantic, Kurt will no longer be captain of this ship."

Erin lowered herself onto the padded bench near the wall. She sipped.

"Is that true?" Rachel inquired, walking over to a chair.

"What do you think?" Erin returned a question instead of giving the simple yes.

Rachel shrugged, then looked curiously at Erin. "I don't want to believe it."

"Why not?" Erin said, folding one leg beneath her and fiddling with the hem of her slacks. "If that's what he wants to do, why don't you want to believe it?"

Rachel returned quietly, "He may be doing it, but I've known him a lot longer than you've known him, and if you tell me he wants to do it, then one of us doesn't know him at all."

Erin fell silent for a moment. She didn't want to stir up bad feelings again with Rachel Lawrence. She didn't want to argue with her, but Rachel's words were upsetting her and she couldn't keep from saying, "He's a grown man, Rachel. He makes his own decisions."

"Like hell he does," Rachel spat out. "He's doing this for you, not for himself. Why Kurt Garisen wouldn't let himself be dragged off this ship in a million years if he wasn't so blindly and stupidly head over heels in love with you. He's the one sure of what he's doing. It's you, Dr. Barclay, who doesn't know."

Erin's neck stiffened. "I think I resent both your tone and your implications, Miss Lawrence."

"And I resent the hell out of you for taking the best, most qualified captain on the oceans today and making a housewife out of him! That's all he'll be to you—someone to fall back on like you've been doing for this past year!"

Infuriated beyond words, Erin jumped to her feet.

"What makes you think I'll tolerate this from you or from any other member of this staff!"

Rachel, too, stood up, but slowly and deliberately. "I didn't come in here to pick a fight with you, but since it seems that's what's happened here, I'm going to finish what I came to say. I know you're a good doctor and I respect your ability. But, my Lord, you are one hell of a dumb woman! You ran away from what you were and you came here, and you did that of your own volition. You walked away from that operating room; it didn't walk away from you. And you would have never done that if you loved it. But you didn't love it, you hated it." Suddenly her voice softened. "In a way I'm sorry for you, because you're too damned proud to admit that you chose the wrong career, and now you're going to take Kurt back into your private hell with you."

"Are you quite finished, Miss Lawrence?" she said impatiently, and began moving to the door.

"No," Rachel went on stubbornly. Then suddenly her tone changed, became soft. "Dr. Barclay, I just don't understand your reasoning. For the most part, haven't you been happy on this ship?"

Erin's hand reached up and touched the frame of the doorway. Slowly she turned around and looked hard at Rachel. Her other hand rubbed her cheek. "I don't expect you to understand this, Miss Lawrence." As she spoke the expression in her eyes changed to that of being tired. "But we do what we have to do."

"No." Rachel shook her head slowly. "It's my belief that we do what we choose to do."

Erin stepped toward the door, already regretting the exchange of words with the nurse, then she heard Rachel mutter under her breath, "Lord, spare me from women with causes."

A few steps and Erin was back in her office where she closed the door and sank down into her chair. Propping her elbows on her desktop, she rubbed her brow vigorously. Rachel was wrong. Wrong. She had never asked Kurt to give up this ship. She had never expected him to do it.

She began clenching and unclenching her fists, her darkened eyes rooted to the wall, while the most intense feelings pounded throughout her body. Frustration seethed on her face, in her eyes. It was useless to wish that something hadn't happened when it already had. She tried to tell herself that it didn't matter, but it did. What Rachel had done in the ship's lounge was to bring to surface thoughts Erin had been struggling with since the night Kurt asked her to marry him, thoughts she couldn't back away from anymore, thoughts pressing to be free. Deep inside she believed, as Rachel did, that she had made wrong choices in her life. If she had lost a hand or an arm, or her vision, or her hearing, she would be forced to give up that career simply because she couldn't function at it anymore. Hadn't she done that? Hadn't she walked away from it because she couldn't function anymore? But the part of her she had lost had been within her heart.

Sinking farther into the cushions of her chair, she faced the truth directly for the first time. She didn't love it; she didn't even like it. She spent all those years to become someone only to discover when she became that someone she didn't like who she was. Why couldn't she just walk away from it and quit, just like others did every day in all walks of life? Why did she feel the guilt for leaving? Why did she feel she must go back? Because she expected it of herself, and self-expectations are difficult to compromise. If she gave in now, would she give in again at some other point in her life when a decision must be made?

For the most part, haven't you been happy on this ship? That question played over and over in her mind. She had spent her entire life thus far avoiding that question. And now it was happening. Alone in her office, alone with her thoughts, she could admit that, yes, for the most part, she had been happy. She began twisting the ring on her finger, Kurt's ring. And she experienced a small chill. The truth was, the choices of her life, concerning her life, had always been there. She chose the path she now walked, and if she found thorns along the way, it was because of her own choosing. No one set her feet there at the start and said, Walk. She took that first step herself and all others since.

She had not been unhappy on the *Royal Princess Star*. There had been times when she felt inadequate, but even then she had not been unhappy. At that precise moment she realized the strength would be in staying. Was she strong enough to stay? Was she brave enough to admit to herself and those she loved, I made a mistake? I don't want to be a surgeon anymore. It doesn't make me happy. Who would understand? Would Kurt understand? Was her love for Kurt clouding all the issues? Now that new thought lurked in the shadows of her overly tired mind. She had not ever dreamed of a Kurt Garisen in her life, yet he was not a dream, he was real. His selfless, giving love for her was real.

Rachel Lawrence had set off a chain reaction in Erin's mind. Tiny explosions of truth waiting to be set free. Strange, of all people, she would have least expected Rachel to be the one to put the torch to the fuse.

She placed her fingers to her lips, unable to conceal the emotions flashing through her. All the questions she had so feared were now being answered.

That night after dinner and dancing she went out on deck with Kurt. Hand in hand they walked close to the railing. Throughout the evening he had eyed her cautiously, studying her face again and again. He had never seen her with such a solitary, isolated expression and he wondered about it, and worried about it.

The full moon shone through a thin layer of wispy clouds and a soft breeze played with their hair as the quiet beauty of the Caribbean flowed all about them. He regarded her expression again, trying in vain to scrutinize the thoughts going on behind those beautiful brown eyes. Finally he turned and stared out at the water. "Would you like to find a table?" he inquired.

She hesitated, then answered softly. "No, Kurt, let's just stand here." She turned and faced him, her eyes wide. She appeared to be in search of words, as if she did not know where to begin or what to say.

He stood a short distance away from her, one hand touching the rail. He could see her face so clearly in the moonlight and he was troubled by what he saw. He tapped his fingers on the rail. "Erin," he finally broke the uncomfortable silence. "Is something bothering you?"

Looking at him, she hesitated before saying, "Kurt, since the other night I have been doing a lot of thinking."

"About us?" He took a step toward her.

She nodded and whispered, "Yes, about us."

His fingers fell away from the rail and searched for hers. She felt the warmth of his hand around hers. "What about us?" His fingers tightened.

"I want what's best for us, for both of us."

He shook his head. "You know, Erin, I've had this fear that you would talk yourself out of marrying me, that you would sit down and rationalize me away." He moistened his lips and inhaled a deep breath. "Is that what you've done?"

"No," she whispered. "I could never rationalize you away. You are the one reality in my life." Overhead the moon moved behind a cloud. "Earlier today Rachel Lawrence and I had quite a heated discussion."

"I'll take care of it," he interrupted smoothly.

"No. It took care of itself. As a matter of fact, Kurt, it's taken care of a lot of things. I'm not upset with her, not anymore."

He stiffened. "Well, if she's talked you out of marrying me, I'll be upset with her! Enough for both of us!"

Erin smiled slightly. "She didn't. Believe me, she didn't."

The expression of concern remained heavy on his face. "Maybe I'm just slow after a couple of drinks, but I—I don't understand what you're saying."

The moon was back and her face was shining in the wavery light. "Darling, what I am trying to tell you is that I am not ready to leave this ship."

His expression was one of complete bafflement.

Smiling, she went on. "Maybe it was just a lucky accident in my life that brought me here, but now that I am here I'm not ready to leave. This past year has been a rare one in my life, and maybe that's because of you, or my love for you. Perhaps I didn't come here to stay, but in coming here I find I don't have the heart to leave. I love this ship. I love being the ship's doctor. I love the ocean and the ports we visit, and the world. You know, darling, I never thought about how beautiful this world is, how privileged we are to see it all and share it with each other."

His lips parted and he whispered, "You don't want to leave the ship?"

She smiled and replied confidently, "No, Kurt. This may sound strange, but I find being happy is the hardest thing I've ever done. It's something I didn't want to admit to myself. I am happy here and why should I sacrifice my own happiness to go back to a career that never made me happy? Why should I go back to something my parents wanted for me, not something I wanted enough for myself? There was a time when I had a sense of satisfaction, of pride, and when I lost that, I lost it all. You were right so many times when you tried to talk to me. You could see me more clearly than I could see myself. My life has been such a storm simply because I wouldn't give up a dream when I discovered it was wrong for me. I wouldn't let go even when I knew it was destroying me. Still, I held on. I had invested my life and my dividends were chaos and dissatisfaction. And still I wouldn't let go of it."

Suddenly she felt her eyes mist. "My grandfather taught me so much, and yet I didn't learn. He was a wise man, Kurt, but I never really listened to what he was saying to me, not then. But now, sixteen years later, I hear him. I know what he was saying, and I understand."

The relief was visible on his face as he drew close to her. "Erin, above all else I want you to be happy. I want us to be happy." He kissed her hair.

"I felt so guilty," she whispered, "for leaving, for quitting. Because that night I walked out of that hospital, I did quit. I felt as if I had betrayed something deep inside me, or maybe that I had betrayed my fellow human beings dependent on my skills. I don't know the exact source of the guilt, I know only that it has been overpowering."

He smiled and murmured close to her lips. "We do that sometimes." He touched her mouth lightly. "When something feels so right, we fight it with the thought, nothing should feel so right." He kissed her again. "I do it, and you do it, and so does everyone else. When we are happy we sit around wondering what we've done to deserve it. We can't just accept it. When you found yourself happy on this ship, you couldn't accept it because you weren't expecting it and you were punishing yourself, saying you didn't deserve it. But, darling, that is the one thing in life we do deserve, to be happy. And if we can't be, then what is our purpose in living? So you quit, so what? There's someone else out there to take your place. And did anyone there ever need you more than John Rainey needed you, or Mark needed you, or Beth Randle? Our passengers are people, too, Erin. And when they're ill they need a doctor, just like those on land."

She leaned her head against his shoulder and whispered, "I realize that now."

Wrapping his arms around her, he smiled and looked up at the stars beginning to appear as the clouds drifted away. Burying his mouth in her hair, he thought, *Dreams perish, yes, they do*. And lucky for him. She had lost one dream and in losing it had at last discovered the meaning of her life, and given real meaning to his.

They would have a while yet at sea, and someday they would go ashore, but they would go ashore together. He could deal with that.

LOOK FOR NEXT MONTH'S
CANDLELIGHT ECSTASY SUPREMES:

CANDLELIGHT Ecstasy Supreme

- ☐ 21 **BREAKING THE RULES,** Donna Kimel Vitek 10834-9-28
- ☐ 22 **ALL IN GOOD TIME,** Samantha Scott 10099-2-28
- ☐ 23 **SHADY BUSINESS,** Barbara Andrews 17797-9-10
- ☐ 24 **SOMEWHERE IN THE STARS,** Jo Calloway 18157-7-20
- ☐ 25 **AGAINST ALL ODDS,** Eileen Bryan 10069-0-16
- ☐ 26 **SUSPICION AND SEDUCTION,** Shirley Hart 18464-9-10
- ☐ 27 **PRIVATE SCREENINGS,** Lori Herter 17111-3-19
- ☐ 28 **FASCINATION,** Jackie Black 12442-5-10

$2.50 each

At your local bookstore or use this handy coupon for ordering:

DELL BOOKS
P.O. BOX 1000, PINE BROOK, N.J. 07058-1000   B173A

Please send me the books I have checked above. I am enclosing $ _____ (please add 75c per copy to cover postage and handling). Send check or money order—no cash or C.O.D.'s. Please allow up to 8 weeks for shipment.

Name _____

Address _____

City _____ State/Zip _____

Candlelight
Ecstasy Romances™